dark star
calling

by julia keller

THE DARK INTERCEPT TRILOGY FOR TEENS

The Dark Intercept

Dark Mind Rising

Dark Star Calling

THE BELL ELKINS SERIES FOR ADULTS

A Killing in the Hills

Bitter River

Summer of the Dead

Last Ragged Breath

Sorrow Road

Fast Falls the Night

Bone on Bone

The Cold Way Home

dark star
calling

Julia Keller

A TOM DOHERTY ASSOCIATES BOOK

New York

This is a work of fiction. All of the characters, organizations, and events portrayed in this novel are either products of the author's imagination or are used fictitiously.

DARK STAR CALLING

A Tor Teen Book
Published by Tom Doherty Associates
120 Broadway, New York, NY 10271

www.tor-forge.com

Tor® is a registered trademark of Macmillan Publishing Group, LLC.

The Library of Congress Cataloging-in-Publication Data is available upon request.

ISBN 978-0-7653-8769-1 (hardcover)
ISBN 978-0-7653-8770-7 (ebook)

Our books may be purchased in bulk for promotional, educational, or business use. Please contact your local bookseller or the Macmillan Corporate and Premium Sales Department at 1-800-221-7945, extension 5442, or by email at MacmillanSpecialMarkets@macmillan.com.

First Edition: November 2019

P1

To Ruth Thornton

FINIS CORONAT OPUS

Somewhere, something incredible is waiting to be known.

—*Carl Sagan*

If I can dream, I can hope. If I can hope, I can fight.

—*Makayla Young*

dark star
calling

Prologue

TIME: 2297

A year has passed since the Intercept rose from the dead—not the complete Intercept, that is, but only bits and pieces of it, a motley montage of broken-off code and partial data and interrupted algorithms. The technology was still capable of harvesting emotions via a chip embedded in the crook of the left elbow of every citizen, but only from a few people at a time. Not from the entire civilization as it once did.

Now even the mini-Intercept is dead.

New Earth is free again.

But freedom has a price. A deadly crisis looms, and this time, New Earth is on its own. There is no Intercept to save the day. No Intercept to keep the peace. No Intercept to scoop up and file away feelings, and then deploy those feelings as weapons when people misbehave.

A world without the Intercept is a world of wild uncertainty, a world ruled by passion and by the vivid potential for catastrophe.

A world where anything can happen.

And usually does.

PART ONE

Searching the Skies

1

The Robot Who Loves Knock-Knock Jokes

"Star number 76.435.7863."

"Negative."

"Star number 76.435.7864."

"Negative."

"Star number 76.435.7865."

"Negative."

"Star number 76.435.7866."

"Negative. Hey, Rez, I'm totally, *totally* starving. How about a lunch break?"

Rez looked up from his computer screen, scowling in the direction from where the remark had come. His scowl was deep and deliberately prolonged—even though it would, he knew, have absolutely zero impact on its intended target.

Not because that intended target was a robot. Robots were fully capable of reading human facial expressions and deducing the emotions generating them, and then initiating the appropriate behavioral change.

No, the scowl was a total waste of time for another reason:

Because this particular robot wasn't about to change *anything*. He was not like other robots. He was not earnest and dutiful. He was not devoted exclusively to service and obedience.

This robot was a rascal. A joker. A screwup. A show-off.

If Rez had had his way, he would've traded in the AstroRob—short for Astronomy Robot—for another. But he couldn't. He had pulled this one out of the scrap heap and, when nobody was looking, put him to work for an off-label use. He needed to keep that fact as quiet as possible. Requesting an AstroRob through regular channels might have caused some nosy supply clerk in NESA—New Earth Science Authority—to get a little too curious about why it was that eighteen-year-old NESA director and chief technologist Steven J. Reznik needed an AstroRob in the first place, being as how the director's job was largely bureaucratic.

"Largely bureaucratic" was another way of saying that Rez spent his days approving *other* peoples' projects. Signing off on *other* peoples' requests for AstroRobs and BioRobs and TechRobs and ReadyRobs and other essential equipment.

Not doing his *own* project.

Yet that's exactly what Rez was up to—privately, that is. Under the table. His actions weren't specifically illegal, but they were . . . highly irregular. For the past three months, he'd been coming here on his nights off, first checking the roster to make sure nobody else had scheduled time on the telescope for the next chunk of hours—and then going to work.

His only companion on these secret shifts was the misfit AstroRob, an orphan from a long-shut-down project in the Dark Matter lab. An AstroRob that nobody missed because, frankly, he had been such an annoying little twerp to begin with.

But Rez needed an extra hand. So he was forced to endure

the robot's completely infuriating and wildly inappropriate sense of humor.

Or what passed for a sense of humor.

A few weeks ago, he had nicknamed this robot "Mickey." He'd remembered, from his Old Earth History and Culture class, an animated character back in the twentieth century whose name—Mickey Mouse—became synonymous with time-wasting nonsense. "That's a real Mickey Mouse thing to do," people would say. Or, "Don't be such a Mickey Mouse."

Perfect, Rez had decided. It fit him. Mickey it was.

Tonight, for the past several hours, Rez had been in a bit of a trance, because this work—while critically important—was also tedious. Rez would call out the names of star after star on a randomly selected grid of galaxies, and then Mickey would check to see if there was any anomaly, any shift, any variation, in the light emanating from that star. Rez would systematically record Mickey's response on the spreadsheet whose ever-changing numbers quivered across his computer screen like a spiderweb trembling in a morning breeze.

And then Mickey had broken the spell with his ridiculous request for refreshments.

"Shut up," Rez snapped back at him.

Mickey answered with a sound that was engineered to resemble a snicker. Robots didn't get hungry. Hence they didn't need food. But sometimes—if they happened to have been programmed by someone who regarded stupid humor as a good thing, a view that Rez found totally bogus—they did make jokes. Groaningly awful ones. Stupidly juvenile ones.

"If you want to know the truth," Mickey added, "I could really go for a bucket of bolts in chipotle sauce."

Rez's scowl intensified yet another degree, despite its futility.

He added an eye roll. He was not amused. He'd been working hard. This was a serious matter. He didn't need the aggravation.

He knew the guy who was responsible for the funny—the *allegedly* funny—robot. It was a programmer named Dave Parkhurst, a.k.a. Dumb-Ass Dave. Spiky yellow hair, baggy trousers, food-stained tunic, big stinky feet: Rez had gone to school with him and could picture him—and almost smell him—to this day. Because of Dumb-Ass Dave's wacky plan, what lived inside Mickey's cranial cartridge was a tiny, telltale wiggle in the otherwise rigidly straightforward lines of instructional code. The wiggle had been put there by Dumb-Ass Dave to enable at least one industrial-use AI machine, normally a bland and predictable variety, to crack jokes at regular intervals.

To be, that is, a first-class, all-purpose goofball.

Dumb-Ass Dave had somehow persuaded his bosses to let him endow a handful of robots with a sense of humor. *It'll help morale,* he had argued. *Lighten things up.*

Rez, on the contrary, believed quite firmly that things did not need to be lightened up. In fact, if he'd had his way, things would be darkened down, not lightened up. But he'd lost the argument. The Dispute Resolution Subcommittee of the Conflict Strategy Division of the Science Committee of the New Earth Senate had sided with Dumb-Ass Dave.

"I told you to zip it," Rez muttered.

Mickey's response was swift and sure: He emitted a noise that was indistinguishable from a human fart.

Rez's irritation flared again. He didn't say anything out loud, though, because he didn't want a back-and-forth conversation. Time was too precious. They could be interrupted any minute by some eager-beaver staff astronomer colleague with actual authorization to be accessing the telescope, and

Rez had a ton more stars to get through tonight to make his quota. His schedule was terribly ambitious.

At least Mickey's latest attempt at humor hadn't been a knock-knock joke. Knock-knock jokes were a favorite of Dumb-Ass Dave's. Last week, the AstroRob had interrupted their labors with the following:

Mickey: Knock-knock.
Rez: (silence)
Mickey: Knock-knock.
Rez: (silence)
Mickey: Come on, Stevie-boy. Live a little. Knock-knock.
Rez: (after a heavy, exasperated sigh) Okay, fine. Whatever. Who's there?
Mickey: Uranus.
Rez: (another sigh) Uranus who?
Mickey: Uranus ought to be pretty sore by now, after all this sitting around!

It was the lamest, lowest, stalest gag in the history of both New Earth and Old Earth and probably a grab bag of other planets, too. But Rez was forced to put up with it. His hands were tied. He needed this shiny metal pile that specialized in turning out lousy jokes.

"Hey, Stevie," Mickey chirped. "If you're running low on chipotle, I'll take honey mustard sauce with those bolts instead. On the side."

"Hilarious," Rez responded. "Freakin' hilarious."

"Wait, I got a question for you. Why did the robot cross the road?"

Rez fumed silently. Maybe ignoring him would work.

"Okay," Mickey said, "so I'll *tell* you why the robot crossed the road . . . to get to the other sidereal motion!"

Rez needed to calm himself down, so he sat back in his chair. He let out a long sigh. He rubbed his eyes. When he opened them again, he took an appreciative look around his lab.

Not even a bothersome AstroRob could diminish his pleasure in this space.

He had custom-engineered it to his exact specifications. Sure, it might be crowded, cramped, and jammed with whatever cast-off and won't-be-missed materials he could scrounge, but it was just what he needed. It was accessible only through a small, half-hidden porthole, and wriggling through that porthole required an intricate series of acrobatic maneuvers, topped off by an ability to twist, leap, and land with abandon. So he never had to worry about uninvited guests.

Rez had quietly carved this workspace out of a forgotten corner of the Sagan Observatory in Mendeleev Crossing. He had installed a long, busy control panel across one wall, a wall broken only by a small niche for the AstroRob and his monitor and screen. The control panel was set into a rectangular slab of shiny chrome; the glass-fronted dials and gauges fluttered with constant activity. From both armrests of Rez's red leather chair, joysticks jutted; with these, he could rotate the chair up and down or side to side or turn it in a circle. Affixed to the ceiling that loomed a bit too close over his head, a row of toggle switches awaited the quick flicks of his fingers.

Out in the real observatory, protruding from the vast gap in the roof, was the giant telescope. It stared unblinkingly into the night sky, its gaze peering deep into the wilderness of stars.

Somewhere within that wilderness was the single star Rez was determined to find.

And so here he sat, muscles tensed, senses on high alert

as he steadily checked the readout from the telescope's night watch. He examined star after star after star. Every night, he traveled millions of miles—but he never left the lab.

The only person Rez had thus far confided in was Violet Crowley, daughter of Ogden Crowley, the late founder of New Earth. She was the closest thing he had to a friend. She was also president of the New Earth Senate and chair of the astronomy subcommittee, and at first, she hadn't understood why he was so obsessed with setting up his own research area.

"You've already *got* an observatory, Rez," she'd said. "With the biggest telescope in the history of . . . well, in the history of really big telescopes. And you're in charge of it, right?"

"Yeah. But other people want to use it, too."

Half-exasperated, half-amused, Violet had shaken her head. "Ever heard of a little thing called *sharing,* Rez?"

He scowled at her. He'd heard of it, sure. He just didn't want to do it.

And then she had asked the obvious follow-ups:

"Why, Rez? Why do you need a secret spot all your own to make your observations? What in the world are you looking for, anyway?"

The answer was right there in her question: The thing for which he searched wasn't *in* the world at all. It wasn't on New Earth, and it wasn't on Old Earth, either, the original planet that now served as little more than the rickety scaffold for the gleaming new civilization that thrived above it.

He had told her the truth because he trusted her. It was a funny feeling—trusting somebody, or at least anybody other than his little sister—and it didn't come naturally to him, but Violet had proven herself to be worthy of that trust.

So had the others: Shura Lu, Kendall Mayhew, Tin Man Tolliver. He just hadn't had a chance yet to fill them in about his project. But he would. Because they were a team. A year ago, they had banded together to keep New Earth from being destroyed.

One by one, the special features of their faces flashed in his mind: Shura's intense dark eyes; Kendall's square jaw; Tin Man's confused frown. And Violet's pale forehead, crinkling with concern each time she asked Rez if he was okay, which she frequently did. He pretended not to like it—"Don't *fuss* over me," he'd snap at her—but he sort of did. It was nice to have somebody care about you, even if you had to pretend that it annoyed you.

There was one more face that he pictured, too: His little sister, Rachel. She had been only eleven years old when she perished in the chop and heave of the dark waters of an Old Earth ocean. Heartbroken but resolute, Rez had overseen the cremation of her body, sending her ashes into space in a small capsule programmed to disintegrate in a matter of days, ensuring that his sister's remains would drift amid the stars forever.

If he'd been antisocial and prickly *before* Rachel's death—and he had, because he didn't like having people interrupt his work with the silly things they said—then he became a million times *more* that way afterward. He was shattered and bereft. But the difference was that now he couldn't control it.

He wasn't mean on purpose anymore, to get people to back off and leave him alone; he was mean because he was hurting.

Outside of his staff at the observatory, the only people Rez interacted with on a regular basis were Violet, Shura, Kendall, and Tin Man. And that's exactly how he wanted it. The fewer people he had to deal with, the better.

They were all doing different jobs now from the ones they'd been doing a year ago. Saving New Earth had made them famous, and New Earth president Ahmad Shabir had insisted that they accept promotions: Rez headed up NESA. Shura was in charge of all government-sponsored research. Kendall became chief of police; Tin Man was his top deputy. Those new roles made sense.

Except for one.

The one upgrade that didn't make sense was Violet's. She had been appointed to the New Earth Senate to fill an unexpired term, following in the footsteps of her father, Ogden Crowley, New Earth's first president. He had died of old age shortly after they returned from their adventure on Old Earth.

Violet, a *politician*? It seemed like a stretch, mainly because she had a quick temper and could be headstrong and impulsive, and she would much rather solve exciting mysteries or hang out with her friends at a club called Redshift than sit through a bunch of boring subcommittee hearings about budget priorities. But Rez could sort of see the logic of it, too. Violet was fair-minded, and she believed in justice. Her last name was the best-known one on New Earth. People, especially young people, respected her.

And New Earth was becoming, day by day, a young person's world. President Shabir himself was only twenty-four. The original settlers were dying off, and the younger citizens were gradually taking over the positions of authority.

Accepting the Senate job meant that Violet had to give up her detective agency, Crowley & Associates. Her assistant, Jonetta Loring, had taken over the firm.

As Rez thought about his friends and the changes in all of their lives, he couldn't help but think about Rachel: If she had lived, what would she be doing now? His sister was brilliant and driven. To what noble cause would she have lent her blazing talents? In what amazing way would she have left her mark on New Earth?

Thinking about Rachel, he felt a familiar ache. That ache was so intense that it made everything stop in Rez's mind. It was a distraction worse, even, than Mickey's bad jokes. And he needed to get back to work.

He took a bite from a half-eaten energy bar—because unlike a robot, he *did* get hungry from time to time. He chewed. He swallowed. He indulged himself in a swig from the nearby canister of water, wiping his mouth on the too-long sleeve of his gray tunic. He almost never thought about his appearance, but occasionally—like right now, when he leaned over to set the canister back down—he'd catch a glimpse in the reflective chrome on the side of a piece of equipment and realize anew that he was nothing special, looks-wise. He resembled thousands of other guys. Millions, really.

Did that bother him? No. But it was indisputably true.

He had medium-length brown hair, milky pale skin, light brown eyes, a nondescript nose, regular ears. Normal, normal, normal. The only special thing about Steve Reznik lay beneath the surface like an underground spring that secretly keeps the landscape alive:

His brain.

He scratched his chin. There was a faint thatch of stubble there. It could've been crusted dirt for all that Rez cared.

He turned his attention back to the computer screen. That screen was home to a rippling hive of orange numbers that roiled against a blue-black background. If he squinted just right and engaged his imagination, he could momentarily persuade himself that he was enjoying an aerial view of an orange grove infiltrated with vermin.

Mickey made another noise. It was quite loud. Because his body consisted of six expandable cylinders topped by a square gray metal box that squirmed with circuitry, sounds tended to expand and intensify as they branched through his layers. If that particular noise had come from a human being, it would have been immediately classified as a belch. An impressively gross one.

Rez had no choice except to put up with it, just as he put up with the farts, wheezes, sneezes, snorts, hiccups, and sighs, not to mention the bad puns, third-rate limericks, and witless wisecracks. He needed Mickey, warts and all. He didn't want to use a human assistant. He couldn't run the risk of word leaking out about his search until he'd gathered all the evidence. Until he'd made an airtight case.

And, most important, until he'd found a solution.

Because if his suspicions were correct, his prediction would start a mass panic across the six cities of New Earth. So he needed to have a remedy, a solid plan, ready and waiting for when he made his revelation. At the same moment he announced the coming catastrophe, he would offer hope. And in this case, he knew, hope came exclusively in the shape of a star.

That star would be a new sun, around which a new New Earth would revolve.

"Hey, Rez," Mickey blurted. "I just flew in from Saturn. And boy, are my arms tired!"

Rez groaned. He grabbed the joystick and tilted his chair forward. He needed to start calling out star locations again. It was the only way to stop the AstroRob from lobbing stupid jokes: Keep the damned thing busy.

"Star number 76.435.7867," Rez said, focusing on the telescope's steady harvest of data.

"Negative."

"Star number 76.435.7868."

"Negative."

"Star number 76.435.7869."

"Negative."

The night wore on.

Rez sifted through the stars.

Shortly before dawn, just as the sun was tipping over the far edge of New Earth's eastern quadrant, flooding this compartment—and all of New Earth—with luscious lemony light, he saw it.

But it wasn't what Rez had been searching for. It was something wildly, disturbingly different.

And it filled him with the most intense and overwhelming torrent of raw emotion he had ever felt.

The Signal

"Hey."

Violet uttered her standard greeting at the same moment her head poked up through the little round porthole in the floor. The first thing she saw was the high back of the big red leather armchair that dominated this impossibly tiny space.

"Over here," Rez said. "Come on in."

She took a deep breath. With a grunt of effort, she managed to hoist herself up the rest of the way. She was able to do that—grasping the heavy iron hinge of the hatch's open lid and using it as a fulcrum so she could swing herself up and scoot through—because she was nimble and fit. Violet's habit was to run several miles each evening across the streets of New Earth. All of those muscles, all of that flexibility, came in handy right now as she popped up and over. Her butt landed on the cold steel floor.

Once Violet was upright again, she dusted off her hands, squared her shoulders, and took the single forward step required to put her next to Rez's chair. She was nineteen years old. A lot of people told her that she was attractive, but she mostly saw only the flaws: She had a narrow face, a nose that was pointy enough to annoy her, brown eyes, a small mouth that frankly looked better with a little lip gloss on it—but she rarely bothered—and short, shiny dark hair that she combed straight back from her forehead each morning because she hated dealing with her hair. She liked to launch herself head-first into her day, with no fuss or bother or forethought.

Sort of like the way she'd launched herself through the hatch into Rez's lair.

"Hey," she repeated. "Got here as soon as I could. So what's the emergency?" She raised her wrist, indicating the communication console strapped there and, by extension, the call he'd made to her a few minutes ago. "You sounded pretty intense. What's going on?"

Before Rez could reply, the AstroRob's square head appeared over the top of his monitor. The flexible material from which his cylinders were made meant that he could grow taller on a whim, extending himself upward to his silicon heart's content.

"Hey, Violet," Mickey said. His singsong tone was sly and playful. "You've heard of the law of gravity, right?"

"Um, sure. I've heard of it."

"So what did we do before that law was passed? " Mickey's guffaw tailed off into a series of high-pitched titters.

"Good one," she said dubiously. Back when she was maybe six years old, that joke had seemed hilarious. Now? Not so much.

Rez had explained to her about his AstroRob's bad habit of making terrible jokes and the reasons why he couldn't replace him with a sedate and more somber machine. Or at least one with some better gags.

Suddenly, with a fury that startled Violet, Rez jabbed a finger at his console, giving it a quick command. The light atop Mickey's head went black. There was a short hum and then a small *beep-beep* as the AstroRob powered off.

"Come on, Rez," she said. "Yeah, it was a dumb joke, but it wasn't *that* bad, right? I mean, you didn't have to shut him down." Despite everything, she liked Mickey. He was better than the vast run of other robots she had to deal with in the course of her day, the dull, plodding, polite, obedient ones. Those robots were, frankly, boring. Mickey was a lot of things, but he wasn't boring.

Rez didn't reply. He bolted from the armchair and started pacing. His hands were clasped behind his back. Pacing was a challenge: The space was so small that he could only go four or five steps in one direction before he had to whirl around and go back in the other direction. And he had to hop constantly over electronic components that he'd stacked up on the floor until he found the time to install them.

His jaw was tight. He was breathing hard. There was a faraway look in his eyes.

"Hey," Violet said. "Tell me what's going on." This behavior was totally out of character for Steve Reznik. Usually the only emotions he showed were irritation and annoyance. She, on the other hand, was known to yell at people when she got mad and even to throw in a few choice curse words if she was *really* upset.

But Rez?

No. In times of stress or high drama—and they'd had plenty of both a year ago—he just got quieter. More focused. Sometimes Violet was half convinced that Rez didn't even *have* emotions—although that was impossible, of course. Everyone had emotions. If they didn't, then the Intercept would not have been as astonishingly efficient as it was, a fantastically powerful tool that had changed New Earth and Old Earth in ways both wonderful and terrible.

The Intercept was gone now, shut down the same way that Mickey had just been shut down—with a single bold gesture, bringing a great deal of relief and peace, as well as a tiny aftertaste of regret. Yet whenever Violet thought about emotions, she couldn't help but think about the Intercept, too.

Rez was still pacing. He lunged forward, came face-to-face with a wall of computers, at which point he had to whirl around and lunge in the other direction, only to come face-to-face with the opposite wall of computers—and then he did the same thing over again. And again.

Lunge, whirl. Lunge, whirl. Lunge, whirl.

Violet had only seen Rez this agitated and upset one other time: when she'd had to tell him about his little sister's death.

"Rez?"

No answer. Another lunge, another whirl.

"Come on, Rez."

Nothing.

"Look," she said. "Whatever it is, you can trust me. I promise I won't breathe a word to anybody. Ever. Not until you say it's okay."

Still nothing. Lunge, whirl.

"Rez, please. Just *tell* me. I'm sure we can—"

"It's Rachel." The pacing stopped.

Violet was aware of a sort of shifting inside her body, as if some of her vital organs had spontaneously decided to trade places. The feeling was a combination of pity and sadness and—yeah, okay, even though she'd hate to admit it out loud—affection and concern for Rez. He had never really dealt with his emotions about his sister's death. Violet knew that, and so did Shura, Tin Man, and Kendall. They'd talked about it from time to time, when Rez wasn't around. About how he seemed to have buried his feelings about Rachel deep inside, in a place almost nobody else could reach.

A place like this lab.

Maybe that's what tonight was all about, Violet speculated. Maybe the loss of Rachel had finally gotten to him. Maybe it was all coming down on him now—a deluge of previously unreleased emotion, plus all the memories and regrets and questions that always go along with anything to do with family.

No wonder he was a mess.

"Listen, we can get you a therapist," she said carefully. Violet wasn't good at the whole consolation thing, and she was hopeless at hugs, but she wanted to help Rez however she could. "They've got a mental health kiosk over in L'Engletown where you can schedule a—"

"NO." His voice was like a bold jolt of thunder. He stared at her. "NO, NO, NO."

"I know you don't like the idea of needing help from anybody, but sometimes just talking it out can really be—"

"NO."

Violet didn't like the way his eyes looked; the white parts were mostly pinkish red. A vein stood out on his forehead. He seemed stunned, as if he'd had a tremendous shock.

"Rez, I just mean that—"

"I shouldn't have called you," he snapped, cutting her off. "Forget it. Just go away."

"I'm not going anywhere. Not until you tell me what happened."

"I *did* tell you. It's Rachel." He dropped his eyes. His shoulders slumped. His voice was so low that Violet had to strain to hear him. "I've checked it again and again. I've gone through all the information backward and forward," he added in a sort of running mumble. "Mickey checked and double-checked my calculations. I've interrogated the signal so many ways, from so many angles, but it doesn't change. It's still exactly what it seemed to be when it first showed up on my screen just a few minutes ago. It—it doesn't make any sense. But it's true. It *has* to be true."

Now he raised his head again. His cheeks were wet and shiny. His nose needed a good wipe. To her shock, Violet realized that in the last few seconds, he'd been . . . crying.

Rez? *CRYING?*

Violet suddenly felt as if she'd somehow landed in an alternate universe. Maybe it had happened when she'd crossed the threshold into the lab. Maybe she didn't know her own strength. Maybe she'd overshot the mark. And maybe, she thought whimsically, she'd ended up in a whole different level of reality—a reality where Steve Reznik, the computer genius with wires and lights and switches where a heart ought to be, was somehow . . . *crying.*

"What do you mean? *What* has to be true, Rez?"

"The signal."

"What signal?"

"*The* signal. The one I just received." He looked straight into her eyes. He really wanted her to understand. "Violet, listen to me. I'm trying to explain it."

"Explain what?"

"I'm trying to explain," he said, pausing for several seconds to drag his sleeve across his nose to mop up the moisture, "that the sensors picked up a signal that originated very far away—at least the other side of the galaxy, and maybe a lot farther away than that."

"And?"

"And it's my sister."

Violet's brain was instantly filled with buzzing uncertainty. She was so confused that she felt as if she'd dived headfirst into a crowded vat of question marks.

"What are you talking about, Rez?"

He didn't answer her. Instead he sat back down in his special chair. He spread his fingers across the tops of the armrests, grasping the red leather in a tight grip as if he needed to hang on for dear life while a ferocious wind blew right through the center of his life.

Anything related to Rachel and Rachel's death, Violet knew, shook Rez to his core—even though he tried very hard not to let it show.

"The signal," he said in an even, careful voice, "came in through the same channel I'm using to measure the light from the stars. I told you all about those measurements. And why I'm doing them. And why I'm keeping it quiet for now."

"Sure."

And so he had. He was scouring the galaxies for a special star.

For *the* star.

The one that would ensure the future of New Earth if the worst happened and its orbit continued to deteriorate.

Rez didn't speak for a few seconds; he seemed to be deciding on precisely the right words that would explain what was going on. Instead of just staring at him, though, Violet reviewed in her mind what he'd told her about his secret quest. And why the survival of New Earth might very well depend upon it.

New Earth had been created a decade ago as a replacement for Old Earth, because by the twenty-third century, the original planet was in ruins. Old Earth's rivers and oceans were poisoned, its soil was contaminated by radioactivity left over from the reckless torrent of bombs, and its landscapes were scraped raw and left to fester. Birds had been erased from its skies. Animal life had dwindled to a few skeletal, desperate species that scavenged for scraps. A few people remained behind on Old Earth, but most of the population had been transported to New Earth.

New Earth was a second chance for humanity. Its orbit was sustained by a system of magnets, wind turbines, and cold fusion. It was a beautiful tabula rasa, a blank canvas upon which a new generation—the generation of Violet and Rez and their friends—was writing its own destiny, creating a future as fresh and clear and promising as a sunrise on New Earth. It wouldn't be defined by the selfish, self-destructive generations that had preceded it back on Old Earth.

Lately, though, during his duties as NESA director, Rez had noticed a troubling trend: New Earth's orbit might be gradually but steadily failing. Which meant that, one day, it would tumble out of the sky, plummeting to Old Earth. The end of New Earth would mean the death of millions of people.

The scenario was so catastrophic that at first Rez couldn't believe his own calculations. He had measured again and again. Checked and double-checked and triple-checked. He ran simulations and projections. Once, in frustration, he even banged his fist on the side of his computer as if to joggle it back to its senses. In a film from the mid-twentieth century, he'd seen somebody do that to a primitive device called a TV set when the picture got fuzzy.

Rez did all that because it seemed impossible to him that nobody else had figured this out. Nobody else saw it coming.

But it was true. He was New Earth's Paul Revere.

New Earth was such a great success—its creation had saved an entire *planet,* after all—that nobody questioned anymore the spectacular technology that had enabled it. They had all grown a little lazy, he suspected, and a little complacent. No other scientist had noticed the terrible fate that lay hidden in the numbers—a future that didn't change, no matter how many times Rez banged his fist on the side of his computer.

I mean, I know I'm brilliant and all, he'd told Violet, *but I'm not the* only *brilliant guy who ever lived. Somebody else sees this too, right?*

Finally, Rez had come around to believing his own calculations. He wasn't ready to share what he knew until he had a solution—but was ready to work.

So at night, Rez combed the skies, quietly but steadfastly, looking for a star. A star that resembled the Earth's sun. A star that would likely have an Earth-like planet orbiting it. Assisted by Mickey, he investigated the light coming from tens of thousands of stars, star by star, to see if the star's light was broken—if, that is, its light wobbled. The wobble would mean that the star was being tugged by the gravitational pull of an orbiting planet.

Such a planet might someday be their new home.

"Okay," Violet said, "so I know you spend every spare minute in here measuring starlight. But what does that have to do with Rachel?"

"Rachel had a chip."

"Of course Rachel had a chip." Violet was impatient, and it showed in her voice. Everyone had an Intercept chip. Until two years ago, the law on both New and Old Earth had mandated the insertion of a tiny receptor in every citizen. Through it, the Intercept could access a person's feelings, first snatching them up and archiving them, and then, if the individual needed to be controlled, sending them back again. The memory of an emotional event—the loss of a parent or a friend, a moment of pain or terror or humiliation—could incapacitate even the strongest personality.

"Right," Rez said. "And when somebody's cremated, the chip stays intact. Same with a replacement hip or knee or arm or leg. Or artificial heart."

Violet nodded. She also winced a bit and wondered why Rez wasn't wincing, too. Why discuss this? She didn't like to think of Rachel that way—as a small, lifeless body, as a bundle of organs and assorted parts, summarily reduced to ash. It was too gruesome. Too sad.

"I still don't see—"

"*That,*" Rez said, interrupting her, "was the signal we picked up this morning while analyzing the starlight. It was a transmission. From Rachel's chip."

Now Violet stared at him. Only one word existed amid the vast universe of words that was an appropriate response to what he'd just told her. And that was the word she uttered:

"Impossible."

"Clearly not."

"But you sent those ashes into space."

"I did."

"So how—"

"That's where the transmission came from. From—best guess—a spot about a dozen light-years beyond the Milky Way galaxy. It showed up on one of the old Intercept channels. I'd repurposed that channel for my star hunt." He shrugged.

"Seemed like a good idea. The Intercept was gone. Those channels are like a bunch of old, abandoned roads that nobody uses anymore. Might as well put them to use. No more Intercept signals will be coming through them, ever again. Or so I thought."

Violet blinked. Suddenly, she was swimming furiously again in that overfull vat of question marks.

"Rez," she said. "I'm not trying to be rude here. I can see you're upset. But I don't have the slightest idea what you're trying to tell me. I mean, are you saying that Rachel is *alive*?"

He gave her a look of pure, Rezian disdain. "Alive? Of course not. My sister drowned a year ago on Old Earth. I made a positive ID of the body."

"So the signal you picked up was from . . . ?"

"Rachel's chip. The chip that survived her cremation."

"But the signal was *transmitted* here. Somebody *sent* it. How can that be? If she's—" Violet paused. She didn't want to say the word. But she had no choice. "If she's dead, then how can the record of her emotions have gotten here? Who's *experiencing* the emotions? And who's sending them? And how—"

"I don't know, Violet. I only know that my sister's Intercept feed just showed up on my computer." He jabbed an index finger toward his screen. "Take a look."

Violet leaned in. She and Rez had once shared a cubicle in Protocol Hall. Their job was to monitor the Intercept feeds back when the technology was still operational, when it was still a part of everyday life on New Earth.

Thus she knew what she was looking at. A moving strip across the bottom of the screen was alight with little orange numbers. Changing by the second, the numbers seemed to zip, shimmy, and twirl, like an agitated chorus line. She knew what they were: the algorithms that constituted the heart of the

Intercept as it riffled through millions of memory-images and selected the one most pungent and persuasive, finding the emotion most likely to induce a desired behavior.

The rest of Rez's screen was occupied by a fuzzy, grainy, pretty much indecipherable picture of . . . what?

Violet leaned still closer. She couldn't quite make it out.

Her cheek almost bumped Rez's shoulder. She was aware of how close to him she was right now.

She squinted. She saw a scattering of black dots like a pointillist painting, but the overall picture was so blurry that she couldn't figure out what she was staring at.

And then, all at once, she *did* know.

"It's a graduation ceremony," Violet said softly.

"It was the day Rachel graduated from law school," Rez clarified. "One of the best days I ever shared with her." Violet had the unmistakable impression that a great deal of emotion was passing through her friend's body right now, wave upon wave. "She was ten years old," he went on in a gentle, faraway voice that was not like anything that Violet had ever heard come out of Rez before. It had pride in it, and affection, too, and something else.

Tenderness, Violet decided to call it.

Tenderness? From Rez?

"Youngest graduate in the history of New Earth," he added, "and she graduated at the top of her class. It was a beautiful spring afternoon. See? Those little black dots—those are her classmates in their black robes and mortarboards. This is Rachel's memory of the day. We're remembering it, right along with her. The old Intercept channel is picking up the signal from her chip."

Violet's confusion was only growing.

"But . . . but she's dead, Rez," she said. This time she said the word without hesitation. She was too flummoxed to find a more sensitive way to phrase it. "Rachel's not alive anymore. How can she be remembering *anything*? I mean, remembering takes a consciousness, right? And Rachel is . . . well, she's gone."

"You're right. She's gone. Gone forever." Rez twirled his seat to face her, so fast that he almost knocked her down. His voice wasn't mushy-soft anymore. It was strong and determined. The tears had vanished. He'd recovered his poise. "But her Intercept chip is still very much alive. And it's trying to tell us something. Something important."

Violet took a second or so to let the awe wash over her. She still had a gazillion questions—give or take—for him.

"So why is this happening?"

"I *told* you," Rez said with a flicker of impatience. He didn't like to stop and explain things, Violet knew, and when you were as smart as Rez, you were always having to stop and explain things to people who didn't get them quite as fast as you did. Or get them at all. "Rachel's chip wasn't destroyed when she was cremated. It's out there in space. The emotions that the Intercept gathered and stored in her chip are coming through on the old channel."

"That's the *how*. My question is, *why*?"

Rez frowned. "Science doesn't do *why*. The *how* is hard enough."

He could definitely be a bit of a know-it-all. But in Rez's case, that was usually justified; he really did know it all. Or at least he knew a lot more than anyone else in Violet's circle of friends—except for Kendall Mayhew.

Kendall. Of course. That's who they needed to consult.

"We have to tell Kendall," Violet declared. "Right away. He'll know what to do."

"No."

"What? Come on, Rez. Kendall *invented* the Intercept. And he shut it down, too. If anybody can figure this thing out, it's Kendall."

"No," Rez repeated. "Point one—she was *my* sister. Not yours. And not Kendall's. So it's my decision. Point two—you promised not to talk about this unless I gave you permission. And I'm not giving you permission. We don't tell Kendall. Not yet."

"What are you waiting for?"

"I need to solve this for myself first. Then I'll bring Kendall into the loop."

"Fine," she said. She crossed her arms and let out a deep, frustrated breath. "So if you already knew what you were going to do—or *not* do, in this case—then why'd you call me in the first place? Why am I even here?"

Rez seemed a little surprised by her question.

"Because," he said.

"Because . . . ?"

"Because you're my friend. And because I needed to talk about it. To—okay, to process what I was feeling. And now I have."

Well, what could she say? They'd been through so much together. Along with the rest of the team, they'd faced death on that stormy night back on Old Earth a year ago. So when Rez played the friendship card, Violet was pretty much obligated to let go of her resentment and to let him handle this in his own way.

"Yeah," she said quietly. "I'm your friend."

"Good." A single nod, as if that settled things. "Now I've got to get back to the sky. It's already daylight. I don't have much time before the observatory staff starts arriving. Jerks."

"No kidding. Those conscientious employees, showing up on time for work—don't you just *hate* that?"

Rez ignored her sarcasm. Or maybe he hadn't even been aware of it. When he focused on his work, the rest of the world fell away.

He grabbed a lever and moved his chair closer to the screen. He punched a nine-number code into his console. In less than a second, Mickey was activated again. With a few clicks and a whirring sound, the AstroRob's pincers slid into the ports on the either side of his computer; he was synching himself with the computer's coordinates. There was a low, rising note as Mickey booted himself up to full power. That particular sound always reminded Violet of a cello string being tuned to match the rest of the orchestra. Her father had taught her to love classical music.

"So what's your next move?" she asked.

Rez didn't take his eyes from his computer screen as he replied, "Collate the data. Analyze the signal. Figure out where it's coming from—who's sending it and why. Come up with an explanation for what's going on."

"Are you sure there *is* an explanation?"

"There's always an explanation. That's called science."

Same old Rez, Violet thought.

His next sentence wasn't aimed at her. "Start another back trace on the signal origin."

"Roger that." Mickey's torso twisted as he executed a series of commands at his keyboard. He emitted a soft chuckle. "Wait. I forgot—who's Roger?"

Rez ignored the robot's little witticism. "I'll do a quick scan of the image from Rachel's graduation day to see if there are any clues about where—"

He stopped. He stared at Mickey.

Something was happening to the AstroRob. Mickey made a very weird noise, a noise so weird that the word *weird* didn't even begin to cover it, even though it was the only word Violet could think of, because she, too, was startled.

She had never heard anything like it before. It was loud and long and terrible. It was a cross between the grinding of teeth and the cracking of bones and the plop of a heavy object dropped in a pond, plus the sounds of a rocket engine revving up to full speed and an elephant's bellow. It was an ear-crunching, jaw-rattling combo of a shriek and a howl and a moan, blended with a husky cough and a loud beep and a harsh hiss and a high-pitched, siren-like *woo-woo-woo-woo-woo* sound that seemed to zip around the room in speedy little circles.

"What's going on?" Violet had to yell so that Rez could hear her over Mickey's caterwauling.

"I don't know." Rez jumped up and peered over his monitor at Mickey. The AstroRob was shaking wildly. Bits of steel stripping along the edges of his cylinders were popping loose because of the massively heavy vibration. The lights along his sides blinked on and off. "Mickey!" Rez called out. "What the hell are you—"

The robot ripped his pincers out of the computer. Dense yellow smoke erupted from the ports. His pincers were black and twisted as if they'd been melted by a tremendously high heat. The burning odor was so intense and so foul-smelling that Violet's eyes watered.

"Mickey," she yelled, "are you okay?"

The AstroRob didn't answer. The obnoxious noise had stopped, but he was still vibrating. He flung his pincers straight up in the air, the telescoping arms locked in tight parallel formation along his torso. He looked as if he might fly apart into a million separate pieces any second.

"Mickey?" Violet repeated.

By now, Rez had resumed his seat and was frantically busy at his computer keyboard, running every kind of diagnostic check he could think of on the AstroRob's mechanicals.

"Oh no," Rez said.

"What's going on?"

"It's a virus. When Mickey accessed his computer, it got him. It rushed into his systems."

"Will he be okay?"

Rez's voice was grim. "He's not built to withstand this kind of multipronged assault. It's as if you or I were hit with tuberculosis, pneumonia, pancreatic cancer, spinal meningitis, a hemorrhagic stroke, a heart attack, and a bad head cold all at the same time."

"But you can get rid of it, right? And repair and restart him?"

He shook his head. "This isn't a regular virus. It's one of the Stratton-Hemlepp Instability viruses."

"You mean it's—"

"Yeah. A jumping virus. I haven't precisely identified which strain yet. And there are hundreds." He continued to punch commands into his keyboard. "I think he extricated himself in time, but we won't know for a few minutes. His circuits are still in spasm."

Violet's mind was drenched by a dark wash of dread. In her computer science class in high school, the phrase *Stratton-Hemlepp Instability virus* was one that her teachers pronounced in hushed, fearful tones.

As computers had grown ever more sophisticated in the

latter stages of the twenty-first century, taking over bigger and bigger swaths of human endeavor, viruses, too, became more clever and diabolical. In 2252, two scientists named Melinda Stratton and Penelope Hemlepp, working in a tiny laboratory outside Paris, identified a "jumping virus"—one that could escape from the confines of written code and take on a tangible form, infecting real things and not just programs. Stratton and Hemlepp isolated several varieties of jumping viruses—one was known to grip, vine-like, the hardwired components of computer systems, and another manifested as a swarm of tiny insects that blocked the cooling vents of large energy-producing turbines, and yet another sent millions of tentacles probing like writhing snakes down the long tunnels containing essential infrastructure. The viruses could leap from machine to human and back again like some kind of evil ballerina doing a series of grand jetés across a stage.

The most damaging of the jumping viruses, Violet knew, was the one known as Graygrunge. It was a sticky, clinging film that rapidly replicated itself, spreading out and wrapping around a computer's circuitry, causing a wholesale destruction of data. Hemlepp had lost two fingers in her quest to isolate and identify Graygrunge. One day in the lab, it jumped from her keyboard to her hand. Had her colleague not been so quick-thinking—Stratton had raced over and used a scalpel to amputate the fingers around which Graygrunge had wrapped itself, fingers already black and dying from the lack of circulation—the virus would have spread across Hemlepp's body in a matter of seconds, killing her.

But maybe this was one of the lesser viruses. There was always a chance.

"I kind of wish he'd tell a stupid knock-knock joke," Violet murmured, while Rez worked relentlessly at his keyboard. "Just to let us know it's still *him* in there."

Mickey was shivering even more intensely now. His arms were still paralyzed. A gelatinous dribble of rusty-red drool yo-yoed down two of his cylinders. Violet knew it was just a liquefaction of the solvent used to lubricate his chassis, escaping from a shaken-apart seam, but she couldn't help but think of it as drool.

"You've got to stop the virus, Rez," she said. "You've got to save him."

Despite all of Rez's complaints, he was, Violet knew, secretly fond of Mickey. And terrified that his robot was toast.

"I'm trying to get a fix on what kind of jumping virus it is," Rez replied, talking fast and typing even faster. "So I can unleash targeted deflection codes."

His fingers seemed to merge with his keyboard as he blasted through the emergency protocols. Rez's forehead was tilted so close to the screen that Violet half wondered if he intended to ram his way right through it. That way, he could dive in and grasp the virus by its roots and destroy it with a wild, *take*-that-*you-bastard* yank.

"It's spreading too fast," he muttered a few seconds later. "It went from the computer to Mickey himself, and now it's flooding the main circuits, because Mickey had total access to the observatory's systems. I've got a real fight on my hands just trying to keep it isolated here in the observatory. If it leaps into the computers handling environmental controls—things like atmosphere and water filtration and orbit maintenance—we're basically screwed."

"Is there anything I can do to help?"

"No. Wait—yes. Yes, there is. When I initiate the tracker

protocol, I need you to watch the screen. Find the third number from the left in the fifth line from the bottom. It'll pop up on my screen in about seven seconds. I need to monitor the deflection codes and can't keep a close eye on the screen."

"Got it."

His fingers flew even faster across the keyboard. Numbers tumbled across the screen. "Protocol initiated."

The moment the numbers stopped spinning, Violet spotted the third one from the left in the fifth row from the bottom.

"Seventeen," she called out.

Rez's face clouded over. "Damn," he said softly.

"So that's bad?"

"That's bad." He swallowed hard. "It means the virus is heading for the old tunnels. The ones that used to start out under Protocol Hall. And from there, it's a straight shot into the operational core of New Earth."

Violet took a deep breath. She didn't know much about computers, but she knew about optimism and how it could help things.

"Well, look on the bright side," she said. "At least it's not Graygrunge."

Rez's fingers paused over the keyboard. He looked up at her. His eyes were filled with the bright fever of focused intensity.

And they were filled with something else, too, an emotion she wasn't used to seeing there:

Fear.

"Thing is, Violet, I'm between 96.8 and 97.4 percent certain that that's *exactly* what it is."

Graygrunge

The tunnels.

Violet shuddered anew each time the words formed in her mind. She and Rez had arrived here mere seconds ago, and she was already creeped out.

If anybody ever needed raw material for a nightmare, this would be a great place to start, she thought grimly. *The tunnels.*

She'd been in this dank, dark, and altogether unpleasant place before. She knew what it looked like and felt like. But knowing those things didn't make the *ick* factor any less intense. If anything, it worked in the other direction—because she knew that as bad as it was in the beginning, it was only going to get worse.

A lot worse.

"Rez?" she whispered.

"Yeah. What?"

"Nothing."

She'd just wanted to hear his voice, to reassure herself that the hunched-over shape that moved a few steps ahead of her was really Rez and not, say, some ghostly hump of something-or-other that was going to turn around any second and devour her.

Devour me. Riiiiight, she chided herself as a little spurt of self-loathing sizzled on her overheated brain. *Drama queen alert.*

She shuddered and pushed forward. If Rez could do this, then so could she.

They were moving through the series of underground tunnels that, once upon a time, had housed the hardware that ran the Intercept. Up on the surface of New Earth, Protocol Hall didn't exist anymore; Violet and Kendall had destroyed it, because it was the headquarters of the Intercept.

But the tunnels were still here. They were dark and silent now, but they were very much present, stretching for mile after mile beneath the streets of New Earth. The tunnels needed to stay intact to preserve the geological stability of New Earth.

The computers in these tunnels weren't hooked to the Intercept anymore—they weren't hooked to anything—and so even if they had been operational, which they weren't, they posed no danger.

But a place could be basically harmless and *still* scare the bejesus out of you.

The corridor was dramatically dim and insistently chilly. The air smelled rusty and pungent. The faraway sound of dripping water—ka-*pock* . . . ka-*pock* . . . ka-*pock*—was like an annoyingly unanswerable question, asked over and over and over again by a bored four-year-old.

Lining both sides of the narrow tunnel, one of a dozen radiating out from a central access point like the spokes of a giant wheel, were the gray, blank-eyed faces of deactivated computers.

Back in his lab, Rez had tracked the path of Graygrunge from Mickey's computer to its most likely destination:

Right here. Here in the tunnels that constituted a pallid subterranean layer beneath the shining surface of New Earth. From this location, Graygrunge could infect all the systems of New Earth—because back when the Intercept was active, it had been attached to every aspect of the infrastructure, tied to every computer.

And so Rez had torn himself away from the thing he most wanted to do—that is, get to the bottom of the mysterious signal from Rachel's chip—to race to the tunnels, with Violet at his side, in hopes of heading off Graygrunge.

They had arrived minutes ago, after a headlong dash across the city. On the way, Rez had sent a console alert to the rest of the team: Shura, Kendall, and Tin Man. He needed backup. He outlined his plan to them on his console.

He and Violet had clambered quickly down the long, skinny steel ladder, jumping from the last rung onto the stone floor of the central access point. The moment their feet touched bottom, they heard, over their heads, the small square access panel automatically sliding shut again, an ominous-sounding *vvvvv-whumpfff.* Instantly, the tender ray of daylight that had guided their progress down the ladder was wiped out.

"Ever been here before?" Rez asked in a hushed tone as they crept along the corridor.

"Twice."

"Twice?"

"Yeah. Both times were with my dad. When I was a little girl. The first time was when he'd just installed the Intercept. It was *so* exciting. They'd finished digging the tunnels and putting all the computers in. My dad had to inspect the job. The second time was right before he ordered the shutdown. He wanted to say goodbye. It was a really sad day for him. He'd thought the Intercept would be his legacy."

"Guess it sort of is, right?" Rez said. "But not in the way he thought."

"Maybe." She didn't want to talk about that. Not with Rez. Not with anybody. "Anyway, the point is, I'm not a rookie."

Which means I ought to be used to this by now, Violet scolded herself. *My heart shouldn't be pounding. My palms shouldn't be all sweaty and gross.* Yet she was barely able to keep her fear at a reasonable level as she scrambled to stay close to him.

"This way," he declared, directing them. "We're just about there."

A minute passed. Her tension level kept inching up.

"A few years ago," Violet said, searching for a topic with which she could distract herself from her agitation, "this place was the nerve center of the Intercept. Running 24-7. Sending out all those Wi-Fi signals. And there we were, in our workstations way up in Protocol Hall, monitoring the Intercept feeds."

But it was this place—not Protocol Hall—that was the true soul of the Intercept, the place where the computers buzzed and hummed, collecting and then deploying emotions.

Now it was . . . nothing. Just an invisible library of lost echoes. Just a series of corridors packed tight on both sides with cold, silent, shut-down machines that ran, shoulder to shoulder to shoulder, across mile upon mile upon mile, under the streets of New Earth.

"Yeah," Rez said. "Pretty wild. Okay, so we need to keep the talk to a bare minimum now. We're close. My tracker says Tunnel Four. And Graygrunge is tricky. It'll pick up on atmospheric changes from spoken words—the extra carbon dioxide when we exhale. And it'll slither away."

"So the plan is to sneak up on it."

"Bingo."

"Got it."

She knew the reason why Graygrunge had fled here: to take advantage of the central access to every computer system on New Earth. But it was aided by the fact that the tunnels were deserted. Nobody watched them anymore. Why should they? When the Intercept was abandoned, these tunnels were abandoned, too.

Violet shivered again. The moment she had realized that this was her third time down here, she'd made a pledge to herself:

Let's try really, REALLY hard to make sure there's not a fourth.

The low ceiling meant that she and Rez had to walk in an uncomfortable, bent-over way. They had to contort themselves into an awkward crouch and still somehow keep driving forward.

The only light came from the illumination app on Rez's console, which he'd turned to its lowest setting.

In a few seconds, he'd have to click it off. They couldn't use a light for very long for the same reason they had to keep the chitchat to a minimum: to stay a step ahead of the wily Graygrunge. It recoiled from light, just as it did from sound. If you hunted it down with a bright light, it would scurry back inside the crevices between the machines, replicating itself wildly as it went, wrapping itself around every gear and sprocket and belt and hose and fitting that it flitted past, choking them off, squeezing them until they became misshapen nubs of uselessness.

The only possible strategy of capture was to ambush a hunk of Graygrunge and blast it with the special jumping-virus retardant that Shura had been working on. It was still in the beta stage, but they'd have to take the chance.

Risks abounded. A too-broad blast might ignite a stray spark and start a fire down here, which would be disastrous. So they would have to be patient and delicate as they hunted Graygrunge, and then, once they'd found it, they would have to turn right around and be the opposite: strong and even brutal when they zapped it back into a dormant stage.

And we have to be and do all those things, Violet reminded herself with a tremor of anticipatory panic, *in total darkness.*

Once Rez shut off his console light, they would have to track Graygrunge using only his instincts and expertise about where it might be hiding. He had dealt with at least four previous outbreaks of Graygrunge that Violet knew about and probably several more that she didn't. Yet this was the first time Graygrunge had made it all the way into the tunnels.

Violet put a hand on her belly. She'd never admit it to Rez—she'd never admit it to anyone—but she had a stomachache from the anxiety.

He lifted his console light to check a small round plaque. It was affixed to the stone wall in a slender gap between two computers:

TUNNEL NO. 4

"Okay," he said. He was still murmuring, and his voice sounded like a faint rustling of papers instead of a human being trying to communicate with another human being. "We're all set. Everything good with you?"

"Fine." She wasn't fine. But she could do this. She hated the idea of weakness.

"Just keep walking in a straight line," he whispered. "Whatever you do, don't touch *anything.* Not even slightly. Keep your arms at your sides."

"Okay."

"I mean it. This is wicked, wicked stuff. All it takes is the slightest contact. If you so much as brush past one of these machines, you'll be making an instant bridge. Machine to skin. They don't call it the jumping virus for nothing."

"Understood. Hey, do the others know that?"

"Of course. Shura's in charge. She'll brief them." His voice grew determined without gaining any volume. "We're going to trap the damned thing in a vise grip. They're coming in through a different tunnel. When we've got it cornered, we'll let loose with Shura's virus retardant. Blast the sucker straight to hell."

"Great."

"Getting ready to go dark," Rez said. He dropped his voice even lower. "Counting backward from three."

"Ready."

"Three."

She took a deep breath.

"Two." Rez's voice sounded a trifle shaky. Was he as nervous as she was? Violet hoped not. She was nervous enough for both of them.

"One." He clicked off his console.

The darkness fell like a solid object, something dense and heavy and edgeless.

A skittering sound.

A rattling sound.

The sounds reminded Violet of leaves being blown along the street in autumn. The engineers who had concocted New

Earth had been careful to add all the familiar accoutrements of Old Earth, especially things like seasons. She'd grown up with the sound of fallen leaves being pushed by the wind, and that was what she heard now.

Except that it wasn't leaves. She knew what it was:

Graygrunge.

The virus was all around them, darting into the computers like a fluttering phalanx of snakes' tongues, probing and elongating. The computers were just shells now, but they were conduits to all the working computers on New Earth, and Graygrunge was quickly colonizing them. Each time she and Rez took a step, she imagined that she could feel Graygrunge oozing forward right along with them, and then a bit more after that. It seeped and it scuttled and it spread. It reached and it engulfed.

A few seconds ago, Rez had risked talking so that he could warn her again: *Don't touch the computers.* Even the slightest physical contact with a computer would allow Graygrunge to slip out of the machine and infiltrate a human body, sliding through the veins, encircling the organs, shutting down vital systems, just as it could shut down a computer's vital systems.

The thought of Graygrunge rooting around inside her was so repugnant to Violet that her toes curled up in disgust.

She was vaguely aware of Rez moving in front of her. She could hear his breathing.

Just keep going, she told herself.

Just keep going.

Just keep—

Violet yelped. She didn't scream—that would've been embarrassing—but she yelped, sending out a sort of high-pitched blurt. She had bumped up against something solid and big.

"Watch out," Rez whispered sharply. "You almost knocked me over. Pay attention to where you're going."

She might be scared out of her mind, but she didn't like his tone. "Well, I can't *see* you," she whispered back. "And why'd you stop, anyway?"

"Because we're here. The rendezvous point. We've got to wait for— *Hold on.*" Rez sucked in a breath. Violet's eye was drawn to what she guessed was the approximate spot where he held his console. No light flashed, but she was sure she'd heard a very, very, very soft click from it. The click was a signal from the rest of the team.

It meant that they had taken up their positions in the next tunnel over.

Violet still couldn't see anything, but she could imagine what must be happening: With a series of featherlight taps, Rez was sending information on his console to Shura.

Violet was still miffed at the way he'd snapped at her. And then she had a quick epiphany: From the moment Rez had scolded her, she'd forgotten all about her fear. He'd taken her mind off it. Being pissed at him was a great distraction. She could tell him later to cut it out. For now, it had done its job.

Thanks for being a jerk, Rez.

She was ready to fight Graygrunge.

Another soft click emanated from Rez's console.

"That's the signal from Shura," he murmured. "They're ready."

"What should I do?" Violet asked. She'd suddenly realized that she was totally in the dark—in more ways than just the obvious one. Rez and Shura had made their plans silently, through console keys. "I don't have an assignment. I'll just hang back and let you guys get on with it."

"Oh, you've got an assignment," Rez said.

"Like what?"

"Like being the decoy. The thing that preoccupies Graygrunge so that we can get a clear shot at it."

"But how can I be the—"

Before she'd finished her question, she felt Rez's hand on her arm. He pulled her to one side—not powerfully, in a way that would have hurt her, but just enough so that she momentarily lost her balance. Her back bounced against one of the computers lining the tunnel wall.

At the instant of contact, she felt something slimy and cold poking into her shoulders. It drilled into her skin, sending forth tiny shoots like a budding plant.

Graygrunge.

"Rez—what the *hell*—" Violet sputtered the words while she twisted around to slap at her back, trying to get rid of the grotesque virus.

"NOW!" Rez roared into his console.

A powerful blast of light suddenly flooded the tunnel, followed by an insanely loud noise that sounded to Violet like a thousand air hoses disgorging their contents all at once.

"AGAIN!"

A second blast of light and another heavy assault of noise made the whole tunnel vibrate wildly as if somebody had picked it up and were shaking it wildly just to hear the rattle. Dense gray-black smoke boiled up, covering the corridor from top to bottom. A flurry of tiny shrieks from the stricken virus careened against the walls and ceiling, bouncing and spinning.

And then came a stone cold silence.

Violet felt the slimy thing sliding out of her back; it reminded her of a strand of pasta being sucked up by a hungry kid. As it withdrew, it made a small popping sound like a soap bubble pierced by a pin. For a moment, she was too grossed out even to demand an explanation. She just stood there, shivering in disgust.

Rez's console beeped.

"Rez?" It was Shura's voice. "Did we get it?"

"Got it," he said. He switched on his illumination app. The only visible evidence of the Thing Formerly Known as Graygrunge was a small puddle of gray liquid on the floor of the tunnel. In another few seconds it, too, was gone, evaporating before their eyes. "All clear, Shura."

Now Violet did try to speak. But she couldn't. Not right away. She was shocked and angry and confused, and the words stuck in her throat.

Rez reached out for her arm. She flinched.

"Don't touch me," she said, almost growling the words. "I'm so mad at you, I can't—I can't—" She had to pull herself together in order to go on. "I can't believe you did that. You let that—that *thing*—attack me. I can't . . . I'll never—"

"Violet. Come on."

"You *used* me."

"I didn't use you. Well, I mean, I guess I did, but it's the same way I used Shura and Tin Man and Kendall, right? We're a team. Everybody had a job to do. Yours was to distract Graygrunge so we could deploy the retardant."

Rez's console was still connected to their friends in the next tunnel over, which meant they could hear the conversation. Kendall's voice came through the console. He sounded concerned and—this might have been her imagination, but it made sense—slightly guilty.

"Violet, are you okay?"

Instead of answering him, Violet posed a question of her own. "Did you know about this, Kendall? Did you know what he was going to do?"

"First tell me if you're okay."

"Yeah. Yeah, sure. I'm fine. After I take about ten thousand showers to get any lingering traces of that creepy crud off of me, sure. I'll be great."

"Good," Kendall said. "Rez said you wouldn't be hurt, but I was still worried."

Violet glared at Rez while she spoke carefully in the direction of his console, wanting to get maximum value from her sarcasm. "So you were worried, were you? Really, *really* worried? Then why'd you let him do it to me in the first place?"

"We had to get Graygrunge to focus on something else," Kendall explained. "Or we'd never have a clean shot. Rez said it was the only way, and he's the Graygrunge expert. He said we had to make it go after another target."

"Meaning *me.*" Violet closed her eyes. She couldn't get rid of the awful feeling of Graygrunge slinking along her skin, poking between her shoulder blades.

"Yeah. Meaning you," came Kendall's soft, regretful answer. "We couldn't warn you beforehand. And you know why, right? You would've automatically steeled yourself against the virus. Even if you didn't intend to. Anybody would have. And Graygrunge would've sensed your resistance and held off. It's canny that way. Our only chance was having you be taken by surprise. Letting Graygrunge show itself when it tried to infiltrate you. Then we could kill it, and you'd be safe. We'd all be safe."

"Great theory," Violet muttered. "I just love being the bait in the little scheme you guys cooked up." She looked around the tunnel. Even without the threat of Graygrunge, this was a dismal, depressing place, dense with shadow, reeking of leftover smoke. It was like every bad dream she'd ever had, rolled into one.

And yet . . .

And yet the truth was, Violet could feel her anger and her fear receding, inch by inch. She didn't want to let her friends off the hook just yet, but the bad feeling was being gradually replaced by another emotion entirely: a sort of *satisfaction*. Yeah, that was it: satisfaction. She'd helped get rid of Graygrunge. Three of her friends—Shura, Rez, and Kendall—were supersmart, and so they were usually the ones who got to solve the problems and save the world. Violet was bright, and she tried hard, but she was no genius.

For once, she told herself, *the regular girl gets the win. Yay, me.*

It wasn't the kind of thing she could say out loud, and it might never happen again, but right here, right now, she was the hero. Without her, the greasy tentacles of Graygrunge would still be whipping through these tunnels, on their way to the operational heart of New Earth, to do catastrophic damage. But *with* her, the menace had been thwarted.

"I wish there'd been another way to divert the virus. I'm sorry," Rez said. Repeating an apology was a very un-Rez-like thing to do, but then again, this had been a day of firsts. "That's what I really wanted."

Violet shrugged. "Yeah, okay. Fine. You know what *I* really want? To get the hell out of these tunnels. Right now."

4

Why Did the Chicken Cross the Galaxy?

Twenty minutes later, when Shura, Tin Man, Kendall, and Rez walked into the observatory's conference room for the debriefing, this is what they saw: an AstroRob lying flat on his back in the middle of the table.

But that wasn't the weirdest part.

Even odder was the fact that Violet was up on the table, too, kneeling right next to Mickey. She had left the tunnels ahead of her friends, pledging to meet them back here; she had to pick something up first, she said. And now she was putting her plan into action. She was using her console to scan the contents of a warped and stained and battered-looking Old Earth book entitled *1,001 Jokes & Riddles for All Occasions* into his main receptor portal. The portal's edges were jagged and fire-blackened.

That constituted only a small portion of his injuries. The AstroRob was in terrible shape. No lights, no perky hum. The linked cylinders that comprised his body were crinkled and askew. Clumps of steel sheathing hung off him like loosened roof tiles after a rainstorm.

"Um, Violet?" Shura said. She had led the others into the room. She was wearing her white tunic, which meant it was a doctor day. Shura was a painter as well as a physician and researcher. On artist days, she wore a paint-spattered tunic. On doctor days, it was a starched white one. "What are you *doing,* exactly?"

"Trying to bring him back to life." Violet turned a page, repositioning her console to a point midway between book and portal. "Graygrunge infiltrated him. If I can remind him of something he loves, he might come around. And Mickey loves to tell jokes. More than anything."

"Mickey?" Shura said, a question mark in her voice.

"It's a nickname."

By now, the others—Kendall, Tin Man, and, at the far end, Rez—had taken their seats around the large oval table. Its blue-tinted top was so shiny that it looked like a precision-cut sample of New Earth sky. This room was where Rez conducted his meetings with the observatory staff. Through the tall glass walls lay a marvelous view of New Earth, its soaring towers and its silver highways, its meticulously planned beauty.

Rez looked at the book in Violet's hand. He made a face. "Hard to believe people ever relied on those things instead of consoles."

Violet ignored him. She turned to the last page of *1,001 Jokes & Riddles for All Occasions* to finish the scan. Her father had maintained a large library of old-fashioned books, but his were literary classics. "I came across this one on Old Earth a few years ago. In the ruins of a library," she said. "Not sure why I kept it, but I'm glad I did. Thought a few bad jokes might make Mickey perk right up. It's a long shot but worth a try. I'm just about finished with the data transfer."

Tin Man piled his big black-booted feet up on the conference table. It was rude, which was why he did it. Tin Man had been born on Old Earth and never wanted anyone to think he'd been tamed by New Earth's rules of decorum. A purple earring drooped from one ear. He shaved his head just often enough to keep the stubble looking sharp and menacing. He'd decorated his arms and his neck in a dense swarm of tattoos. He did all of those things, Violet knew, just to reinforce the point: He was Old Earth, all the way.

"A robot who likes jokes?" Tin Man asked with a snort of disdain.

"Yeah." Violet's tone was firm. "I think it's pretty cool." She was feeling protective of Mickey and didn't want anybody to make fun of him. Especially not while he clung to life by a couple of singed wires.

Kendall peered more closely at the AstroRob. "Looks like a lost cause. I think it's time for a trip to the recycle pod." Kendall was lean but muscular, with short dark hair and gray eyes that watched everything. He was the only one around the table who sat up straight in his chair. He was the chief of police, and he never let his posture forget it. "Where'd he come from, anyway? And why keep him around?"

Violet glanced at Rez. Was it time to tell them about his secret search for a promising star and how it had led him to find Rachel's chip?

With a barely perceptible motion of his head, Rez answered her: *No.*

Okay, Violet thought. His secret, his call.

But she still had to deal with Kendall's question. "Oh, you know. It's . . . um . . . spare parts for the observatory's other AstroRobs." Technically not a lie—because if Mickey didn't recover, that's exactly what he *would* be.

Kendall nodded. He'd already lost interest in the robot and was checking his console feed. Tiny holographic jewels—black, brown, white, red, yellow, blue, and intricate blends thereof—rose at different rates from the console face, creating a sort of iridescent ballet. A slight tap on the desired jewel opened a message, viewable only by the console-wearer. Onlookers saw a blur.

Rez cleared his throat. He was ready to start.

Violet shoved the book in her back pocket. She patted Mickey's shoulder—or what might be reasonably construed as a shoulder—and hopped down from the table. To her dismay, he remained comatose. She pulled out a chair between Shura and Kendall. She looked around the room.

She'd been here several times before. In her role as a senator, she often had to huddle with Rez and his staff to discuss budget overruns and research priorities—gatherings that she didn't enjoy but had to somehow get through without yawning or doodling on her console. Violet had originally thought that politics would be about helping people, and sometimes it was, but—surprise!—it turned out to be mostly about meetings and signing documents.

On a high shelf in the corner was an orrery—an ornate, beautiful instrument made of wood and tin and brass that represented the movements of the planets of the solar system. It had been created centuries ago on Old Earth. Tin Man had rescued it from an abandoned Old Earth museum when he was a small boy. Last year, he had presented it to Rez as a tribute to Rachel. Tin Man had lost a little sister, too—Molly, back on Old Earth—and he knew what Rez was going through, even if Rez never acknowledged his pain out loud.

Violet had recently realized just how much she and her friends were linked by their losses: She and Shura had each said a final goodbye to a parent. Rez and Tin Man grieved for Rachel and Molly. And Kendall had lost his brother, Danny.

It made it all just a little bit easier to bear, maybe, if the people around you knew what you were feeling without you having to say anything. You didn't have to worry about finding the right words. The words didn't matter. Only the feelings.

By now, it was early afternoon, and the sunlight gliding into the room seemed to make a special point of picking out the orrery first, as if it recognized an old friend and wanted to gift it with sparkle and mystery.

Violet was glad the orrery was here. She was very worried about Mickey, and for some reason she didn't understand, seeing the orrery cheered her up. It wasn't a computer or any other sophisticated, high-tech gadget that would fit in with the numberless wonders of New Earth. In fact, an orrery was about as basic and low-tech as you could get, with its primitive clockwork mechanics, its tiny hand-painted globes, its minute gears that softly whirred and gently clicked as they engaged, its round wooden pedestal. It was almost as anachronistic as a book. But it was always the first thing she looked at when she came into this room and the last thing she looked at when she left.

Rez addressed the table. "Status reports."

They examined their consoles. Virus control was Rez's domain, which was why no one questioned his authority. Had it been a medical or artistic issue, Shura would have taken the lead. Any law enforcement question was handled by Kendall and Tin Man. Political issues were automatically placed in Violet's lap.

"The final sweep of the tunnels," Kendall said, "revealed no residual traces of Graygrunge." A tiny green jewel rose from his console. He touched it, opening a screen that he quickly reviewed. "I did a quick sweep for other viruses, too. Negative. For now. But you never truly get rid of Graygrunge. It goes back into hiding. Lies in wait until the next chance it gets to attack."

"Like a human virus," Rez said.

That drew a frowning rebuke from Shura. "Not *like* a human virus," she said, making air quotes with her fingers around the word he'd used incorrectly. "It *is* a human virus. And it's a computer virus, too. As Stratton and Hemlepp proved, at this point, there's no essential difference anymore—at the cellular level, anyway—between the two. The transformation is complete."

"So how do you know when it's coming?" Tin Man asked. "I mean, we've cleared it out of the computer systems before. Any way to predict when an outbreak's imminent?"

"Not really," Shura replied. "It's opportunistic. The minute it senses a weakness, an opening, it strikes. And the triggers are always changing."

"Thanks goodness you developed that retardant," Violet said to her. "I hate to think what might happen if—"

"Can we move on?" Rez snapped, interrupting her. "Let's save the back-patting for later. Speaking of the retardant, Shura, how's our supply?"

"Low," she answered. "I'll have to start on a new batch right away."

Rez turned to Tin Man. "We got lucky, right? No alarms sent out to police or fire departments. Nobody was hanging around the entrance to the tunnels, wondering why a bunch of people suddenly pried off the hatch and dived in."

"Not a peep," Tin Man replied. "The tunnels are mostly forgotten these days. Just like the Intercept."

"Already?" Violet said.

Tin Man shrugged. "Doesn't matter if it was four years ago or four seconds ago. Ancient history. People are busy. They have other things to think about."

Rez rapped his knuckles on the table. He wanted them to get back to business.

"Tin Man, you always monitor the public channels, too, right? News feeds on consoles?"

"Nobody's mentioned it," he answered. "So far, so good."

"Okay. Let's keep it that way. I don't want people to know how often the jumping viruses actually show up. They'd freak out, for sure. If our computer systems crashed—which is what would happen if we didn't stop Graygrunge and the others—a lot of critical functions would be compromised. But so far, we've been able to contain the viruses when they attack. So let's make this our little secret. Agreed?"

There was a murmur of *Yeah, sure* and *Okay* from around the table. Plus Tin Man's *Whatever.*

"So . . . thanks," Rez said matter-of-factly and in an ice-cold, impersonal way.

The Rez way, Violet thought. He seemed a little too comfortable with secrets.

But then she realized that he'd stopped talking.

He was looking at the four of them. One by one. And not casually. Not as if they were just a glaze of faces that didn't matter to him except for when he specifically needed them.

No. He was really *looking* at them.

At Tin Man, whose nicked-up, tough-guy boots were still stacked on the tabletop and who was using a short penknife to dig a splinter out of his right palm.

At Shura, who was studying the recumbent robot and whose pale, round face had bunched into a frown as she imagined the internal schematics of the machine, trying to figure out how she might help restore him to a robot version of consciousness.

At Kendall, who was still checking his console every few seconds, tapping out replies to messages from his officers and keeping an eye on his news feed.

At me, Violet thought. Rez's gaze had finally alighted on her. She spotted something in his eyes that she'd only seen there a few times before, and only when he was interacting with Rachel:

Gratitude.

Violet felt as if she could, just for an instant, read Rez's mind and his heart.

These are my friends. I needed them this morning, and I called, and they came. It's only fair that I tell them what's going on. Either I trust them or I don't—and if I do, then they deserve to know.

"One more thing," Rez said, "before everybody takes off."

Violet gave him a brief, pleased nod. She was pretty sure of what he was going to say next.

No more secrets. Not the kind you keep from your friends, anyway. It was time to bring the others on board.

Now it was Violet's turn to do a quick scan of the room—at the faces gathered here, the faces of the people she cared about, the people she sometimes argued with and got mad at but that she'd faced danger with, and even death. And would again, in a heartbeat, if the need arose.

Get ready, guys, she thought. And even though she was worried about Mickey, she felt a flicker of excitement. *Here we go.*

Rez's Big Reveal

I know everybody's crazy busy," Rez declared, "and so I'll make this as brief as I can while not leaving out any essential aspects. For the past few months, I've been using the telescope here at the observatory to—"

Suddenly, the sad heap of almost-dead robot in the middle of the table performed a very undead-robot-like maneuver: He sent forth a sound that might best be described as a long, wheezy fart. It smelled of fried wires and overheated plastic.

Violet couldn't resist a small giggle.

"Wow," Shura said. "Kind of makes your eyes water."

"Yeah. Wow," Tin Man added, fanning the air in front of his face.

Rez waited. His silence had a subtext; clearly, he found the entire incident undignified and had decided to ignore it. When no more comments and no further fart-like emissions were forthcoming, he continued, "Anyway, I've been using the telescope on my own time to conduct a clandestine search for a planet that might be able to serve as a new location for New Earth. Our orbit is diminishing ever so slightly. Nothing urgent right now, but someday, it might be. I've been looking for an exoplanet that would suit our needs. The thing is, I didn't want to incite a panic. Same motive for covering up the Graygrunge attack.

"So I found an unemployed AstroRob—the unfortunate Mickey you see before you here—and started making an inventory of stars. We look at the light from star after star after star, trying to spot a wobble. Because the wobble means—"

"—that a planet is orbiting that star," Kendall said, finishing his sentence with an eagerness he couldn't hide. "The planet's orbit interrupts the light. It breaks the path of the starlight."

"That's exactly right." Rez nodded approvingly. "Before his accident, poor Mickey here even came up with a name for the kind of star we need. A broken star. A star whose radiance has been interrupted—or 'broken'—by an orbiting planet. And it was while I was searching for the exoplanet that I found her."

"Found who?" Tin Man asked.

"Rachel. She's back."

The room was still.

An instant later, it was the opposite of still as Kendall, Tin Man, and Shura all tried to talk at once, their voices clashing and tangling and overlapping.

Kendall's was the first to separate itself from the babble.

"What do you mean?" he asked.

"Just what I said," Rez replied. "It's Rachel."

"Rachel's dead." Kendall said it gently but firmly.

Violet recalled having made the same point herself earlier that morning, back in Rez's lab.

"Of *course*," Rez snapped at him, just as he'd snapped at Violet. "It's a signal from her Intercept chip, not Rachel *herself.* The chip's trying to communicate with us. I was attempting to pin down its origin point when Graygrunge showed up. My speculation is that Rachel's remains have reached a distant galaxy and were swept up in a meteor swarm, and then the swarm was rerouted by solar winds and then somehow the chip got separated. And now I'd like to get back to my work, so that I can—"

"Hold on." Tin Man's tone was skeptical. "Just a quick question here, Rez, before we go on."

"Ask away," Rez said.

"Okay, here goes. Are you nuts?"

Rez's reply was swift and sharp. "I am not *nuts,* as you so *charmingly* put it." He sent forth the words in a chilly voice. "And by the way, that's a totally insensitive term with which to refer to people with mental instabilities."

"Call 'em like I see 'em, pal."

"You don't know what you're talking about."

"I know enough not to jump to conclusions based on some silly signal. Which might be anything. From anywhere." Tin Man grinned sardonically. "Maybe you've been staring at the stars too long. Maybe you oughta try keeping your eyes right down here on New Earth for a change. Just like the rest of us."

"You're an idiot," Rez declared.

"Oh, yeah?"

"Yeah."

They glared at each other across the table, Tin Man with his muscles and his shaved head and his spider tattoos and his deliberately torn and raggedy Old Earth tunic, and Rez with his pallid, washed-out skin, which stayed that way because he spent too much time indoors squinting at a computer screen, and his messed-up hair and his mismatched tunic and trousers because he didn't give a damn what he wore.

Watching them, Violet wondered if this quarrel was more than just a simple bout of name-calling. When Rez brought up Rachel, Tin Man was forced to think again about Molly—and to cover up his pain with a show of bravado.

"You don't know *what* that signal is," Tin Man declared. "You could be making a big deal out of nothing."

And then, just as Rez was about to issue a snarling retort about Tin Man's intelligence—or the lack thereof—something happened:

Mickey woke up.

The AstroRob twisted. He shivered. A humming sound ensued, followed by a beep and a series of clicks. A light popped on, popped off, popped on again. This time it stayed on.

Rez and Tin Man forgot all about their argument. They leaned forward in their seats along with Shura and Violet.

Mickey made a noise that sounded like *dee-dee-dee-dee-dee-dee.* Then he made another noise that sounded like *eh-eh-eh-eh-eh-eh.* And yet another: *ya-ya-ya-ya-ya-ya.*

Hinging himself at what had been designed to resemble a waist, the robot sat upright and surveyed the room. He swiveled the flat side of his topmost compartment—the one designed to vaguely mimic a face—from side to side as he took note of the people around the table.

"Hey," Mickey said. "I've got a limerick."

"NO," Rez declared, his voice rising in protest. "I absolutely *forbid* it."

The AstroRob made a noise that had been calibrated to resemble a throat-clearing and then embarked upon a recitation in a singsong voice:

A daring young spaceship commander
Was nervous and just couldn't land her.
As his orbit diminished,
"I fear I am finished!"
He cried with incredible candor.

"That's great," Violet said. Pleased at Mickey's recovery, she laughed. "More!"

"It is *not* great," Rez muttered. "Do *not* encourage him."

Shura opened the portable medical kit that she kept in the breast pocket of her white tunic. She drew out three gossamer-thin threads attached to small triangular pieces sheathed in copper plating and used them to test Mickey's receptors. Finally, she aimed a penlight into the diagonal slashes in his top compartment. The perforations weren't actually eyes, of course, but their placement was intended to suggest them.

She lowered the penlight and clicked it off. "He's back," she concluded.

"Too bad," Rez said with a groan.

Mickey chuckled and started up again before Rez could intervene.

A rocketship captain must fly
Amid dangers of planet and sky.
Asked why he cavorts
Through space, he retorts:
"It's a whole lot of fun, that's *why!"*

"Fantastic!" Violet said. "Love this guy."

"Okay, that's enough." Rez tapped his console. "Rise and shine, Mickey. Time to get back to work." The AstroRob executed a complicated rolling maneuver that brought him to the edge of the table; the cylinders shifted and tilted, enabling him to slide off. He landed upright on the floor. The cylinders reassembled in their original position. "I'll be in my lab," Rez added, "trying to get to the bottom of that signal."

Tin Man mumbled. It sounded to Violet like *gut lump.*

Gut lump?

"What?" Rez said.

Now Tin Man sighed deeply. His pride was making it hard for him to say what he needed to say, which is why he'd mumbled it in the first place. "Okay, fine. *Fine.* What I said was, 'Good luck.' With finding the signal, I mean. I'm sorry I questioned you. It's just that when you mentioned Rachel, I started thinking about Molly, and thinking about Molly always makes me feel kind of—"

"No problem." Rez cut him off, but not in a mean, you're-a-dope way. It was more of a I've-got-to-get-to-work way. "I don't blame you for doubting this. It's pretty crazy stuff. All I know is that, somehow, Rachel's Intercept chip is still functioning."

"Could it be a false signal?" Kendall asked. "An echo, I mean?"

Rez frowned. "What?"

"An echo. From an original Intercept transmission—one that was collected and then deployed years ago, perhaps. Maybe it's not a new transmission. Just a repetition of an old one."

Rez pondered the idea. Kendall had invented the Intercept years ago in a laboratory on Old Earth, thus his ideas carried extra weight.

"I don't know," Rez finally said. "That's definitely a possibility. I need to get back to my computer and start running tests."

Violet made eye contact with Kendall. She had something she wanted to ask Rez, too, but she wasn't a scientist. So she hesitated. Kendall gave her an encouraging nod.

She took the plunge. "Hey, Rez. What about the exoplanet search? I thought that was pretty important, too."

"It is." He stood up abruptly. "But not as important as Rachel. So I'd better get to it."

"Need any help?" Kendall asked.

Of all the people present, Violet knew, Kendall was the only one with the technical expertise and raw brainpower to be of any service whatsoever to Steve Reznik. But she knew something else as well: Rez liked to work alone.

Well, except for his AstroRob. A necessary nuisance.

"I can handle it for now," he answered. "But thanks." He addressed the table at large. "I'll keep everybody posted on how it goes. And I know I don't have to say this, but I will, because it's so damned important. Just like with the Graygrunge attack, this has to stay confidential. Okay? Nobody talks about this *at all.* With anybody. For now, it stays in the group."

He looked around the room. Kendall nodded.

Tin Man grunted.

Shura murmured, "Okay."

Violet said, "You bet." Her voice had a slight edge to it, but not because she doubted the need for discretion. None of the others seemed to notice. She had a funny feeling in the pit of her stomach. It was a vague, fluttery wisp of a thing, a flicker of anxiety. Once more, something momentous was beginning to stir in their world, something extraordinary and exciting, but also challenging.

She sensed that they were about to make another great leap into the unknown—a place she loved and feared in equal measure.

6

Senator Crowley

When Violet awoke the next morning, she realized it was still there: the funny, fuzzy, flipping feeling in her stomach.

Maybe she was just hungry.

Now, that's *a problem I know how to solve,* she told herself, cheering up. *Even though I'm not a genius.*

She shuffled into the kitchen of her small apartment, the same one she'd had since she was sixteen and had left the home she'd shared with her father. The basic elements of the place were nothing special—living room, bedroom, bathroom, kitchen. Gray carpet, gray drapes, white walls. What made it extraordinary were Shura's paintings. Over the years, her friend had given her dozens. Some of them showed scenes from Old Earth, but not the blasted-out, radioactive, rubbed-raw parts. These depicted roller coasters and Ferris wheels suspended high over the deserted landscape, bits and pieces of the half-finished amusement park that Rez had dreamed of creating down there before a crisis had shut it down. Some were portraits of their friends: Kendall, Tin Man, Rez, Shura herself. And Molly and Rachel.

The artwork made Violet's apartment dazzling. Not because every single painting was beautiful—some of the paintings, in fact, were deliberately *not* beautiful—but because they were true. And truth was another kind of beauty, Violet had discovered. A beauty that went beyond pleasing shapes and pretty colors.

She wasn't thinking about art right now, however.

She was thinking about breakfast.

Hash browns and scrambled eggs sounded good, and so she waved a ReadyMeal across the blue rectangle embedded in the counter and fumbled around until she found a fork. When she was a kid, she'd visited the Technology Museum over in Mendeleev Crossing and was fascinated by a funny square box dating from the twentieth and twenty-first centuries called, if she remembered it correctly, a "microwave." It was hard for Violet to imagine a world in which you had to stick a meal into a black box and shut the door and wait several minutes for it to be done.

Sometimes she tried to picture a nineteen-year-old from back then—somebody a lot like herself. Did that person wonder about the future just as Violet wondered about the past? One person looking forward, the other person looking back?

Before she settled down at the table to eat, she touched a small red spot on the wall next to the window. The curtains parted, revealing a fine, sunny day. No surprise there. Most mornings on New Earth were fine and sunny. The truth was, they *all* could potentially be fine and sunny, because the specifics were created each morning at the Environmental Control Center right next to Violet's workplace, the Central Administration Building.

Color Blenders mixed the hues that determined the tint and texture of the sky. Atmospherics Specialists selected air temperature, wind direction and velocity, the barometric pressure. Subspecialists in the Weather Corps checked the algorithms and decided whether it would rain or not rain today, or snow or not snow, or if fog would roll in or not roll in. If a fair day came up on the rotation, they further decided whether the sunlight would be at full strength or whether it would be filtered through an assortment of clouds.

Variety was the key. Too many beautiful days in a row could be as dreary as too many overcast, drizzly ones. Violet's father had explained that to her when she was a little girl. She hadn't really understood it then—*Why can't it always be sunny and nice, Daddy?* she would ask him—but she understood the concept now. Sort of. She still longed for sunny days. Who wouldn't?

There was no dome over New Earth. A dome, Ogden Crowley had theorized, would come to feel oppressive. *Ants in a jar,* he'd said to Violet, explaining his reasoning. *That's how we would see ourselves.* Thus the environment was maintained through a system of massive magnets that delicately calibrated each aspect of life in this world suspended above Old Earth, echoing its orbit. The magnets were augmented by wind and solar power, as well as by the controlled chaos of nuclear fusion.

This had been Ogden Crowley's great inspiration: to create a world that was tethered to Old Earth but completely different from it, too. As Old Earth had sunk deeper and deeper into the morass of poisoned oceans and ruined cities and dead landscapes, many people had advocated the wholesale relocation of the population to a new planet. Mars topped everyone's list. But Violet's father fought that idea. *We need to maintain our sacred tie to the Earth,* he would declare, over and over again, in every forum that would have him. *Leaving for a new planet would be too much, too soon. The psychological trauma caused by a complete break with Earth would be devastating. Later, perhaps. After we've gotten used to a New Earth that hovers above the Earth we know*—then *we can make the move to an entirely different planet. But not now. Not yet.*

He had supervised the construction of New Earth, harnessing the brilliance he saw in people, a brilliance that the people themselves often weren't aware of until Ogden Crowley pointed it out. He inspired engineers to create stupendously effective new materials for New Earth's streets and structures; he challenged the physicists to perfect the staggeringly complex systems of magnets and hydraulics and fusion that would whip up the necessary energy to maintain the orbit; he rallied the population to share in his vision of a breathtakingly new civilization that prospered atop the old, dying one.

And then, to ensure that New Earth never fell victim to the forces that had doomed Old Earth—the madness and greed and bloodlust of too many of its people—Ogden Crowley installed the Intercept. That was his only stumble. And Violet had forgiven him. He had only been doing what he thought was right. Once he'd realized his mistake, he had shut it down, leaving its hollow shell: the long, dark tunnels that ran in straight lines from a central hub beneath the streets of New Earth, filled with unplugged computers.

And occasionally—she shivered at the memory—filled with Graygrunge, too.

While she ate, Violet checked the news feed on her console. Still no mention of yesterday's Graygrunge attack. Which was a good thing, because Rez was right: If the average citizen ever knew how close they came to disaster each time a jumping virus made its way into a computer system, the panic would spread like . . . *Well, like a jumping virus,* she thought ruefully.

She spooned up the last forkful of crunchy hash browns. She'd need the energy; she had a busy day ahead. Committee meetings; long, boring hearings; briefings by staff members. Reports to read and assimilate. Hands to shake. Papers to sign. Sometimes Violet looked at her life now—a life of responsibility and regimentation—and she wondered, *How the hell did I get here?*

A year ago, she was a half-bankrupt private detective well on her way to becoming a *fully* bankrupt one, staying out too late at night, dancing at her favorite club—Redshift—and drinking too many Neptunia Nodes in hopes of washing away her troubles. She was, according to what most people saw at the time, a mess. Not even her brush with death on Old Earth had made her change her habits.

But then six months ago, her father died, and something happened to Violet Crowley.

She grew up. Just like that. It had taken a little longer than it should have, probably, but she'd always been a late bloomer. Once her grief for her father had gone from being a fierce daily pain to a quiet now-and-then ache, she realized that she had a destiny to fulfill—a destiny that didn't have anything to do with running a detective agency.

She would carry on Ogden Crowley's legacy. She would make sure that New Earth continued to run smoothly, that decisions made by the government were in the best interests of all the citizens. And there was only one way to guarantee that her father's dreams for New Earth would stay true:

She had to become a politician herself. Work from the inside.

When she told her friends what she intended to do, they were shocked. Shura offered to check her for a concussion. Each time Violet turned around, there was Shura, trying to shine the penlight in her eyes. *I'm fine,* Violet would declare, more than a little annoyed at Shura's joke as she ducked away from that stupid light. Kendall tried to initiate long, late-night console conversations about it. *You've never worked in a big bureaucracy before, Violet,* he said multiple times. *But* I *have. And it's no fun. Everybody at the police department's got their own agenda. Trust me, it's a friggin' nightmare.* Tin Man was even blunter: *Girl, you're nuts.*

Violet had tried to reassure all of them that, um, yeah, she knew it wasn't going to be easy. But her mind was made up.

A senator had retired early. Violet asked President Shabir to appoint her to the seat, and he was happy to comply. The Crowley name was a glittering one on New Earth. When the term was up, she'd run for the seat. She'd win. No question.

Which would mean, of course, more meetings. More briefings. More reports to read. More staff members to confer with. More hands to shake.

Yet on some mornings—like this one—when she sat at her kitchen table and recalled those ragged, super-fun nights at Redshift and the crazy, totally irresponsible life she used to lead, Violet was aware of a small doubt in the center of her soul.

That doubt seemed to have grown just a little bit bigger since yesterday, because she'd been thinking a lot about Rachel.

Rachel had never had the chance to find out what her destiny was. What it should have been, that is.

Violet *did* have that chance—she was living it, right now—but she wasn't totally sure about the choice she'd made. How could you ever *be* sure?

How, that is, did you find the path you were supposed to be on?

She liked what politics *did*—that is, help people get what they needed. She simply didn't like what *she* had to do to make it happen:

Be a politician.

Her father had been a natural at it, but she wasn't. Not by a long shot. These days, she had to tamp down her normal inclination to argue and to lose her temper on a regular basis, storming off and slamming doors or firing off nasty console messages when she didn't get her way. She couldn't behave like that anymore. Being a rebel wasn't an option. She had to act polite, even to people who pissed her off. She had to work on her smile in front of a mirror. She couldn't wear the same tunic two or three days in a row because she hadn't been home to change. She couldn't live for weeks at a time with one half-eaten ReadyMeal in her apartment. She couldn't stay up all night to work on a tough case. She couldn't call people names and tell her creditors to go screw themselves.

No more Violet the Wild.

She'd become Violet the Mild.

It was worth it, though, because it was for a good cause, right?

Right?

"I've checked all the extra places you suggested. No luck so far."

The young woman who had addressed her from the doorway of Violet's office continued to stand there. Her name was Evie Carruthers. She was one of three assistants assigned to Violet. She had a springy halo of black hair, thick glasses, mahogany skin, and a please-like-me smile. She radiated nervousness.

That was one of the things that Violet detested about political office: Power made people treat you differently.

She had watched it happen over and over again to her father. When people found out who he was, all at once they began to sweat and stutter and fret. They tried to come up with clever things to say to make him laugh. Even as a little girl, Violet had been perplexed by this behavior; later, she was annoyed by it.

Okay, so he's president of New Earth, she'd think. *Big deal.* Somebody *has to be, right?*

Now that she had power, it was happening to her. She was only a senator, and so people only tried half as hard to impress her, but still.

"It was a long shot," Violet replied to Evie's news. "But thanks, anyway." She went back to the document she'd been reading at her desk. The proposed bill was about water conservation in L'Engletown. Important, yes. So why couldn't she focus on the particulars of the legislation?

Why did she find herself wanting to jump up, hop on a tram to L'Engletown, and tackle the problem single-handedly?

When she looked up again, Evie was still standing there.

"Yeah?"

"I—I was just wondering."

Violet waited.

"I was just wondering," Evie said, starting again, "if maybe . . ."

The second delay was too much. Violet was desperate to get out of here. She spent as little time as possible in this stuffy beige box of an office, and her assistant was prolonging it. "I've got a lot going on today, Evie. Could we move this along?"

The young woman flinched, even though Violet's words had been delivered gently.

"Oh! Sure, yeah. Sorry, Senator." She gulped some air. "You asked me to help you find your father's console, right?"

"Right." Ogden Crowley's personal console had vanished after his death. Violet had scoured his apartment in Starbridge, the assisted living community where New Earth's older citizens ended up, but couldn't find it. She had asked Evie to interview the Starbridge staff. If someone had taken it, she didn't want to get them in trouble, but she wanted it back. She had very few keepsakes from her parents' lives.

From her mother, she had only Lucretia Crowley's black leather medical bag. Violet had given that to Shura when Shura graduated from medical school. Her mother would have approved, Violet knew. But from her father's life, she had very little except for his books.

"Well," Evie continued, "we've been going on the presumption that the console was either misplaced or that somebody took it."

"Yeah."

"What if President Crowley deliberately hid it? What if he didn't *want* you to find his console? I mean, that would be a different kind of search."

Violet was stunned. And then embarrassed. It had never occurred to her that her father might have had something to hide on his console. But why hadn't it?

Because she loved him. And trusted him.

She nodded. "Maybe. Good point. I'll take it from here."

Evie gave a little wave as she backed out of the doorway, her HoverUp making its usual *shhhhh* sound as millions of air currents were pushed through an equal number of tiny coils, coils which in turn shifted and manipulated her limbs in response to her brain's commands, enabling her to walk upright despite a spinal cord injury suffered when she was twelve years old. After many experiments, Shura had vastly improved upon the original design of HoverUps. Nowadays, the movements were so natural that you could occasionally miss the fact that someone was using a HoverUp; only a faint murmur revealed its presence.

Violet massaged the back of her neck. She'd been at work for an hour now, and all she'd managed to do was sign a few papers and reply to outraged messages from New Earth residents who wanted something. Because *everybody* wanted something, and they wanted it now. No wonder her father had always been so tired when he came home at night.

Why had President Shabir stuck her in this job? It wasn't her style at all.

But wait—she'd sought it out. *She* had asked *him.* Not the other way around.

Because being a senator is what a daughter of Ogden Crowley ought to do.

And so here she sat.

She yearned to be back in Rez's lab while he tried to discover the origin of the chip's signal. Not here in the Central Administration Building, surrounded by other senators and their assistants—instead of being surrounded by stars.

She signed a few more papers. She answered a few more console messages.

A colleague popped up in the doorway, a woman named Amber Chandler, who wore a shimmery-green, gold-trimmed tunic that fell to her ankles. Her jewelry was the noisy kind: clanking bracelets, clicking earrings, a necklace whose many facets scraped and rang as they met and mingled. Her skin was trimmed with wrinkles.

She asked Violet if she'd heard about the rumor about the Graygrunge attack.

"The what?" Violet said. She tried to look surprised.

"A virus. There's some gossip about unauthorized activity in the tunnels yesterday. Might've been a virus. One of the jumpers," said Chandler. She was ancient—at least forty years old, Violet speculated. Impossible to imagine being that old.

"Haven't heard a thing," Violet replied. She felt guilty about the lie, but only for a second, because it was for the greater good: preventing a mass panic.

She gestured toward the stack of documents on her desk so Chandler would get the hint: *I'm busy.*

As soon as her visitor left, Violet put in a console call to the best detective she knew: Jonetta Loring. She told her about the missing console.

"I'm sure you searched his apartment thoroughly, right?" Jonetta asked.

"Four times. No, wait—five."

"Okay, so if your father *did* hide it, he didn't hide it there." Jonetta paused. "I'll check some other places and get back to you, okay?"

"Thanks."

"Least I can do. You taught me everything I know."

Violet was tempted to murmur, *Not exactly a ringing endorsement, girl,* but she didn't. Truth was, Jonetta had hauled the detective agency up out of all-but-certain doom. Crowley & Associates—she'd kept the name so she wouldn't have to buy a new sign, she'd told Violet, who suspected there was a little more to it than that—was thriving.

But swamped or not, Jonetta always found time to help her mentor and former boss.

More bills to sign. More reports to read. More console calls. More and more and more and . . .

Finally, it was noon. Violet had made plans to have lunch with Shura. She jumped up from her chair and looped around her desk, heading for the door. Once again she was desperately hungry, but this time it wasn't for food.

She was hungry for freedom.

7

Rescuing Rez

The door to Shura's lab was wide open, which was highly unusual. Violet spotted the gap the moment she turned the corner in the hall and made for the threshold. As she came even closer, she suddenly understood the reason the door had been summarily flung open:

Shura was trying to air out the space, which meant the world at large was now forced to suffer right along with the room's sole occupant.

An epic stink barreled out of the lab. It was caustic enough to clear a sinus passage or scour a sink or eliminate the rust from a rocket hull. The smell was a blend of rotten eggs and rancid meat and hairy armpit and infected toenail, topped off with singed tennis shoes and rat droppings, with a rich bottom note of swamp goo. It was the kind of odor that seemed to have recently solidified, achieving a critical mass of nastiness that could not be contained by scent alone. It had a shape, a weight, a density.

"Shura?" Violet said, adding a gasp as she thrust her head

in the door. She assumed her friend was in there somewhere, even though she hadn't seen her yet.

"Sorry about the smell!" Shura called out.

At least it sounded like Shura. There was no immediate evidence of the speaker's identity. The lab was drastically crammed with her friend's ongoing experiments—with, that is, oily engine parts, metal vats whose contents heaved and popped, quasi-assembled robots, gizmo-choked shelves, stacks of solar energy panels in assorted shapes and thicknesses that awaited testing, rows of partially disassembled wind turbines, boxes rattling with test tubes and beakers all packed tightly in straw, glass tubes, thick bundles of copper wire, curling strips of steel cladding, spectrometers and chronometers and scales of every size and variety, broken-off antennae and ruptured replicators and water-damaged oscilloscopes—as well as Shura's art equipment, from easels to canvases to jars that sprouted with old brushes to rolled-up, crinkled-ended tubes of paint.

"Come on in!" called the still-invisible Shura from somewhere within the conglomeration.

Violet fit a hand over her nose and mouth, bent almost double at the waist, and plunged into the laboratory. The obnoxious odors seemed to pull back just the slightest bit, allowing her to take several steps forward without collapsing in a gagging heap.

Just as Violet breached the first barricade of outsized odds and ends, Shura stepped out from behind a mountain of mismatched computer parts. She wore goggles, a head scarf, and a lab apron covering her tunic. In her right hand, she held a clamp that was attached to a cloudy test tube from which purple smoke rippled and seethed.

"What the hell's going on?" Violet asked. She coughed,

rubbed her eyes with her knuckles, and coughed again. "Does this have something to do with your experiments for that new vaccine?"

"Um . . . no," Shura replied. She pushed up her goggles and blinked several times. "The smell is actually . . . Well, I'm trying to find an antibiotic to use against a jumping virus like Graygrunge. Which means it's got to work in both humans and computers. A retardant is one thing, but I'd like to stop it before it has a chance to get going. I think I know the answer—I need to come up with some lines of code instead of a regular antibiotic. The code will function as an antibiotic. But I was taking a chance with this last mixture. Unfortunately, it caught fire. There's no immediate danger, other than the stink. The trouble started when it spread to a nearby vat and the chemical reaction was just the worst—"

"So it's settled. We're going to a café."

"Yeah."

"What do you think? I mean, *really*." Shura took a bite of her sandwich. They sat at a green metal table in the giant plaza outside her lab.

"Rez is under a lot of pressure." Violet looked at the salad on her plate with zero interest. The smell from the lab had done a number on her usually robust appetite. "He's worried about the orbital decay, and he doesn't want to make a general announcement about it. So it's all on his shoulders. Plus there's the threat of Graygrunge and the other jumping viruses."

"So he might be mistaken about the signal? Is that what you're saying?"

"Maybe. Maybe not. I just don't know, Shura. He's brilliant. You know that."

"I do. And I also know that everybody needs a break now and again." Shura sat back in her chair. "That's one of the reasons I paint. I mean, yeah, there are things I want to say that I can only say through art. But it does other things for me, too. When I'm working on something really intense in my medical practice or my lab experiments, and I feel like my head's going to explode, that's when I pick up a paintbrush. Works wonders."

"I don't think Rez has anything like that in his life." There was a touch of sorrow in Violet's voice.

Shura peered at her friend. "You really care about him, don't you?"

"Of course. We all do."

"That's not what I mean."

Violet gave her a look. "I don't want to talk about it right now, okay?"

They had been friends for so long that they knew every nuance, every detail, every wrinkle of each other's emotional histories. Violet had helped Shura get over Samantha Bolivar, a medical school classmate and her first major crush; Shura had been there when Violet was obsessed with Kendall Mayhew. Finding out Kendall's secret had changed Violet's feelings toward him, and Shura had been there for that ordeal, too, as Violet had to deal with the opposite of a crush:

What to do when you aren't in love with somebody anymore, but *he's* still in love with *you*. In some ways, that was even harder than the other way around, when you were the one who cared more.

Emotions, Violet thought, *can be a pain in the ass sometimes.*

Emotions had taken on an exaggerated importance for them because of the Intercept. They had grown up with it as a daily part of their lives. Their feelings from moment to moment had been monitored, collected, tagged, archived, sliced, and diced a thousand different ways, and then, suddenly, the Intercept was gone. They were free to feel whatever they wanted to feel without the Intercept looking over their shoulder. That freedom brought its own problems.

Through it all, Violet and Shura had remained steadfast friends.

"The only reason I was asking," Shura said, "is because he's sometimes kind of rude and mean. I know it's because he's so focused, but I don't like it."

"Me neither."

"But you've still got a thing for him, right?"

"Yeah. No. Maybe." Violet put her head in her hands. "I don't know." She lifted her head again and grinned. "I guess." She started to remind Shura that she'd expressed a desire *not* to talk about this, but whatever. "He wasn't that way before Rachel died."

"Well—"

"Okay," Violet corrected herself. "Maybe he was a *little* bit that way before Rachel died. But not like this."

"Agreed."

"So we have to cut him some slack."

"If you want my opinion," Shura said, "it sounds like he's one of your rescues."

"My what?"

"You know what I mean. Your rescue projects. You like to save people."

"Is Rez really that bad? I mean, sure, he can be pretty snippy. But he's basically a decent guy."

"Yeah. But you deserve more than just a decent guy, right? How about somebody totally hot who treats you well, too?"

Violet shrugged. "We can talk about my love life later. Back to the chip. If it turns out not to be Rachel's, Rez will be devastated."

"Not to mention embarrassed in front of all of us."

"Everybody makes mistakes."

"Not Rez. Just ask him."

They laughed, and the blended laughter made both of them feel better. For a moment, Violet considered telling Shura about her father's missing console and about the troubling possibility that it wasn't lost at all—that he had deliberately hidden it.

But she didn't. It might not be true. And they had enough to deal with right now, from Graygrunge to the mystery of Rachel's chip.

Anyway, there would always be time later to bring it up with Shura. That was the thing about a best friend: Next time was a given.

Warmed by that thought, Violet felt some stirrings of appetite returning to her. Before she could get back to her salad, though, her console signaled an incoming call. The rising white jewel—in jewel-speak, the equivalent of a siren—told her it was critically urgent.

Rez's worried face appeared in the tiny translucent pearl.

"Can you come over here right away?"

"Another attack of Graygrunge?" Violet asked.

"No."

"What is it, then?"

"Just come to my lab as quick as you can. There's something you have to see." He sounded thoroughly rattled, even more so than during his last summons, when he'd told her about finding Rachel's chip.

"I'm having lunch with Shura."

"Bring her. That's even better. But come now."

"Okay, Rez, but if you could give me a hint about—"

"Please."

In all the years that Violet had known Steven Reznik, through crises and emergencies and issues and problems and snafus and screwups aplenty, she had rarely if ever heard him say, "Please." Or anything remotely close to "Please."

Until right now.

A Cry in the Night

Rez wasn't in his big red chair. He was standing upright, leaning over the computer keyboard. His hands were balled into fists, and those fists were balanced on either side of his computer keyboard. He stared at the screen.

"Hey," Violet said.

She had shimmied up through the hole in the floor first and then put a hand down and helped Shura up.

Rez didn't answer her. Violet looked over at Mickey. The AstroRob had yet to say a word to her—no bad jokes, no unbearable puns, no ridiculous riddles, no groan-worthy plays on words. He was focused on his own screen, which featured a rich orange circus of cartwheeling numbers.

The tiny room seemed to tremble with a dizzy strangeness, trailing sparks of confusion.

What was going on?

"Rez?" Violet said. "Is it Rachel's chip? Did you figure out where the signal's coming from?"

"No." His voice had a peculiar quality to it. If Violet had been forced to define it, she would have called it . . . *haunted,* maybe. As if it were caught between two worlds and didn't quite know where it belonged.

"Then what is it?"

He slowly raised a hand and pointed to the screen. Violet and Shura moved closer so that they could see what had affected him so deeply.

And instantly, Violet understood why Rez was behaving this way. She and Shura didn't speak—the room was silent except for the thrumming *swish-swoosh swish-swoosh* of machinery and the low murmur of the fans that kept the computers cool—but Violet was sure that her friend understood it, too.

On the screen was a snippet of video that repeated itself over and over again: There was a frantic sizzle of lightning, a flashing of bottomless blackness, a tumbling fall, a fierce cataclysm of water, an immense and terrible pressure that nothing as fragile as a human body could possibly withstand; and then an absolute emptiness.

Somehow, on a level of understanding that existed apart from thought, a level that involved pure instinct, they knew exactly what they were looking at:

The chip was transmitting Rachel's view of the last few seconds of her life as she plunged from the top of a half-built roller coaster track into the swirling, churning waters of an Old Earth ocean. It repeated over and over again. The feed was terrifying to watch because as you watched, your consciousness merged with hers, Violet realized, and suddenly you knew what it felt like to be falling, falling, falling, into the heart of terror and black panic.

You knew what it felt like to be helpless.

You knew what it felt like to be doomed.

You knew what it felt like to die.

In a hushed voice, Violet asked, "How long has this been coming in?"

Rez tried to speak, but couldn't. He tried again. This time, he was able to answer.

"It started five minutes before I called you," he said. "At first, I didn't know what it was. I'd been working on the signal all morning long, trying to track it. When that didn't work, I tried to intensify it, and clarify it. And then—" He faltered. "And then this video feed started up, replacing the graduation scene. It repeated several times before I realized that . . . that it was still Rachel. It was still her perspective. It was Rachel's Intercept feed. Rachel's feelings as she perished."

The video had repeated twice again while he talked: the lightning, the flashing, the tumble, the water, the pressure.

The end.

And again: lightning, flashing, tumble, water, pressure. Death.

"Can't you make it stop?" Shura asked.

Rez swallowed hard. He tore his eyes away from the screen. "That's the thing, Shura—I don't *want* it to stop. I mean, I *do,* but I don't. It's excruciating to watch, yes, but it's still Rachel. It's as close to her as I can get now. It's the last thing she knew. The last thing she saw. The last thing she felt. The last thing she *was.*"

His eyes were pulled back to the screen. Their eyes went there, too:

Lightning. Flashing. Tumble. Water. Pressure. Death.

Violet looked at Shura. Shura slowly shook her head. Violet understood what her friend was saying. *I don't know what to do, either.*

The image had no sound, which only added to its surpassing strangeness. *We're filling in the sound with our own imagina-*

tions, Violet realized, *and that probably makes it ten thousand times worse than the sound as it really was.* Or *is.* She was certain she could hear the screeching howl of the wind, the moan and roar of the storm-whipped ocean, and Rachel's cries as her fate became terrifyingly clear to her.

Yet the room was silent. Only the occasional chirp from Mickey as he ran through his progressions in his continuing search for the signal's origin interrupted the vast, momentous quiet.

And so there they stood, the three of them, mesmerized by the final seconds of Rachel's life as it unspooled in front of them, over and over again.

Finally, Rez took a deep breath. The spell was finally broken.

"Wherever that signal is coming from, we've got to find it," he declared. "Look, I know you guys have your own stuff to do, but I could use some extra help for a few hours, okay? Mickey and I can't make much headway by ourselves. I'd like to expand the search parameters. What do you say?"

"Absolutely," Violet said.

"Count me in," Shura said.

Hearing that response, anybody else would've high-fived them or fist-bumped them or even just offered up a brief but heartfelt, "Hey, thanks." But not Rez.

He nodded.

Because Rez is Rez, Violet reminded herself.

Now he was talking again. "Mickey, fix them up with laptops, okay? And assign them quadrants." He dropped back down in his big red chair. Each hand clamped around a joystick, he rotated the chair forward. "We'll find her."

Violet thought about correcting him; there was no "her" to find. They were looking for a chip, not a person. A signal, not a little girl.

But Rez had already returned to his own world, a world of auditory trace programs and numerical analyses and probability fractals. A world of rigor and resolve. He wasn't listening anymore. Because he was working.

"Hey, Violet," Mickey said. "What did the astronaut want for Christmas?"

"Mickey, I'm not sure this is really the time for—"

"Missile-toe!"

She laughed. She was glad to have something silly and lighthearted to think about for a minute, something to act as a counterweight to the grim obsessiveness in Rez's eyes. Her affection for the AstroRob, goofy as he was, was growing. Maybe it was the fact that Mickey had almost been destroyed by Graygrunge, and she pitied him. Or maybe, Violet thought, she just had a weakness for bad jokes.

"Why did Saturn turn down a marriage proposal?" Mickey asked.

It was Shura's turn. "I don't know," she said. "Why did Saturn turn down a marriage proposal?"

"Because it didn't need another ring!"

Shura and Violet both groaned. Then they settled down to work, tracing the elusive signal. Each of them claimed a corner of the lab, sitting on the floor, backs against the metal shelves, laptops balanced on their upraised knees. They scoured their assigned quadrants.

The only sounds in the room were the breathing of the humans and the slight humming of the robot.

An hour later, Shura stood up.

"I'm taking a quick break." She did a few deep-knee bends to get the kinks out of her legs.

"Good idea," Violet concurred, standing up next to her. "This is pretty tedious work."

Rez glared at them. Violet didn't take it personally

"Yeah, fine, take a break," he groused. "But make it short. We've got twelve more galaxies to get through before—"

He stopped. His attention had been jerked back to the screen.

Shura and Violet looked, too.

The picture of a dark ocean and a wild night had vanished. Across the screen, unrolling in bright yellow letters, was a simple, haunting plea:

HELP

PART TWO

Rachel's Return

Trillum, Nogg, Waw

The five friends gathered in the shadow of the great telescope.

Beyond the telescope was a glittering wash of stars, a swipe of light that looked like a brushstroke across the vast black canvas of space.

Beyond those stars were more stars. And beyond those stars, more stars still. And more and more and more.

From somewhere far beyond the limit of all that these five people knew, all that they understood about the universe, something was stirring. Something as yet undreamed of.

Whatever it was, it was trying to communicate with them, sending forth a single word across distances too immense for the human mind to envision.

It was good that the five of them were together in this moment, Violet thought, a moment that filled her with a sense of bright, burning wonder. When Rez had asked them to come, they came: Tin Man and Kendall had just joined Violet and

Shura here in his lab. They put aside their petty feuds and their minor grievances, and they looked toward the stars.

They had been through so much together already. They had known pain. They had faced down the possibility of disaster. They had weathered storms—real storms, like the one on Old Earth on the night that Rachel died, and other kinds of storms, too: storms of the heart. They had dealt with grief and with love and with all the troubles that grief and love could bring. They had quarreled the way all friends quarrel, but they always came back together again stronger, and sometimes wiser, too.

They had seen death.

And they had survived.

Everything they had been through had brought them to this moment.

Violet was not a mind reader, but she was fairly certain each of them was feeling roughly what she was feeling as they stood beneath the motley, magnificent array of instruments with which Rez had stocked his secret lair:

They were on the threshold, once again, of a grand adventure.

But first they had to solve a baffling mystery.

They stood in a ragged half circle, facing the screen upon which **HELP** had continued to pulse in yellow letters.

The small lab felt even smaller with so many people—and one AstroRob—crammed in the space. It seemed cold, the sterile, metallic cold of scientific instruments, but the chill was mitigated by the presence of the five friends and the comradeship they shared and by the amazing, astonishing thing that seemed irrefutable now:

They were being contacted by the inhabitants of another planet.

They stared at the message. They pondered it. Compared to the sophisticated equipment all around them, the word on the screen was about as simple and primitive as could be:

HELP

For several minutes, no one spoke. The silence was finally broken by Tin Man.

"Where's it coming from?"

"I don't know." Rez's reply was sharp. "If I knew, I wouldn't have asked you guys to come right over, okay?"

"Don't talk to him that way," Violet said. "Calm down."

"We're under a lot of pressure here," Rez muttered, "and I don't have time for stupid questions."

"It's not a stupid question," Kendall countered. "It's the perfect question. Who's asking us for help?"

"And why?" Shura put in.

Rez didn't answer. He wouldn't snap at Shura and Kendall the same way he'd snapped at Tin Man; he thought of them as his intellectual equals, whereas he considered Tin Man his inferior. Violet didn't like the snobbery, but she knew that was how he felt. Rez assessed people according to their brainpower, and he had little respect for Tin Man's.

Or mine.

She pushed the thought away. There was too much to do right now to sink into self-pity.

"It's coming in on the same transmission as Rachel's chip," Shura added after checking the numbers at the bottom of the screen. "I'm not sure, but I think the chip is being used as a sort of surfboard. The message just rode in on the chip's back, you might say." She was thinking hard. Violet could tell because her friend's lips were drawn up into a thin line, and her dark eyes had a faraway cast. She had seen the same expression on Shura's face when she was finishing up an especially difficult painting or attempting to make an elusive medical diagnosis or bumping up against a daunting challenge as she upgraded an oxygen synthesizer or a neural trigger for a cold-fusion initiation sequence.

Or—Shura being Shura—trying to make lunch. Domestic skills had never been her specialty.

"But it can't be from . . . well, from Rachel," Shura concluded.

They still tiptoed around the name when they were in Rez's presence. They weren't sure what he was feeling about his sister's death.

Hell, we're not sure what he's feeling about anything, Violet thought.

"Because she's dead," Rez said. "Understood."

"So who's making the request for help?" Kendall asked. He seemed to be addressing his question as much to the screen itself as to any individual in the room. "There's got to be some sort of consciousness behind the message. Asking for help is a specific, urgent action. Someone's in peril."

Shura shook her head. "Not 'someone.' It's not a 'someone,' remember? The signal's not really coming from Rachel. It can't be. It's her chip, but it's not *her.*"

"Whatever." Kendall's attention switched to his wrist console. Calling up jewels and then swiftly rearranging them in an elegant dazzle, like a juggler with a collection of colored balls, he performed a series of calculations. "Okay. So given the triangulation theorem I just used, Shura's right. The message came in simultaneously with the chip's signal. But that's also the same frequency Rez has been using to measure the orbital parameters of New Earth." He turned to Rez. "Can you send me those coordinates? I want to cross-reference the numbers. See if there's any symmetry between those parameters and the angle of incidence of the incoming call for help."

"That'll take *days,*" said a disgruntled Rez. "My numbers go back to the founding of New Earth."

"So I'd better get started." Kendall didn't take any crap from Rez. There had always been an edge of competitive tension between the two of them, dating back to when Rez and Violet worked together in Protocol Hall—and Rez had a crush on Violet, while Violet was obsessed with Kendall. All of that was different now; Violet's feelings for Kendall were strictly those of friendship. If she had a crush on anybody these days, it was Rez—a fact that she didn't like to think about too often, because it was so . . . well, so *weird.* And it probably didn't mean anything at all. She'd sort of convinced herself that maybe it was just a temporary glitch—like a short in a computer keyboard. It would sort itself out soon.

Meanwhile, Kendall and Rez treated each other with a kind of mild, keep-your-distance wariness. They collaborated on projects, and they respected each other's minds, but they didn't socialize.

Come to think of it, Violet reminded herself, Rez didn't socialize with anybody. Rachel had been his only real friend. And she was gone.

"Maybe whatever entity found Rachel's chip is the thing asking for help," Shura said. "Either that or it's an automatic distress beacon of some kind." She looked over at the AstroRob. "Hey, Mickey. Even if we can't tell where the signal's coming from, can we at least pin down if it has a true source or if it's just a random distress beacon that got mistakenly triggered?"

Mickey jammed his pincers into the sides of his keyboard.

"Give me twenty-one seconds," he said. His pincers vibrated ever so slightly, and his central processing unit thrummed as he synched himself up with the computer's hard drive.

While Mickey finished his calculations, Shura leaned closer to the screen. "Look at the words and how they're formed," she said. "Must be the nature of the signal. Those letters are kind of . . . *tentative.* Like whoever sent the message wasn't sure which letter was supposed to come next."

Violet leaned in, too. "Yeah. They're sort of rickety. Like maybe they were made by a kid who just learned how to spell."

Rez made a *humfph* sound, a small noise that seemed to start in the back of his throat and then move into his nose. It was filled with skepticism bordering on ridicule. Not even his reverence for Shura's tremendous brain could override his natural inclination to scoff. "I think you're both seeing things. They're just regular letters."

Mickey spun around and addressed the group. "Inconclusive," he said.

"Great. Thanks," Rez said.

"I don't think robots get sarcasm," Tin Man murmured.

"Oh, we get it, all right," Mickey said cheerfully. "We just choose to ignore it. Rise above it."

Rez slammed a hand on his control panel. "One more word out of you," he said to the AstroRob with a snarl, "and I swear I'll throw you back in the recycle pile. You'll be a rail at a tram stop before the night's out. Or maybe a toilet-paper dispenser in a public bathroom."

Kendall moved to the center of the room. Because the space was so compact, the entire journey required only a step and a half.

"Guys, *come on,*" he said. He made eye contact with each one of them: Violet, Shura, Tin Man, and finally Rez, who brooded in his big chair. He even included Mickey. "Do you see what's happening here? We're arguing and squabbling like a bunch of kids. We have to stop—and stop *now.* We're dealing with important things. Crucial things. Things that might affect the fate of New Earth. So can we stop sniping at each other? And remember that we're all friends here?"

No one spoke for a few seconds.

"Everybody's tired," Shura said. "Tired and frustrated and confused. That's the problem. But yeah, you're right, Kendall. It's time to quit picking on each other. Time to focus." She gestured toward Rez's screen, where the **HELP** message still hovered. "I want to figure this out. So, yeah. I say we start over."

"Me too," Violet declared. She looked at Tin Man, who nodded.

"Okay, then," Shura said. "From now on, we remember why we all became friends in the first place. Because we're a great team. And okay, I've got to say it, even though it's corny—because we love each other. And because we know that if this mystery is going to be solved, it'll be solved by somebody in this room with help from the others."

Kendall looked inquiringly at Rez. "How about you? Are you with us?"

Rez shrugged.

That was the best they were going to get.

The message changed.

They had just settled down to work again. Rez was running his calculations on the probabilities of signal origin. Kendall stood next to Mickey, joining forces with the AstroRob as he ran multimatrix analyses through his computer, and Shura and Violet continued their search through the assigned quadrants on the laptops. Like before, the two of them staked out a corner of the lab and settled in, computers propped on their knees. Tin Man had noticed a loose fitting on the porthole door in the floor and was busy fixing it so that the next person who entered or exited didn't find herself dropping unexpectedly into the storage room just below, holding a ripped-loose fitting in her possibly broken hand.

And then, after several minutes of companionable, work-filled silence, Shura glanced up at Rez's screen.

"Hey," she said.

There was no immediate response from her friends, because *Hey* lacked any real drama.

"Hey!" she said, raising her voice.

Now they lifted their heads from their own work. They followed the direction of Shura's finger, which meant that their gazes landed on the screen.

The message still read **HELP.** The letters were still yellow. They were still all caps. But now the word seemed to be squirming, getting bigger. The letters themselves were fluttering uneasily. The picture wavered. Fuzzy static gathered in the corners of the screen like lint in a pants pocket.

"What's happening?" Violet asked.

Rez scowled. He punched a series of buttons on his control panel. He twisted a dial next to his keyboard. His scowl deepened until it seemed to swallow up his face.

The message continued to shiver. The fuzz in the corners was moving slowly toward the center.

By now, Kendall had relocated from his spot next to Mickey to a spot behind Rez's chair, watching the message as it twisted and shifted.

“The signal is—well, I don’t know what to call it,” Rez said. Bafflement had turned his usual sharp tone into something softer. “The letters are getting *thicker.* That’s the only way I can describe it.”

“Thicker.” Shura repeated the word.

“Yeah,” Rez said.

Kendall leaned forward. “Mind if I try something?” he asked. Nobody touched Rez’s keyboard without his permission.

“Be my guest.” Rez tipped the joystick, moving his chair back and to the side about a fraction of an inch so that Kendall could have easier access to the control panel.

Kendall’s fingers flew over the keyboard as he entered a series of commands.

“Dammit,” Kendall said under his breath.

Whatever was happening on the screen was still happening, despite his efforts. The letters continued to swell. They were almost unreadable now: The spaces between the **H** and **E**, and the **L** and **P**, had nearly vanished. The letters were so large that they constituted a single solid block.

“You’re right, Rez,” Violet said. “It’s like the letters are out of control. But why? What’s going on?”

The answer came a few seconds later, and when it did, it hailed from a most unexpected place.

Tin Man was probably the least likely person anywhere on New Earth—or Old Earth, too, for that matter—to solve a highly technical problem. Violet knew it, and she knew her friends knew it, too, including Tin Man himself. He’d had no formal education on Old Earth, unless you counted his rough life on the streets down there, when he ran with a cruel, ragtag gang that used violence to stay alive. Once he arrived on New Earth, he refused Violet's offer to help get him into a school. He'd held up his fists and declared, "Got all the education I need right here."

But he was the one who figured out why the message was changing.

"Can I suggest something?" he said.

Rez ignored him, but the others didn't.

"Sure," Kendall answered. "Whatcha got?"

"Go for it," Shura put in as Violet nodded.

"Those letters," Tin Man said, "remind me of a jacket I used to have back on Old Earth."

"A *jacket.*" Rez crammed a ton of disdain into his repetition of the word. "Right."

"Shut up," Tin Man said. His voice was hoarse with suppressed anger.

Shura touched Tin Man's arm. "Hey. Come on." She lightly tapped the top of Rez's head. "Cut it out. Lose the attitude. Let him finish, okay?"

Rez didn't reply, but Violet could tell he was miffed. And she could tell, too, that Tin Man wasn't feeling any more kindly toward Rez than Rez was feeling toward him. The reason for Rez's petulance was obvious: He thought Tin Man was a dope.

And the reason for Tin Man's prickliness?

Molly, Violet thought. When Tin Man talked about Old Earth, naturally he thought about Molly. He missed her fiercely. Grief gripped him and shook him and turned him into another kind of person. He had to fight to find his way back to who he truly was.

Tin Man crossed his arms. He'd try again. "Yeah. A jacket. It was this old, dirty, smelly, torn-up thing. Just a rag, really, but it was all I had. I'd found it in a pile of junk in an alley. Wadded up in the corner. Covered with dirt and leaves and all kinds of crap. The best part was, it didn't fit. It was way too big for me."

"And that was good because . . . ?" Kendall tried to keep the impatience out of his tone. Violet could tell that he was edging over to Rez's side: How was any of this relevant to the critical mystery that lay before them?

"Because it meant I could carry a bunch of stuff under it," Tin Man replied. "Stuff I didn't want people to know about until I *wanted* them to know about it. Until I decided to show them."

Shura nodded vigorously. "I think I get what you're saying. You mean the letters in the message are expanding because there's something *underneath* them. Pushing them out. Something we weren't supposed to know about until now. Now that whoever sent this message thinks we're ready."

"Exactly." Tin Man uncrossed his arms so he could give Shura a thumbs-up. "You got it."

"That could be right," Kendall said. "Shura, Rez, Mickey, let's unweave the signal, strand by strand. We can go back to the search for its origin later. Right now, we need to find out what's beneath it. We'll take turns at the keyboard so we can establish a rhythm. Violet, start a recording log, will you? So we won't lose whatever pops up."

They crowded in closer around Rez's chair.

It was tedious, painstaking work that involved trial and error and bizarrely creative mashups of computer commands, but they systematically isolated the separate threads of the signal, picking them out one by one and setting them aside, relegating them to another part of the screen. Each time they removed a thread, whatever was behind the signal loomed a little bigger, throbbed a little brighter, became a bit more prominent, as if it could finally breathe.

"There," Kendall said. "Last one." He punched in a flurry of numbers.

"About time," Shura added. She stood up straight again,

releasing a long breath and shaking out her hands. "That was rough—coming up with commands so delicate that they could take apart something as thin and flimsy as that signal. It was like trying to floss a flea's teeth."

"Yeah," Rez said. He sat back in his chair, also weary from the effort. Too weary to make a crack about too many cooks spoiling a stew.

"Fleas can't floss," Mickey piped up. "They don't have teeth. Although it does make a great tongue twister. How many teeth can a fine flea floss?"

"Shut up," Rez said. "It was a metaphor."

"What's a metaphor?" Mickey responded and then answered his own question. "It's for whatever you *want* it to be for."

Rez groaned. "Would somebody pull his plug?"

"Guys, guys," Kendall said, trying to keep them focused on the business at hand. "Let's see what we've got. Violet, would you please read us the log of what came up when we freed the hidden message?"

Violet looked dubiously at her console. As each word had been released from beneath the **HELP** signal, she had recorded it on her console log. Her friends had been too focused on the torturously cumbersome task of signal separation to deal with the hidden letters they were liberating.

Now they were ready to behold the wonders uncovered by their work.

But there was a problem.

"Um," Violet said.

"Come on. Tell us what was under the signal." Shura's impatience showed in her voice. She kept a hand on her lower back, which ached from the posture she'd been forced to maintain, bending over the keyboard.

"Um," Violet repeated.

"Why are you stalling?" Kendall asked.

"Because it's gibberish. Nonsense words." There. She'd said it. Their hard work didn't matter, after all.

"Really?" Rez asked. He'd been just as eager as the rest of them to find out the secondary message. "Are you sure?"

Violet nodded glumly.

"Well," he said, "at least read the words aloud. Even if they don't make any sense."

Kendall and Shura and Tin Man signaled their approval of that plan by creating a casual symphony of *Yeah* and *Why not* and *Might as well* and *Got nothing to lose* and then back around to *Yeah.*

"Okay," Violet said. She cleared her throat and spoke:

"Trillum. Nogg. Waw."

She had pronounced the words as best she could. It was a guess. Just for good measure, to drive home the point that the words made no sense, she repeated the list, faster this time. "Trillum. Nogg. Waw."

Silence. They were nonsense syllables.

From Shura came a bleak smile. "Maybe if you chanted that over a bubbling pot by the light of a full moon, some evil spirits would show up."

Nobody laughed. They were too frustrated.

"So we're back to square one," Rez said. "We've got a signal that appears to be coming from Rachel's Intercept chip from somewhere on the far edge of the galaxy. We've got three meaningless words embedded below the message. And the message itself, which appears to be asking us for help—which we can't respond to, mainly because we don't know who sent it or why or from where."

The lab had gone silent again, aside from the faint hiss and gurgle of machinery.

"Hold on." Violet made some quick sketches on her console, using a light pink jewel to do so. "What if."

"What if . . . what?" Rez asked impatiently.

Violet looked up from the jewel. The idea that had just come to her was thrilling.

That, she decided, was the only word for it: *thrilling.*

"What if," she went on, "we're not supposed to understand the words?"

"Huh?" Shura said.

"Yeah, I second that 'huh,'" Tin Man put in.

"Okay, listen," Violet continued. The more she talked, the faster the words came to her. "When the Intercept was running, the chips collected emotions, right? It was data, sure, but the data came in the form of feelings. Memories of how you felt at a particular time in your life. Anger or sadness or happiness or regret or anxiety. Whatever. And back when we monitored Intercept feeds at Protocol Hall, we could see the source of those emotions—the specific incidents that prompted them."

"Right," Kendall said. He had invented the Intercept and was still defensive about its operation. His motives had been pure. "It created a stockpile of weapons that the government could deploy against people who threatened the peace. The emotions gave the state leverage."

"So the Intercept relied upon emotions," Violet said.

Kendall nodded. "Exactly. What are you getting at? You *know* all of this, Violet. All of us do. The Intercept needed emotions."

"Yes," she said. "*Human* emotions."

No one moved. No one spoke.

Rez took the plunge. "Well, of course the Intercept used human emotions. What other kind of emotions *could* it have used?"

Violet tried to keep the excitement out of her voice. "Alien emotions."

Her friends stared at her.

Shura blinked several times. "At the risk of repeating myself—huh?"

"What if an alien civilization found Rachel's chip?" Violet said, her voice rising with excitement. "And figured out what it was for? And they're trying to use it to communicate with us? They realized that the Intercept runs on emotions that it collects. Emotions like love and hate and fear. And they're using Rachel's chip to access their own emotions. But they call *their* emotions by different words—*trillum* and *nogg* and the other one."

Rez tilted forward in his red armchair. He didn't look impressed. "Okay, right," he said. "So where's the revelation? An extraterrestrial species would have its own language. Naturally they wouldn't have the same words for feelings that we do. I mean, jeez. Pretty obvious."

Violet waved her hands as if she were clearing a windshield. "No, no, no. You're not getting it, Rez."

He frowned. She could guess his thoughts: *Nobody* told Steven Reznik that he wasn't getting something. He always got everything, and usually long before anybody else got it. Or even knew there was anything to get.

"What are you talking about?" he said.

"I don't mean just the words. I mean the emotions themselves."

Before Rez could respond, Shura made an *mmmmm* noise. It sounded to Violet like somebody enjoying an ice cream cone. Shura's face seemed to grow brighter as she caught the essence of Violet's idea.

"So you're saying," Shura said, "that human emotions might not be the only ones in the universe. If life developed on other planets, those life-forms would have their *own* emotions. Different from ours. Our emotions—things like jealousy and joy and ambition and empathy—well, those might not even *exist* in other worlds. They could have whole new mixes of feelings. Like colors we've never seen before. Colors outside the visible spectrum. Our eyes don't even have a means of seeing them."

Violet nodded. "Exactly. And these words—the ones they put underneath *HELP,* like a message in a bottle—are just attempts to use *our* language to capture *their* emotions. They're not very good at it yet. They've got a long way to go. So we have no idea what these particular words mean because we don't know what emotions they're linked to."

"Wow," Kendall said. "I never thought—" He was still trying to come to grips with Violet's theory. "They may have tried to contact us before but didn't know how. And then they found a chip—Rachel's chip—floating in the stars. I bet they were *ecstatic.*" His voice was suffused with enthusiasm. "I mean, it must've been like having a raft wash up on a desert island where you've been marooned for years. And you've been desperate to communicate with other civilizations that you know—you just *know*—are out there, out past the horizon. And here's a raft! Suddenly, you have this conduit. This vessel. You have a way of crossing the ocean of the galaxy *if* you can figure out how to use it."

"Except," Rez said, breaking in, "we don't have a friggin' clue about what they're trying to tell us. And no way to find out. At a *minimum,* they're hundreds of millions of light-years away. We can't get there, and they can't get here. It's hopeless."

A frustrated silence dropped like a big ugly rock in the middle of the room. He had made an excellent point.

On Rez's screen, the newly uncovered words—*trillum, nogg, waw*—pulsed and surged and wriggled in what looked like mute desperation as if trying frantically to explain themselves.

Even with all the brainpower in this room, Violet realized, even with all the elite education and unprecedented brilliance and scintillating intuition, there were still vast secrets locked away in unknown corners of the universe, secrets that eluded their understanding. Of course she already knew that—it was a mighty big universe, after all—but never before had she been forced to really *think* about it.

They were like little kids in a room where all the good and interesting stuff was stored on a high, high shelf. They could see it, but they couldn't reach it. All they could do was get up on their tiptoes and *reach* and *reach* . . . and yearn.

Rez fumed. Shura shook her head in frustration. If Kendall's face were a painting, Violet thought, she would've titled it *Defeat.* He rubbed a palm across the top of his head. That was his tell; it meant he was fresh out of ideas.

The only one who still seemed upbeat was Tin Man. He swept a meaty hand through the air, indicating the lab and its sleek array of blinking equipment. His gesture took in the wall of computers and the rows of monitors and the little red lights and the little blue lights and the bundled wires and the spinning gauges. It even included Mickey.

"Hey," Tin Man declared. "Come on. You're smart people. Really, *really* smart. And you work damned hard. You may not know what those guys way out there are trying to tell us—for now. But I'd bet everything I have that you're going to figure it out."

Violet's Idea

F its great."

Violet lifted her arms straight out from her sides, the better to prove to Shura that the pink-and-aqua-striped pajamas she'd borrowed from her best friend would do just fine. Shura's kitchen was tiny—barely bigger than the lab they'd just left, as well befit someone with no time or inclination to cook—and so when Violet lowered her arms with an equally dramatic gesture, she almost knocked over a stack of ReadyMeals on the counter.

"Really?" Shura asked.

"Really."

Never mind that the sleeves only reached to Violet's elbows or that the buttons down the front were in imminent danger of popping off or that the simple act of raising her arms threatened to rip open a series of fragile, newly beleaguered seams.

"If you say so." Shura sounded dubious.

"Let me put it the way a politician would. Ready? Okay, here goes: The top fits as well as the bottoms do." Violet grinned and deftly executed a leg lift. The hem barely cleared the middle of her calf. She'd already uttered a silent prayer that the strained material across the backside was up to the challenge.

They laughed in unison. It really didn't matter how Shura's pajamas fit; Violet was too tired to care. Only a few hours remained until sunrise, when they'd have to get up, get dressed, and return to the lab to continue their work.

Would they be able to fulfill Tin Man's prophecy? Would they figure out the meaning of the message in Rachel's chip?

Violet didn't know.

All she *did* know was that she was completely exhausted. Her head felt too heavy for her neck. Her eyes burned. And so when Kendall had suggested that they break for the night and start fresh in the morning, Violet had pumped a fist in the air and said *Yes!* so fast that she cut off the end of his sentence.

Shura's apartment was much closer to the observatory. It made more sense for Violet to hang there for the next couple of hours than to go all the way back to her own apartment in Hawking. And there was, moreover, a pleasantly retro feel to the idea of a spontaneous sleepover at Shura's. It stirred up good memories.

When they were kids, and both of them still lived at home with their parents, Violet and Shura had spent the night together almost every weekend. They'd talk and laugh and listen to music on their consoles until late in the night. If they were at Shura's house, Shura would sometimes show Violet a painting she was working on; Violet loved to see her work, especially a work in progress, but she never asked. She waited for Shura to offer. And then, lying side by side in Shura's bed, they would discuss, hour after hour, how art was a way of stopping time, of lifting a moment from the ceaseless flow of eternity and setting it aside and sort of scribbling your name on it. Leaving your mark on the universe.

They didn't do that much anymore. In fact, Violet couldn't remember the last time she had spent the night at Shura's. They were both too busy. They had jobs now, and responsibilities, and other friends. Besides, they were adults now. Adults didn't spend the night at each other's houses, did they, giggling or listening to music or talking about eternity? Violet missed those weekends more than she could say, but like her desire to see Shura's work, she wouldn't bring it up first.

"I think I've got a bigger pair somewhere," Shura said. "I'll go look for them."

"Don't bother. Really, I'm fine." If she did end up ripping a hole in the backside, Violet thought, Shura would probably just call it a ventilation panel. She once told Violet that there was no such thing as an unsuccessful experiment. Every experiment told you something new.

"Are you hungry?"

"Of *course* I'm hungry," Violet replied. "Trouble is, though, I'm too tired to eat."

"Me too."

Shura's bed was narrow—too narrow, really, for two people—but they made do. Violet could have slept on the couch, but this struck them both as a better idea.

Violet scrunched up on her left side, hoping she wasn't crowding Shura. She could hear her friend's breathing, a sound she knew as well as she knew the sound of her own. She'd forgotten how comforting that could be: that familiar rhythm, the soft rise and fall. The sound of somebody breathing was like the sound of the ocean. There weren't any oceans on New Earth, just lakes and canals. But Violet knew about the oceans on Old Earth.

Humans arose from the oceans, she mused, her thoughts drifting like a ghost ship moving through the fog. She'd learned that in her biology classes. And her father had reminded her of it over the years. It was one of the reasons he insisted on locating the new civilization within sight of Earth, echoing Earth's orbit and not migrating to another planet. *We need to keep the oceans next to us, Violet,* he'd said, his husky voice rising with the purity of his certitude. *We need to stay attached to Earth.*

Why, Daddy? That's what she had asked him. She was a wide-eyed, eternally curious seven-year-old.

Because, Ogden Crowley answered, *Earth is our home. And always will be.*

What had made her remember that conversation? The sounds of Shura's breathing, yes—but there was another reason, too. Maybe it had to do with the message they were trying to interpret. The one from deep space. From somebody else's home.

Yeah. That made sense.

She lay there awhile longer, hoping to fall asleep. But as tired as she was, it didn't happen.

Oh, great, Violet thought. *What a terrific time to have insomnia. I've got a huge day ahead of me—we all do—and I'm going to be dragging. There's not enough coffee on all of New Earth to keep me going when I'm this beat.*

Dammit.

Well, stewing about it wasn't going to get her anywhere. She could at least get up and read something on her console—but not in here, where the light from the dancing jewels might awaken Shura.

Carefully, trying very, very hard not to disturb her friend, Violet put a leg over the edge of the bed. Then the other leg. She stood up. Stepping slowly and gingerly, she moved from the tiny bedroom into the equally tiny living room.

And then she saw it.

In the frail, gray, predawn light that seeped in from the small window behind the couch, she found herself staring at the portraits that covered all four walls from baseboard to ceiling. She had seen the portraits before, of course. Many times, over the years. At first, Shura had been self-conscious about displaying only her own paintings. Violet had finally persuaded her that there was nothing wrong with living in the middle of her creations—that it was, in fact, incredibly cool and incredibly inspirational and incredibly right. It was one-of-a-kind décor. And so now Shura kept dozens of her pictures here in her home, rotating them each time she finished a new batch like a shifting kaleidoscope of scenes from her inner life.

Violet turned in a slow, mesmerized circle. The room was too dim to enable her to catch every nuance of every painting or to burrow into the rich heart of each color, but she was able to feel the grand sweep and theme of these works, to see the way that each brushstroke described a thought as well as outlined a shape.

There: That one was a portrait of an old woman whom Violet and Shura had seen in Perey Park, a yellow scarf tied around her head. From the sideways tilt of the old woman's neck, from the apologetic hunch of her shoulders, from the unraveling hem of her scarf, Violet could sense how it would feel to be an old person in a young person's world. You were forgotten.

And there: It was a landscape portrait of a high hill on the outskirts of L'Engletown, one of the least populated cities of New Earth, where the terrain was rugged, surprising you at every turn. Violet could almost feel the dizzy enthusiasm of the grass as it grew in wild profusion, or the stubbornness of the burly rocks as they brooded and lurked. In the meticulously planned world of New Earth, having a place like this—tricky, unpredictable—was exciting, a necessary contrast to all the smoothness and regularity.

And over there: It was an abstract painting, a series of black-and-white circles and squares and triangles and exclamation points that didn't feel abstract at all, but instead reminded Violet of the way her mind leaped and sizzled when she suddenly got a mathematical concept that she'd been struggling with. The picture captured the joy of making connections in her brain, the *snap* of revelation.

She kept turning. A picture in the corner showed one of the massive turbines that powered New Earth; it spoke of power and ferocity, and the longer Violet studied it, the more aware she was of her own heartbeat, relentlessly pumping the blood through her body 24-7 with marvelous but unsung efficiency.

In another corner was a portrait of a big black dog running full speed through a meadow, ears pinned back, pink tongue flapping from the side of its mouth like a flag flying, its whole being aimed like an arrow at some distant point. The dog was pure purpose. She would've sworn that the wind ruffling the dog's fur was moving along her own arms and that the dog's sense of freedom and adventure stirred in her blood, too.

Shura's paintings, she realized, were as much about feeling as they were about seeing.

Feeling...

In a flash, Violet was absolutely certain she had the answer. Yes! She knew how they could discover what that faraway civilization was trying to say to them.

11

Protons and Picasso

"You want to do *what*?"

Rez squinted and frowned, the better to make Violet feel as if her idea were the most ridiculous, asinine, outlandish, delusional, and downright cockamamie one ever concocted by a human being who wasn't drunk, stoned, stupid, confused, depressed, distressed, hallucinating, or simply prone to making very bad jokes—in other words, a carbon-based version of Mickey.

"Hold on," Kendall said, stepping between them. "Give her a chance."

"Fine." Rez rotated his chair and stood up. Now he faced Violet head-on, not at an angle.

She kind of wished he'd stayed sideways. And seated. This was a little intense.

Across the room, Tin Man was trading jokes with Mickey. He wasn't paying attention to the argument. Shura, who stood just a little bit behind Violet, looked perplexed. Violet had explained the rudiments of the idea to her on their way back here, but Shura wasn't clear on the particulars. That uncertainty showed up in her face. She wanted to be loyal to Violet, but then again, the idea was . . . strange.

Very, very strange.

It was also bold and quite possibly nuts.

But it has as good a chance of working as anything Rez has come up with so far, Violet thought, trying to psych herself up as she stared him down.

Seconds ago, she'd presented her brainstorm to him in a brief, four-sentence summary. "Let's skip words altogether and rig up a Virtual Tether between Shura and the signal. She'll have her brush and easel. She'll be the conduit. She'll *paint* the alien emotions."

Virtual Tethers had been developed in the early 2260s. They were used to link computer systems by means of a signal far more durable than traditional Wi-Fi. Their roots lay in the cloud-computing concept of the early twenty-first century. They were also used for long-distance communications. The link was a form of bodiless teleportation, similar to a face appearing on a console screen.

But a Tether had never been attached directly to a human being.

"I'm going to give you the benefit of the doubt, Violet," Rez said, his tone drenched in skepticism. The frown dug even deeper. "I'll assume you didn't get much sleep during the break we just took. And you skipped breakfast. And *that's* why you're talking nonsense." He peered at her. "*Did* you get any sleep?"

"As a matter of fact, no. No, I didn't." Violet knew she sounded defensive, but she didn't care. She couldn't let herself be intimidated by Rez. Her idea wasn't crazy. It deserved a shot. "But that's not the point. The point is—"

"The point *is,*" Rez broke in, "we've got a lot of work to do here. We don't have time for your little schemes. So please, just let me and Shura and Kendall get back to work." In other words: Let the smart people solve the problem.

Violet seethed. How could she ever have been attracted to this guy? What in the world had she ever seen in him? Yeah, maybe they'd had some fun times when they worked together at Protocol Hall, but there was such a thing as *politeness,* and there were such things as *kindness* and *respect,* and there was also such a thing as not making your friends feel like boneheaded fools when they were just trying to . . .

Wait.

Rez hasn't always been like this, she reminded herself. Losing his sister in such an abrupt and violent way had changed him. Rez had always lacked social ease or personal warmth; the *hi-how-are-you?* part of life eluded him. But he'd never been this . . . well, this angry before. Preoccupied, yes; nasty, no. He was different now. Bitter, driven. When Rachel died, it was as if Rez lost his ability to care what anybody else thought of him. He was sad and lonely, and he'd built a hard shell around himself.

But that didn't mean she had to take any crap from him.

"No way, Rez," Violet snapped. "I will *not* stand down. Not until you listen to me."

He made a show of sighing. "Okay. I've got a few more seconds before my coffee's heated up and I can get back to my computer to do some *real* work. So go. Convince me."

"Great." She was up to the challenge. "First, we tried all the translation apps that we could get our hands on, right?"

Rez nodded. "Let's see. The total we tried last night—and that includes languages that haven't been spoken or written since Old Earth's first century, plus all their dialects—was

481,467. Whatever the aliens are speaking, it's not in our language database."

"Right. So if we want to get to the bottom of their language, let's forget about words."

"Even though words are commonly understood to be that from which language is comprised."

"Yeah. But they're not the *only* things from which language is comprised. They're not the *only* way we communicate," Violet stated.

Rez's attention was now officially snared. Kendall's, too. Shura and Tin Man had moved closer.

"Explain," Rez said.

"We don't have any way of interpreting the alien language, but we know they found Rachel's Intercept chip somewhere out in space and were intrigued by it. They must have realized that it collects and stores emotions. So this transmission from them—these words we don't understand because we don't have access to their language—is their way of trying to communicate their emotions to us." Violet pointed toward Rez's computer screen, where the words *trillum, nogg, waw* continued to pulse like an odd version of a screensaver. "They tried to use our language, our alphabet, but it's not working. There's no common point. No bridge."

"So no matter how many words they send us," Shura broke in, thinking out loud, "we don't know what they're really trying to say. And we can't, because we don't know what the individual words mean."

"That's the key," Violet declared, growing more excited. "We don't *need* to know their words. What they're really trying to communicate aren't their words at all but their emotions. So we let them."

"How?" asked Tin Man, although Kendall, Rez, and Shura were only nanoseconds behind him, and so a series of *Hows?* seemed to ripple through the tiny room like a runaway echo.

"Through *another* conduit for emotions," Violet said. "Something other than words."

Kendall's eyebrows rose as he posed the question. "Which is . . . ?"

"Art."

The expressions on her friends' faces continued to reflect bafflement, so Violet went on, "Shura's painting."

"But how can we do that?" Kendall asked.

"It's what I suggested to Rez right when we got here today," Violet answered. "We use a Virtual Tether. We establish a link between the incoming signal and Shura's consciousness. The aliens—whoever they are, wherever they're from, whatever they're trying to tell us—can communicate their emotions through Shura's painting. She'll be a sort of simultaneous translator. But she won't be turning one language into another language; she'll be turning one form of language into another form of language. She'll be turning *their* words into *her* art—into the colors of emotion."

A moment went by.

Rez said, "Wow." His voice was softer than Violet could ever remember it being. And for a moment, he didn't say anything else.

Tin Man scratched his ear and muttered, "Holy shit."

Kendall's face showed that he was thinking. He was thinking hard. And then slowly, slowly, he began to nod. He gave Violet a brief smile.

"That's . . . that's amazing," he said to her.

Now he addressed Shura. "Before we go too far down the road with this idea," he said, his voice grave, "it's all up to you.

You're the only one with the artistic ability to pull this off, but it makes you a guinea pig. Are you willing to take the chance? I mean, we don't know the full extent of the risks yet. We'll be hooking you up to a foreign transmission. We don't know where it's coming from or why. Anything could happen. Including... well, you know." He didn't want to say the word *death,* but he didn't need to; they all knew what he was getting at.

Shura nodded. She'd made her decision even before Kendall had outlined the stakes.

"You know what? When Violet first told me about this, my reaction was, '*Nooooo* way.'" Violet winced, and Shura gave her a light punch on the shoulder. "It's true," Shura continued. "No offense, buddy, but I sort of figured you'd gone batshit crazy. And then something occurred to me." Deep breath. "Ever since I was a little kid, I've been fighting a battle."

"Against who?" asked Tin Man.

"Against myself. It's like I'm two different people, okay? Half of me is a doctor. A scientist-inventor. These days, I lock myself up in my lab for days at a time, and I try to create new antibiotics and vaccines for jumping viruses. Or I try to design better HoverUps. Even when I leave the lab, I'm still thinking about viruses and vacuum tubes and vaccines.

"But I've got this other half, too. The half that loves to paint. To create pictures that make people feel. And *see.*" She looked at her friends one by one, starting with Violet and ending with Rez. "The problem is the art half of me. It's easy for people to appreciate the science part; I mean, I'm saving lives. I'm easing pain and suffering. Who doesn't understand *that*? But my paintings—those are important, too. Even more important, I think, than the science. But when I'm working on my art, I feel like I'm letting the world down. Like I'm playing instead of working.

"When Violet told me about this wild idea of hers"—Shura paused to smile at her friend—"I realized that it was the perfect way to put the two halves together. I'll be using science and technology to figure out what the alien civilization wants from us, but I'll also be doing it through my art. We'll need computers *and* colors. Protons *and* Picasso. I'll be translating new emotions—emotions we don't even know about yet—through shapes and colors. So I won't be divided anymore. I won't have science on one side and art on the other side. For the first time in my life, I'll be a whole person."

Violet tried to swallow but found she had a big lump in her throat. She'd never understood just how conflicted Shura was about her art. To Violet, her friend's blazing talent was wonderful, period; she had never considered the possibility that it also caused Shura some torment.

How could you not know such an important thing about your best friend?

To Violet's surprise, the next person who spoke was Rez. "I think Rachel sort of felt that way, too," he said. "She was really good at math, but it was the law she cared about. Some of her teachers were disappointed when she picked that. They didn't understand her. Why can't people be a lot of different things? Why do we have to choose?" He ran a finger across the bottom of his keyboard, buying time while he formulated his next sentence. "I'll do whatever I can to help. In memory of Rachel."

From across the room, Tin Man broke in grumpily. "Well, make up your mind, guys. We're either going to do this or we're not." Violet had noticed something odd; when Rez mentioned Rachel's name, Tin Man frowned. Maybe he was tired of hearing about the brilliant little girl. Or maybe he was just tired, period. They all were, even after the short break.

Kendall had already started punching buttons on his console. Violet could tell by the colors of the rising jewels—blue, black, gray—that he was doing high-level mathematical calculations.

He looked up. His eyes gleamed with excitement as he spoke.

"You know what, Violet? Your idea is completely original and totally ridiculous and makes no logical sense whatsoever, but that's basically what people told me when I was creating the Intercept, too." He grinned at her. "So it just might work."

Countdown to Danger

"Receptors in place," Kendall called out.

With a thumb and an index finger, he snatched up one of the wires leading from the tripod into the Signal Enhancer, tugging on it to make sure of the connection. The tugging was only for show, of course; the connection was secure. It had been secure the first dozen times he'd tested it after rigging up the tripod and placing it in the center of the lab, and nothing had come along since to dislodge it.

"Once the transmission is initiated," he added, "it'll undergo a ton of stress, but it'll hold. Mickey? Can you give me a signal level?"

"I *can,* but will I?"

The AstroRob snickered at his own wisecrack. Kendall ignored him, whereupon Mickey cleared his throat and, in a flat voice that was more in keeping with the cold, soulless machine that his designers had intended him to be, said, "Signal level is 140.7 and holding."

It was just after noon. They were packed so tightly in the

small lab that if anybody moved too fast or gestured too dramatically, she or he ran the very real risk of accidentally kicking, elbowing, head-butting, or chest-bumping somebody else. Every inch of space was occupied by either a person or a chunk of equipment.

And yet somehow, it didn't feel crowded. Improbably but magically, everything fit.

They had worked feverishly all morning long, each at her or his specific task, getting ready for the most bizarre undertaking of which any of them could conceive. The roles were clear: Mickey would monitor the incoming signal from the aliens. Rez would keep an eye on the energy level of the Virtual Tether. Tin Man would attend to Shura—watching her vital signs, making sure she was comfortable. And Violet was in charge of easels, brushes, and paint, the raw materials through which Shura would speak for whatever distant species had tried to contact them.

"Okay," Kendall said. "Rez? Ready at your end?"

All Kendall could see of Rez—all any of them could see of him from their vantage point in the center of the lab—was the wide back of his big red chair. But they all knew he was there. They could hear the low, running mumble of Rez talking to himself. Which is what Rez tended to do at the start of any new project that had not been his idea; he continued to badmouth it, but instead of doing it out loud, he took it underground. *This is a highly dubious proposition,* is what Kendall imagined Rez was murmuring over and over again, even though he couldn't tell for sure. Followed, perhaps, by *Probably won't work, anyway.* Pessimism seemed to settle Rez down. Negativity was his favorite mood stabilizer. But he'd agreed not to bother the others with his doubts, so all they got was the mumble. It was a kind of poem.

"Affirmative," Rez said blandly.

The next sound Kendall heard was a slight click, and then another, meaning that Rez had flipped two toggle switches on the control panel. "Virtual Tether synched," Rez added. "Online migration in three, two, one. Got it. Synching confirmed. Tether is online."

Kendall leaned down and tapped Violet's shoulder. "All good at your end?"

She gave him a quick thumbs-up from her position on the floor, where she knelt in front of a wooden crate with an open lid. She didn't reply out loud so as not to interrupt her counting of the closely packed rows of tubes of paint. She'd already counted them twice and was doing it a third time.

Violet had gathered every color she could think of on such short notice: the obvious ones like blue and red and green and brown and yellow and black, but some not-so-obvious ones, too, like gravel and sassafras and butterfly wing and raincloud and eggshell and mud puddle, plus combinations like red gold and blue orange and peach white and gray black and lime white. The tubes came from the Color Blenders, the team responsible for creating the revolving constellation of hues that adorned each night's sunset and each morning's sunrise on New Earth. Because the request had come from Senator Crowley, the Blenders had been happy to oblige—and without asking a lot of pesky questions.

A few minutes ago, a single-wheeled, self-driving Uni had pulled up to the observatory. Out popped the wooden crate. Two ReadyRobs had delivered the crate to Rez's office. Violet had fetched it there and brought it up to the lab by herself. She didn't want Rez's staff to know what was happening just one floor above them. Heaving it up through the porthole—even with Tin Man helping at the other end—had left her with a nice little memento: an ouchy twinge in her shoulder.

"Just about ready," she replied.

"Okay." Anxiety crouched in Kendall's voice. No one else would have noticed it, but Violet did. He never sounded nervous, not even when he was truly frightened; he had mastered the art of covering up his emotions. Back in the days of the Intercept, it had been a critical skill. "Remember, though," Kendall added. "We can't keep Shura hooked up too long. No one's studied the effects of it on a human being."

"Got it," Violet replied a little testily. Why was he telling her that? She *knew* that. They'd already discussed it. She knew the danger her scheme might pose to her best friend.

They'd be uploading a live Tether feed directly into Shura's consciousness, and the results could be magical—or cataclysmic.

The circuits could overload.

Or the Tether could overheat.

Or the alien signal might be corrupt, injuring Shura's brain.

Or the energy vectors—set to levels that were pure guesswork, because nobody had ever done this before with a human—could explode, and the observatory itself be demolished.

But this was their best shot at getting to the bottom of the mysterious **HELP** message. And so, risk or no risk, Shura had signed on to be the channel for the alien emotions.

"Hey," Shura said.

Violet looked up. "Hey, yourself."

Shura smiled. She'd positioned herself in the center of the room, encircled by three large blank canvases arranged on three identical wooden easels. Just beyond the ring of easels was Kendall's tripod, bristling with wires and seething with electrodes. Shura herself wasn't attached to anything because she didn't need to be—all the signals were wireless—but standing in the designated spot was key. It had been chosen for maximum signal receptivity.

Violet thought her friend seemed a little self-conscious, just standing there while everyone else worked. Shura swayed, shifting her weight from one foot to the other. She crossed and uncrossed her arms.

"Those colors look amazing," Shura commented, inclining her head toward the crate.

"How can you tell? All these little white tubes look exactly the same."

"I can tell."

Bet she can, Violet thought. Shura had once explained that she could intuit the presence of color, even if she couldn't see it. She could close her eyes and run her hand over a painted surface and know—through her fingertips, through a kind of hypersensitivity to the visual—what color it was.

And Violet totally believed her.

"Are you scared?" Violet asked. She had finished sorting and counting the tubes of paint. She stood up. She was outside the ring of easels; when she looked at her friend, it was almost as if Shura were imprisoned inside some magical forest, courtesy of a spell put on her by an enterprising witch.

That wasn't really true, of course. Shura could step out at any moment. But Violet knew she wouldn't.

"A little bit."

"I get that." Violet reached between two of the easels and put a hand on Shura's arm. She gave it a light, affectionate squeeze. The arm felt so thin to her. Was there any flesh there at all, or was it just hard bone covered by a bit of skin? Shura was the kind of person who forgot to eat when she was in the throes of a science project or a painting—or anything, really, that fully absorbed her attention. Violet had found her in her lab once, just before she'd announced a major breakthrough on a new antibiotic, so woozy and light-headed from not having eaten a bite for five and a half days that she could barely stand. Violet had quickly made three peanut butter sandwiches and stayed there until Shura ate them, one right after the other. *But I have work to do!* Shura had moaned as Violet handed her the next sandwich. And then the next. *Yeah, you do,* Violet had countered, *and your work is to finish this sandwich, or else I'll stuff it in an IV and feed you intravenously. Think of the mess.* That made Shura laugh. It also made her eat.

"What did your office say when you told them you weren't coming in today?" Shura asked.

Violet shrugged. "Not much. I think they're pretty used to me by now. If a constituent wanders in, they just give them a form to fill out."

"And then what happens to the forms? Do you read them?"

Violet winced. "I try to. I really do. I mean, I know it's important. But sometimes I think I'd be better off at a protest rally than sitting behind a desk reading forms. It's hard to figure out what you're supposed to do with your life, right?" She smiled at Shura. "For everybody except you. You've always known. Art and science."

Shura shook her head. "Don't change the subject. Tell me what you do with those forms after you read them. Or not."

"I recycle them. Of course."

Shura laughed. Her laugh was soft and almost musical. Violet thought about how many times she'd heard that laugh across all the years of their friendship. In a way, they were oddly matched and always had been: Shura Lu, the scientific genius and magnificently gifted artist, and Violet Crowley, the restless, headstrong rebel and former detective who was now a hopelessly mediocre politician. But somehow it worked. They'd been best friends since they were in kindergarten together, members of the first generation to grow up exclusively on New Earth. She loved Shura, and she knew that Shura loved her.

If anything happens to her because of this idea of mine, then . . . then I'm not sure how I'll live with myself, Violet thought. She felt a sudden clutch of panic.

"Hey, you two," Kendall said. "We're almost ready to crank it up." He checked some last-minute equations on his console. "Rez? Tin Man? It's just about time, everybody."

"How about me?" Mickey uttered a sound that resembled the squawking of an outraged chicken.

"Okay, Mickey," Kendall said. "Forgive me. Are you ready?"

"Sonny boy, I was *born* ready." The AstroRob spun his head around and flashed a few lights.

"Show-off," Rez muttered.

Violet picked out three tubes of paint from the crate. She uncapped them and arranged one on the tray of each easel. She wanted Shura to have a primary color within easy reach as a place to start; later, as the alien emotions and ideas that rushed into Shura's mind grew ever more complex, the other colors would be retrieved for her use by Violet, the blends and the swirled compounds.

"Signal level," Kendall said.

"Holding stable at 140.7." Mickey's response didn't include a single belch, fart, snort, snicker, or knock-knock joke. This was serious. The experiment would be underway in seconds.

"Shura? Are you ready?" Kendall asked. Once again, his voice shook just the tiniest bit. A casual acquaintance would not have detected the small quaver, but Violet did. She tried to catch his eye, but he looked away. *You can't even* look *at me, Kendall? Are you THAT worried?*

"Ready," Shura responded. Her voice, unlike Kendall's, didn't shake at all. It was solid and sure.

Violet was very proud of her friend. Rez had tried to get them to consider some sort of sedation for Shura, but Shura and Violet had said, in unison, *No.* Clarity was key. Sedation might impede the signal, keeping it from flowing from her brain into her brush hand.

She wanted to be as open as she could be, as receptive as possible to the alien transmission.

Mickey started up the Signal Enhancer. The next sounds they heard were a *whoosh* and a series of dull thumps and then a louder, longer *whoosh.*

It was set.

As Shura picked up her brush, Kendall continued with his final checklist. "Rez? Tin Man? Violet?"

The answers came in a flurry: *Yes. Yes. Yes.*

Everyone was ready.

Violet took a last glimpse at Shura. Her best friend looked as she always did when she was starting a new painting; there was excitement in her dark eyes. Her feet were spread. She squared up her body in relation to the canvas in the middle and leaned forward as if she couldn't wait for the very next moment of her life to arrive. She gripped the brush firmly in her right hand. With the fingertips of her left, she stroked the bristles just once. Violet could almost feel the bristles herself; they were soft, pliable, but also firm.

Shura picked up the palette with her left hand. Then she gave Kendall a quick nod, her head barely dipping forward at all. It was enough. He understood and nodded back.

"Go," Kendall said.

Mickey punched in the coordinates that switched the signal's destination from Rez's computer screen to Shura. Violet was so nervous she felt like throwing up; she wanted to be here, but part of her also wished she were a thousand miles away, because if something went wrong, if Shura ended up injured or, God forbid, if she ended up . . . *No, I won't think about that, I* can't *think about that . . .*

Violet spun around, looking for something, anything, to hang on to, but the room was too small. No room for extra chairs. There was nothing. She had to stand up straight and deal with the consequences of her idea.

Shura, she thought desperately, *I never meant to hurt you. I just have to know what the aliens are trying to tell us. We* all *have to know.*

A rapid series of metallic clicks. The signal was switching, intensifying. Rez's computer screen went blank. The words were whisked away. And then the screen was overtaken by a bright blue light as the signal swelled and prepared for its jump. The receptors in the tripod that Kendall had rigged up began to hum and glow; they were gripped by a frantic vibration as the signal flooded them, on its way to infiltrating Shura's brain through the Wi-Fi channel. The power drawdown in the lab was so monumental that the lights flickered.

As the signal hit her brain and skittered across both lobes, Shura gasped. Her brush hand jumped.

This was it.

Wonderstruck

They waited.

They waited longer.

They waited and . . .

Nothing happened.

At some point in the first few seconds of the changeover in the signal's destination, when the alien transmission was reaching Shura's brain, Violet had closed her eyes, pinching them shut. If something terrible happened to her best friend, she didn't want to witness it.

Now she opened them.

And she saw that . . . nothing had changed.

Shura still stood in front of the blank canvas, brush raised and ready, palette poised. Mickey's attention was locked onto the incoming coordinates. Rez was focused on his computer screen. Kendall was stationed next to the tripod and its bevy of receptors, watching for the tiniest twitch or fizz, while Tin Man watched the device that monitored Shura's vital signs.

Still, nothing happened.

Absolutely . . . *nothing.*

"Told you it wouldn't work," grumbled Rez. He smacked the desk upon which his keyboard resided. "Friggin' waste of time." He bolted up from his chair, stretching out his arms. "Geez. Trying to turn alien emotions into *painting.* That's about as stupid an idea as I've ever—"

"STOP IT." Shura's voice sounded like a lion's roar crossed with a rocket engine. "Just *stop.* We're all in this together, Rez. We don't make fun of each other's ideas, okay?"

Rez looked a little stunned. He was used to being reprimanded by Violet or Kendall. Even Tin Man had taken shots at him. But Shura? No.

"I just meant—"

"I don't care *what* you meant," she said. The outrage in her voice still hadn't subsided. "Nobody made fun of you last year for Olde Earth World, right?" She was referring to Rez's plan to create an amusement park on Old Earth, complete with roller coasters and a variety of rides related to the fate of that tattered planet.

"No." He said it simply and quietly. Because she was right. "No, they didn't." He sat back down in the red chair.

"So let's cut Violet a little slack here," Shura went on. "She's doing her best. We're all doing our best. And besides—" She turned to face the others. They'd been watching the confrontation with surprise and—it had to be said—more than a little bit of satisfaction. "I think I know why it didn't work. And what we can do to *make* it work."

"You do?" Violet said.

Shura nodded. "I do."

Tin Man was at her side in an instant. "What do you need?"

"My medical bag. It's in my apartment." She told him the access codes required to enter.

"Anything else?"

"Um . . . yeah," Shura said. She looked a little embarrassed. "While you're there, could you make me a peanut butter sandwich? I'm so hungry I swear I could eat this brush."

By the time Tin Man returned with the battered black-leather bag—and five peanut butter sandwiches, one for each of them—Shura had explained her idea to Kendall, Rez, and Violet.

"Where's mine?" Mickey asked in a pathetic-sounding whine as Tin Man passed out the sandwiches.

Tin Man hesitated. Mickey giggled. "Come on," the AstroRob said. "I'm not serious. Those don't appeal to me at all."

"Because robots don't eat sandwiches?" Tin Man said.

"Nope. Because you didn't put any jelly on 'em."

The chorus of groans ended only when Rez spoke. "If I ever run into Dumb-Ass Dave, that guy's in *big* trouble." He had explained to them earlier why Mickey was the way he was: bursting with bad jokes and silly bits of wordplay that rained over his circuits like confetti. "I'd rewire him myself if I had the time."

"Me—or Dave?" Mickey said, chortling at himself.

As soon as she polished off her sandwich, Shura retrieved what she needed from her bag. It was a vial half filled with a white powdery substance. She held it up to check the level of the contents.

"Looks like there's just enough," she said.

"What is it?" Rez asked.

Before Shura could answer, Kendall stepped forward. His body language indicated that he'd like a look at the vial. Shura handed it to him.

"I know what this is," he said quietly.

"I thought you would." Shura accepted it back from him. With her free hand, she touched Kendall's forearm.

"Yeah," Kendall said.

Addressing the rest of her friends, Shura said, "It's deckle. I keep a small supply in my bag, in case a patient is anxious or frightened."

Deckle.

Now Violet got it. She knew why Kendall had reacted as he did to the sight of the fine white powder.

Deckle was a substance found exclusively on Old Earth. It was harmless, but for many years, it was believed to be a dangerous drug, fiercely addictive. And it topped the list of illegal drugs bought and sold on the ragged streets of Old Earth by desperate people. Actually, deckle had only one significant effect: It rendered the user immune to the power of the Intercept.

Kendall's brother, Danny, had been killed on Old Earth by a drug gang in search of deckle. Seeing the substance, Violet realized, must have evoked a flurry of memories in Kendall, memories of his life with the last family member he would ever have. And now Danny, too, was gone. Kendall was alone.

He has his friends, Violet thought. *He has me and Shura and Rez and Tin Man, but that's not the same as family. As blood.* She knew that very well. She had learned it six months ago, when her father died. *Rez knows it, too, after losing Rachel. Even though he never talks about it. And Tin Man's no stranger to that kind of loss, either.*

There was no substitute for the people whose blood you shared.

"How's deckle going to help us?" Rez inquired. He was still a bit cautious around Shura after her takedown. "It just calms you, right? And barely that?"

"Yeah," Shura replied. She'd poured a few grains into her palm while she talked. "But 'barely' is all I need."

"You don't seem nervous to me," Tin Man observed.

"I'm not. But my mind is resisting the alien signal. That's why Violet's plan isn't working. The plan is just fine; the problem is *me.*" She put the grains of deckle on her tongue and then put the stopper back in the vial. "That'll do it."

"Can't you just tell yourself not to resist the signal?" Tin Man persisted.

"I'm an artist. I paint what *I* want to paint—nobody else. I paint what I feel. It's the strongest part of me. The most powerful element in my whole being. I can't be a passive conduit for the alien signals. My will is too fierce for that."

"You don't seem fierce to me. You always seem kind of—well, kind of quiet and polite," Tin Man said.

Shura laughed. "I *am* quiet and polite—everywhere except when I'm in front of a canvas. Just ask Violet. She's the troublemaker, the rebel, and I'm the little voice in the background going, 'Um, Violet? Should we, like, ask permission to do that? I mean, the sign says *No Admittance.*'"

Violet grinned.

"But when it comes to my art," Shura went on, "everything changes. My art is the one place where I'm this pure, primitive, furious force."

"So true," Violet murmured. "I've watched people try to tell you how and what to paint. I've seen you kick some ass."

"And deckle," Kendall said, nodding as he followed her logic, "will let you relax enough to be that conduit."

"Right." Shura closed the clasp on her black medical bag with a crisp *snap!* and handed it back to Tin Man.

"If we're finished with all the explanations," Rez said, more than a little impatiently, "can we get back to work?"

They returned to their former posts: Shura stepped into the middle of the ring of easels; Rez hunched over the control panel; Kendall stationed himself next to the receptor-laden tripod; Violet sat cross-legged on the floor next to the crate of paint tubes and stacks of extra blank canvases; Tin Man stood vigil in the corner, his eyes on the monitor that measured Shura's heartbeat and respiration.

"Mickey, initiate the signal changeover," Kendall ordered.

"Roger that." The AstroRob couldn't help himself. "Although to tell you the truth, I'm not really sure who Roger is." He coughed. "Sorry. Bad habit."

Rez ignored the indiscretion as he checked the readouts on the panel. "Energy vectors online. Signal level stable."

"Materials ready," Violet declared from her spot. "Shura?"

"Ready." Shura examined the brush in her hand one more time. The slender wooden stalk looked so old-fashioned, Violet thought, here amid the dazzle of twenty-third-century technology, and the bristles were like a throwback to a world of simple tools. But there was magic in the brush, a lively and robust magic that enabled it to float above all the gleaming marvels in the lab. It reminded Violet of a truth she'd come to believe in the last few years: Methods, techniques, and technology might change, but human beings didn't.

"Ready," Shura repeated in an even stronger voice.

Once again, the room was invaded by a *whoosh* and the dull thuds and a faint rumble and finally another *whoosh.* The lights flickered once more.

Shura uttered a soft but audible gasp. Her shoulders moved to one side as if she'd been slightly jostled in a crowd.

She closed her eyes.

She lifted the brush. She angled the palette. Her brush hand trembled, and then, as her friends looked on with rising excitement, she leaned forward and began to paint, at first carefully, but after the first few seconds, feverishly. The picture burst forth upon the canvas, blossoming like a flower.

The moment was so intense, so captivating, that none of them noticed one small detail:

Tin Man was no longer in the room. He had taken advantage of their keen, absolute focus on Shura and slipped out through the porthole in the floor.

14

Strokes of Genius

It was the most amazing thing Violet had ever seen. She assumed her friends were equally stunned, because no one moved—only Shura.

And Shura was doing enough moving for all of them.

Now that her own imagination had moved over to make room for another, she was a tornado of pure painting energy. She was a whirling circus of creativity. Her brush danced across the canvas, skipping and sweeping and then engaging in large circular swoops, sending forth sparks of colors. The blues were fantastic and ethereal; the greens were a living thing, wet and lush; the reds and yellows popped and sparked. The grays and blacks had a haunting quality to them, a sense of deep time and the slow emergence of wisdom.

Kendall was the first of the onlookers to break free of the spell.

"Mickey, check the signal strength," he said.

"It's at 152.8 and rising."

"Too fast," Rez muttered. He was clearly worried. "The

aliens—they don't know our capacity. I think they're turning up the signal intensity at their end. It's too much. But they realize they're getting through, and so they're a little reckless."

"Yeah," Kendall said. "They are. But it's not too much. Not yet, anyway. She can handle it." His voice was riven with awe. He took a quick look down at Violet, who was resupplying the paints as fast as Shura needed her to, which was very fast indeed. Astonishingly fast, as a matter of fact. Violet uncapped tubes and jammed them into the easel trays with deft, rhythmic motions. Then she swept up the empty tubes, getting them out of the way. Shura snatched up the new tubes and squeezed the fresh colors onto the palette.

"It's *working,* Violet," Kendall declared. "It's really working. You were right. They don't know our words, but they're desperate to communicate their feelings. I mean, just *look.*"

He swept a hand toward Shura's canvas. She had just finished with the one on the second easel and was moving on to the third. Her eyes were still closed, but she seemed to know instinctively where each canvas was located and precisely where she wanted to place her brush upon it, and with which colors. As she completed each canvas in mere minutes, Violet yanked it away and immediately replaced it with a fresh one, angling the finished canvases against the wall.

She couldn't answer Kendall. Not right away. She was too moved, too overwhelmed by the breathtaking spectacle of what Shura was doing and how she was doing it.

And what of the paintings themselves?

The paintings . . .

They exploded across Violet's consciousness. They told of impossibly distant worlds brimming with fantastic spectacles. They described planets made of pure glittering ice, planets that burned with sinuous flames, planets surging with volcanoes, and planets that were nothing but writhing tendrils of smoke and fog.

They depicted galaxies that spun so fast they were mere blurs against the blackness of space.

One painting looked like rage; it was black and harsh. Another looked like melancholy; it was slathered in gray, the gray of lost hope and thwarted ambition. A canvas slashed with red made Violet think of passion that had changed into hatred.

Every stroke of Shura's brush conveyed a distinct emotion.

Occasionally, a word would form at the edge of the canvas, the letters shifting and tentative, a word added before Violet was quite aware of it. Only in retrospect was the word visible.

Trillum, one said.

Nogg was another, followed by *waw.*

And there were other words, too, words that had not been part of the first transmission: *foxol* and *lunti* and *cawbon* and *siggul* and *pompf.* It was as if the aliens were still trying to grope their way into human language, still grappling with the alphabet—even as emotions, bold and blunt and florid, assumed visible form across painting after painting.

The paintings leapt out ahead of the words, communicating much more swiftly and directly than if they had to rely upon the cumbersome journey of language.

"This is—this is *fantastic,*" Rez gushed. He kept switching his attention from Shura's canvases to the control panel, going back and forth, back and forth, as fast as he could. He needed to monitor the signal, because that was his job, but he was drawn to the paintings. "And it's coming to us through Rachel's Intercept chip."

Violet, leaping about as she replaced paints and canvases, was astonished. Gone was Rez's cynicism. Gone was his sour smirk. The old Rez had fled, at least temporarily. Instead he seemed filled with . . .

Wonder.

Yeah. That was the only word for it, Violet decided; he was wonderstruck. *And I'm pretty wonderstruck myself,* she thought as she switched a new tube of bright scarlet for a used-up one.

Hours passed. Or was it minutes? Violet didn't know. Nor did she care. The tiny lab was bathed in a radiance that seemed brighter and truer than any light yet known on New Earth. It was a light beyond light, a light that purified as much as it illuminated.

And then it disappeared.

There was a brief sizzling sound, and suddenly Rez's computer screen was filled with fuzzy gray blobs. They had replaced the sharp, beguiling blue. Another signal had overridden the alien transmission.

"What *happened*?" Rez yelled.

The room was dominated by a loud burst of static and then a halting, ragged voice: "*This . . . this is Tin Man. I need help.*" The transmission was fitful and weak. It quickly disintegrated into snatches of words: *Need . . . trapped . . . hope . . . please.*

"Hey!" Rez called out angrily. He punched buttons on the panel with a rising fury. "We've got to get the alien transmission back."

"Hold on," Violet said. She had grabbed the back of Rez's chair and spun him around so that, for the moment, he couldn't switch the signal. "That's Tin Man. We can't just cut him off."

Behind her, slumped over on the stool, Shura took several deep breaths. She'd been painting with such passionate intensity that she was totally exhausted.

"We're in the middle of an important experiment here," Rez countered. "We're making incredible progress."

"I know that. And we can go back to it after we figure out what's going on with Tin Man. He's asking for help."

"No," Rez declared. "We have to keep going." He scowled. "Where is he, anyway? He was here just a second ago. Over there in the corner."

"I don't know," Violet said. "But we can't ignore him. Kendall? You're with me, right?"

Kendall was torn. Violet could see that. He was deep into the interpretation of the signal, totally focused on the challenge at hand. Like Rez, he was desperate to figure out what the unknown civilization from beyond the stars was trying to tell them.

But Tin Man was his friend.

"Okay," Kendall said reluctantly. "We'll find Tin Man and see what he needs. And then we'll switch back to the alien signal."

Rez uttered a howl of protest and sputtered a profanity, but Violet was already at the control panel, twisting dials to try to clarify the image.

"Tin Man," she said. "Hey, where are you? Where are you transmitting from?"

The reply was garbled and weak.

"What?" Violet said. "Can you repeat that?"

"We can't hear you!" Kendall yelled.

The gray screen turned a hazy, mottled brown. Finally, it resolved into an image of a small, windowless room with slimy walls and a dirt floor. In the center of that floor—lying on his side, curled up and moaning while he clutched his stomach—was Tin Man. There was a deep gash in his forehead. Blood had dried on his neck and hands.

"You're hurt," Violet said. She knew she was stating the obvious, but she couldn't help herself.

"Oh my God," Rez muttered. "What's that jerk gotten himself into *this* time?"

Violet started to tell Rez to shut up. Instead she raced over to the control panel, her gaze taking in all the dials and switches that she didn't know the first thing about. "Where's that signal coming from?" she demanded.

Working at his own computer, Mickey located the transmission coordinates. His answer stunned them all:

"Old Earth."

Tin Man's Betrayal

Violet checked her console three times. And then she checked it a fourth, because if she and Kendall became separated—which might very well happen, given the chaos and unpredictability of any visit to Old Earth—they'd need a means of keeping in touch.

Old Earth had a way of taking even the very best plan and turning it upside down, shortly before shredding it to bits and setting the scraps on fire.

"Console's testing fine," she said.

"Mine, too," Kendall verified.

They walked side by side along a winding path that might once have been a road. In the distance was a pus-yellow smear that might once have been a city. A tangled mass of thick vines seemed to reach at them from both sides, and behind the vines, there was a tightly furled block of dark woods that was, Violet felt, pushing hard against them. If they didn't keep going, they might very well be crushed. Or maybe just suffocated to death.

Overhead, the sky was the brownish-red color of an infected

wound. The sun was somewhere up in that rusty haze, too. You'd have to part the layers of heavily polluted air with two hands, though, to actually see that sun, Violet knew, like somebody peeking out through a thick dirty curtain.

"His console signal's coming in at north-northeast," she said. "Another mile or so and we'll be there."

"Okay."

"No telling what we'll find. Need to be ready for anything."

In a weary voice, Kendall responded, "We always are, right?"

Neither one of them wanted to be here. They wanted to be back at the observatory, watching Shura paint her marvelous paintings, trying to figure out what the aliens were saying and why a distant civilization had asked for their help. They wanted to be solving the greatest puzzle of their lives.

Instead they were trudging along a weed-choked, mud-clotted, barely discernable path on Old Earth, following the distress signal from Tin Man's console. Of course they were in a hurry—he had appeared to be injured, and they still didn't know how badly or why, because he hadn't answered direct questions—but they couldn't go any faster across the rugged terrain. The wind blew straight in their faces, and it brought the hot, rancid smell of decay along with it.

The argument back in the observatory had been quick but tense. Rez had tried to argue them out of their decision to track Tin Man. He wanted them to continue channeling the signal through Shura and her stupendous paintings. Violet told Rez he was being callous. She and Kendall won the argument, but the truth was that part of her didn't want to win.

Indeed, part of her thought Rez was right. *My God, we're actually seeing the emotions of an alien civilization!* Hesitating, even briefly, was excruciating.

Finally, they'd all agreed that Violet and Kendall would go

to Old Earth and look for Tin Man, while Rez and Shura stayed in the lab. Shura needed to rest; she was dizzy with exhaustion, and the hand with which she'd held her paintbrush was twisted into a cramp.

Rez, meanwhile, would watch for a new message. The aliens would surely wonder why their signal wasn't going through anymore. Rez wasn't sure how he'd do it, but somehow he would explain:

Hang in there. We'll be back.

Violet was furious with Tin Man. Why had he sneaked out of the lab? And gone to—of all places—Old Earth? That difficult, forbidding place had been the site of the worst moments of his life. He'd lost his sister there, and sold drugs on the street, and been arrested, and served time in prison. Coming to New Earth had given him and his mom a new start. Why would he throw all that away, and why would he do it right *now*?

Now, when they were on the cusp of an amazing discovery?

As angry as she was at Tin Man, though, she would help him. He was her friend. No matter what he'd done, that was the most important thing.

"Give us two hours," Violet had said to Rez, her voice steady, implacable. This wasn't a negotiation. "We'll bring him back, and then we can restart the connection again."

"Two hours," Rez had said glumly. He winced, because he hated the idea of waiting even two *seconds* to resume the grand experiment. "I've got your word on that."

She nodded. "Ready, Kendall?"

"Here."

She stopped. The silence created in the wake of that pause was eerie. They had not seen another living soul or heard a sound other than their own footsteps for the past twenty minutes. Neither of them had felt like talking. And so after double-checking the signal direction, they had marched along, silent but resolute, while fallen branches and dead leaves crackled and crunched underfoot.

Kendall checked his console. "I'm getting an ID confirmation for Tin Man. He's in there, all right."

They could barely see it, mired in the woods: a small, dilapidated cabin. Violet and Kendall had to thrash and flail their way through a natural latticework of thick branches to get there, stumbling numberless times into bogs hidden by hedges and unruly bushes swarming with thorns.

"He's gotta be in there," Violet said.

She had a foot on the broken-down porch and was almost at the door, a slab of wood that bore the marks of an ax blade as well as the claws of wild animals, when Kendall grabbed her.

"Wait. I'll go first."

"Why?"

He couldn't think of a good answer, so he shrugged and released her arm.

"Let's go in at the same time," he said.

Only after Violet had started to lift the wooden latch did she wonder if maybe it was some sort of trap. What if Tin Man had been forced to summon them here and they were about to be attacked? Old Earth was a wild, lawless place that seethed with people who had nothing to lose. Violet's and Kendall's consoles could be melted for scrap; scrap metal could be traded for food and shelter and weapons.

Well, if that happens, it was a pretty good life overall, even if it was damned short, she thought. Worst-case scenarios always brought out the smart-ass in her, instantly improving her mood. *Nothing to do now but go forward.*

The door was heavy, and its hinges were so rusty and stubborn that all of Violet's strength was required to heave it open just a tad, even with a massive assist from Kendall. They slipped sideways into the cabin.

The first thing they saw was the image that had been transmitted from Tin Man's console. He was lying on the floor in the fetal position, bleeding profusely from a long gash across his forehead.

"Tin Man!" Violet called out. She rushed toward him.

Kendall, suspecting an ambush, sent his gaze flying around the room. It was dim, lit only by the shaft of daylight allowed in by the half-opened door. "Anybody else in here?"

Tin Man moaned and shook his head.

"Don't think so. They dumped me here and left."

Violet was down on her knees now, peering at the head wound. "Who? Who did this to you? And why?"

"Yeah," Kendall said. He was checking the corners, despite Tin Man's assurances. "What the hell's going on?"

Tin Man coughed. The effort to do so made him yelp in pain. "It's my ribs," he said, gasping out the words. "I think at least two of them are broken. They kicked me pretty hard." He tried to sit up. Another yelp. But he stayed up, blinking mournfully first at Violet and then at Kendall, who by this time was looming above him. "I'm really sorry, guys."

"If you're so sorry," Kendall answered, with no kindness in his voice, "then tell us what happened. Your distress call interrupted the alien transmission. Rez is livid. Let's put it this way—the fact that you're not actually dead may be only a temporary state. Because he wants to kill you."

"Come on," Violet said, trying to get an arm around Tin Man's waist to help him up. At first, he wouldn't budge, but when Kendall leaned down to help, taking an arm, he seemed more inclined to rise.

With a few more yelps and a piteous-sounding moan, Tin Man stood up. He still kept a hand on his chest, holding his injured ribs in place.

"I was looking for Molly," Tin Man said.

An astonished Violet stared at him. "But your little sister is dead. Why were you—"

"Yeah," Tin Man said, interrupting her. "And Rachel's dead, too. But she's back. Sort of. Because we've got her Intercept chip. So Rez gets to see her again. Or at least her memories. Rachel's graduation day, remember? Well, it's not fair. If Rez can have *his* sister back, then why can't I have *mine*? I want to see Molly's memories. I loved my little sister just as much as Rez loved his. So why can't I have her? Why?"

"I get it," Kendall said quietly.

"You do?"

"Yeah." Kendall looked at Tin Man. "You came down here to find Molly's chip, right?"

Nodding slowly, Tin Man said, "There's an old cemetery just behind this cabin. It's all overgrown with weeds now; you can't see it from the road. Most people wouldn't even know it's back there. But I know. Because that's where I buried Molly."

He put a hand to the gash on his forehead. He pulled his hand away again and saw the blood slathered on his fingers. The sight made him wince.

"Bunch of guys jumped me," Tin Man explained. "They came from out of nowhere. Old Earth's worse than it's ever been. Gangs don't just stick to the cities. They hang out on the back roads, too, waiting for somebody to come by so they can rob them." He poked gingerly at a rib and caught his breath as the pain sliced him. "They beat me up and threw me in here. They didn't take my console—only my money. Good thing, because that's how I reached you guys. The console fell out of my pocket when they dumped me here, and it skidded over there." He tried to incline his head toward a dark corner. "I used voice activation and put it on panorama, and I—"

"And you interrupted the signal from the aliens," Violet said, cutting him off. "*That's* what you did." Her voice had lost its concern. Now that she knew he was basically okay, she was angry. "So let me get this straight. You were going to get Molly's chip? From her *body*? Good God, who *are* you? Dr. Frankenstein? What were you *thinking*?"

Tin Man closed his eyes and shook his head. "I know. I know. I'm the world's biggest dope. As soon as I got here, I realized how insane it all was. I just . . . I just went a little nuts. When I thought about Rachel's chip transmission coming back to us, I couldn't help myself. I want Molly's chip back, too. I miss her so much. Sometimes I can't . . ." His voice thickened. Violet could tell he was fighting the urge to cry.

Which was a totally weird spectacle even to contemplate: Tin Man, the biggest, strongest person she knew, his muscular body stamped with tough-looking tattoos—*weeping.* Or almost.

Kendall had heard enough. He didn't want to deal with tears. "Okay. No more self-pity. Let's get out of here before some *other* gang comes out of the woods and all three of us end up with busted heads and broken ribs instead of just one of us. Can you walk?"

"Yeah." Tin Man coughed and winced. "But one more thing. I need you to know something." He gulped. "She gave me my nickname. Did you guys know that? Molly's the one who started calling me Tin Man. She was only five years old. She'd found an abandoned console and she watched an old, old movie called *The Wizard of Oz.* She loved it. And her favorite character was Tin Man because he was the only character in the story who really *worked.* That's what she said. The scarecrow just hung there in a field, and the lion blustered and bragged, but Tin Man *worked.* With his ax. And Molly knew how hard I worked to protect her. In the end, though, I failed. I lost her. She died." Once again, he seemed close to tears.

"Let's go," Violet said. She nudged him. "We have to get back."

"I'm sorry," Tin Man blurted. "I'm so sorry, you guys. I just lost it. The thought of Molly's chip and being able to see those good times again, all these amazing times we had down here, was too much. As hard as life was down here, we had fun. She was such a great kid. So filled with life."

Finally, he let himself be drawn along. Violet and Kendall stationed themselves on either side of him, ready for the journey back to the transfer point at Thirlsome.

They had barely cleared the door before Tin Man murmured, "I was kind of hoping you'd bring Shura. I mean, she's a doctor, right? And these ribs really hurt."

Kendall let out a long, pissed-off sigh. "Yeah, well, I'll tell you what, Tin Man. I'll make note of your *preferences*"—he pronounced the word with a shudder of distaste—"for the next time you sneak off and jeopardize a project that could hold the key to the survival of New Earth, okay? I'll do that. Yeah. *Sure.*"

Violet totally understood Kendall's attitude. They'd forgive their friend—because you had to forgive your friends when they screwed up. Sometime, though, you could take a little while to do it. He might not have meant to betray them, but that was what he'd done.

Shuffling along between them, his head hanging down, Tin Man didn't say anything else for a long time.

By now, the preliminary sounds were familiar to them—the *whoosh,* the rumbles, the second and even louder *whoosh*—as they linked up the wireless connection between Shura's brain and the signal cruising in from the distant reaches of space.

Once again, she stood in the middle of a circle of blank canvases. Once again, Rez and Mickey monitored the computers, keeping a close eye on the signal strength. Kendall secured the tripod and the receptors. Violet returned to her spot on the floor by the crate. She'd hurriedly counted the tubes yet again, making sure they wouldn't run out of colors—which, in this case, would be like running out of life. The supply of canvases made her smile with satisfaction. There were plenty.

The only thing different about the booting-up process this time was the absence of Tin Man. Violet and Kendall had taken him home, to the small house he'd once shared with his mom. Violet called Jonetta Loring and asked her to take care of him. Jonetta had readily agreed, and with a blessed lack of pesky questions.

And now they were all back in Rez's lab, ready to pick up where they'd left off.

After the second *whoosh,* Shura's eyes fluttered shut, just like before.

She lifted her brush, just like before.

She picked up her palette, just like before.

Kendall adjusted the row of sparking receptors along the tripod, just like before.

And just like before, the canvases began to explode with great arcs and whorls of color as Shura painted, her body swaying slightly as she dabbed her brush on the palette and mixed the colors and then lunged forward and—

Suddenly, Shura froze. The brush plummeted from her newly opened hand. It fell to the floor with a clatter. Next, the palette fell, too.

Eyes still closed, she began to tremble. Both hands were drawn up into tight fists.

"What's going on?" Violet cried out.

Shura didn't answer. Her moan widened out into a wail of intense pain.

"Kendall? Rez?" Violet said, her voice urgent. "*Do* something. Cut the signal! Pull the plug! Just *do* something! Anything! She's hurting!"

Rez was already on his feet. He'd rushed over to Mickey's computer. One look at the robot's screen gave him the grim news.

"The signal booted up too fast after the break," Rez said in a helpless-sounding voice. "It's too much for her. Her body can't absorb the energy at this intensity."

"Shut it down!" Violet screamed the words. "Shut it down!" She lunged toward Shura, intending to gather her in a tight hug and hold her, trying to make the vibrations stop.

"NO!"

Kendall, Rez, and Mickey yelled the word simultaneously.

Violet halted. Her hands were inches from Shura's trembling body. "What? Why can't I—"

"Don't touch her!" Kendall yelled, yanking Violet back out of the circle of easels and out of reach of her friend. "You'll be caught up in it, too. It's like when someone grabs a live electrical wire; you can't make contact. Or you die, too."

Die? Violet felt sick and dizzy. Shura couldn't die.

That cannot happen.

But Shura was shaking even harder. Her entire body was racked by spasms—her shoulders, her torso, her arms, her legs, her feet. Liquid trickled from her mouth. She clearly couldn't speak, just as she couldn't break free from the signal's escalating grip.

"Shut it down! Cut the signal!" Violet said, almost hysterical now. Her best friend was in total distress and apparently there was nothing—*nothing*—she could do to help her.

"We're trying!" Rez yelled back. He and Kendall worked furiously at the control panel, rushing back and forth, wrenching dials and flipping switches.

"We've cut it at our end," Rez explained as his fingers flew over the panel, "but the aliens have to cut it at *their* end, too. And I can't tell them that. I don't have any way to communicate with them. When we shut it down for you to go after Tin Man—and then booted back up again just now—they didn't recalibrate. They just started where they left off."

"They're killing her!" Violet cried out.

"Yeah, but they don't *know* that," Kendall muttered. He slapped at buttons and slammed toggle switches. "They're clueless."

"Look at her!" Violet cried out. "Guys, you've got to do something *now*."

The spasms had intensified. Shura's eyes had flown open, and they revealed a great, helpless, fathomless fear.

More dials. More switches. More yelling from Violet and also from Rez and Kendall as they tried everything they could think of, calling out to each other when another idea occurred to one or the other and then trying the new idea, a desperate frenzy in every gesture.

Nothing worked.

Mickey's voice sounded even more frantic and agitated than the human ones.

"It's getting worse! The circuit's at full capacity! It's overloading!" came his rattling, metallic squawk. "She's burning alive! She has approximately eight seconds until death."

Silicon Heart

*ight seconds.*

Seven.

Six.

Five.

Violet made up her mind. No matter the cost, she would leap forward and embrace Shura. If it killed her, at least she'd die with her best friend.

And that was something, right?

It was. It was *more* than something. It was a hell of a lot.

She readied herself for the jump.

Four.

Three.

Two.

All at once, Violet felt herself being knocked out of the way. Mickey rushed past her and spun into the circle, snatching up Shura's right hand with one of his pincers. He squeezed tightly. With his other pincer, he reached forward. All Violet could see was a blur of robotic motion, a flash of translucent panels, and a geyser of sprung wires.

A flash of sparks leaped high in the air. A giant trident of flame burst forth from the receptors on the tripod, which initiated the noisy release of the black, spongy, fire-canceling foam that was packed into the walls and floor of every lab on New Earth. The foam expanded wildly, doubling and tripling and quadrupling its size as it engulfed the space, suffocating the flames.

The shouts and cries of Violet and her friends were instantly muffled. And then, there were no cries at all anymore.

Only a terrifying stillness.

A few seconds passed. Just as quickly as the foam had been deployed, a small door in the wall opened. Out scurried a unit of ReadyRobs to vacuum the foam. To Violet, who was watching the world reemerge from under the thicket of smoke and foam, they looked like tiny, efficient versions of Mickey.

Mickey.

He lay on his side, charred and blackened and shrunken. Wires had sprung loose from between his cylinders and lay in ratty, tangled heaps around his prone chassis like seaweed draping an oddly shaped and translucent rock.

Shura stood over him, breathing hard, her face wet with tears.

Violet rubbed her eyes and coughed. Her mouth and throat felt as if they were coated with a gooey version of the anti-flame foam. She had breathed in a great deal of it when the small room was enveloped in chemicals.

"Shura," she said. "Are you—"

"I'm okay," her friend replied. "But Mickey—" She gestured

helplessly toward the AstroRob. "He saved my life. He diverted the current from me and took it into himself." She dropped to her knees, uttering a sob as she did so.

Rez and Kendall were there, too, kneeling over Mickey.

"Is he—?" Violet asked, barely trusting her own voice.

Rez checked the numbers on his console. He nodded solemnly.

"But I thought robots were built to withstand a power surge," she said.

"They are, and they can," Rez said. "Under ordinary circumstances. Mickey, though, was already weak from the Graygrunge attack. He wasn't back up to full strength yet. He was vulnerable."

Shura's voice sounded stricken. "Did he know that? When he grabbed me, I mean, and took on the current?"

Rez reached out a hand and placed it on the AstroRob's central chamber. It was partially melted from the fierce heat of the current, a heat that been supercooled by the foam. "Of course he knew it."

And then they all stopped talking to let the reality seep into their souls:

Mickey—the Mickey they knew, the wisecracking, infuriating robot who wouldn't stop making bad jokes—was gone.

The small room had been cleaned in seconds by the ReadyRobs, and the air instantly sanitized, so what hung in the air was not smoke or ash but . . . grief, the surpassing strangeness of the realization that this heap of metal, plastic, and silicon on the floor was all that was left of their friend.

Violet lifted her eyes so that she could look around the room. As upset as she was, she had another concern: the paintings that Shura had finished as the aliens' emotions flowed into her. If the paintings were damaged or destroyed, Mickey's death would be meaningless.

Well, not exactly meaningless. He had saved Shura's life. But his sacrifice would matter less.

"Hey, look," she said to her friends. She pointed to a spot in the corner. The paintings were secured under a flame-resistant tarp.

"How did he *do* that?" an astonished Shura asked. "How did he get the paintings out of harm's way and wrap them up and keep them safe like that? It all happened in *seconds.* Total chaos. How did he . . ." Her sentence trailed off.

They all knew the answer:

Because he was Mickey, and because he was their friend, and because he understood how important the paintings were to them.

Rez still had a hand on the AstroRob's ruined torso. With a gentleness that Violet had never seen before from him—a gentleness, in fact, that she did not even know he possessed, except when talking about Rachel—Rez slowly peeled back a flap of mangled plastic sheathing and reached inside the portion of Mickey's anatomy roughly analogous to a human chest.

He slowly and delicately pulled out a small triangular hunk of a hard bluish-gray material. The edges were singed, and the surfaces were pitted and gouged.

"It's his heart," Rez explained. "The melting point of silicon is 2,577 degrees Fahrenheit. The heat from the explosion must've stopped just before reaching that temperature, and so it didn't completely destroy it."

"So they use silicon for the heart?" Violet asked. "I don't know a thing about how robots are put together."

"Yeah," Rez said. Then he realized that he needed to modify his answer. "Well, let me put it this way. Every robot has a heart made of silicon. But not every robot has a heart like Mickey's."

17

Requiem for a Robot

Violet awoke to a beautiful sunrise. The color was a beguiling blend of honey gold and soft peach, with shimmery white tendrils dancing at the edges. Some sunrises were too harsh—the yellow was greasy-looking and congealed, like a fried egg in a ReadyMeal left on the heat too long—but the best ones were light and airy. The Color Blenders had to be extra delicate to achieve this kind of effect. Sometimes they didn't bother; they just dumped the requisite colors in the Color Wheel and activated the computer and—*presto*: There's your sunrise. Enjoy it, okay?

But this one—this one was a keeper. The windows in Violet's apartment gradually absorbed the sunrise like a gracious person accepting a compliment.

Yet she hardly noticed. When she opened her eyes and saw that morning had arrived, right on schedule, she wanted to cry. Not even a sunrise as casually magnificent as this one could help.

Nothing helped.

She'd fallen asleep in her living room, fully clothed. She was lying on her stomach, halfway on the couch, but mostly on the floor; at some point during the night, she'd shifted her position, probably turned or kicked or flailed, and slid part of the way off the couch. She either hadn't been aware of it or she just didn't give a damn.

Mickey's dead.

The fact hit her in the center of her soul. She knew, of course, that robots technically couldn't die; they were recycled and repurposed, but they didn't "die," not the way humans did.

Screw that. Mickey was dead.

She checked her console. No messages. That was unusual; on a typical morning, she had at least three dozen, from fellow senators or constituents or her friends.

Then she remembered. She'd turned off the notifications. She had been so bereft last night that she didn't want to talk to anyone. About anything. She didn't want any messages, and she didn't even want to know that she *had* any messages, either, because that meant she'd have to deal later with the people who'd left them. Better to shut the whole thing down.

But now it was time to return to the world, no matter how bad she felt. There was no escape.

Especially because today was Mickey's funeral.

Through the crowd in the observatory lobby, she spotted Rez. He was frowning at his console.

"Hey," she said. "Anybody else here yet?"

There were plenty of other people present, of course. But Violet didn't mean people in general. She meant Shura and Kendall and Tin Man.

"I don't know," Rez answered. "Haven't been looking. Not even sure I want to be here myself. I'd rather be in the lab, but there's a lot of repair work to do before we can try to access the signal again." He peered around the lobby that churned with scruffy-looking astronomers who worked at the observatory, preoccupied-looking scientists from other labs, and an impressive number of shiny AstroRobs and BioRobs and TechRobs.

Only a handful of these creatures, human and robot, could have known Mickey firsthand. The others were here because the word had spread that an extraordinary AstroRob had suffered an accident and had to be repurposed. They were here to honor an ideal, if not a specific machine. While Rez had kept his use of the AstroRob a secret, once Mickey passed away, he had to report it; the recycling protocols on New Earth were absolute. Mickey's parameters had changed, and the size and energy requirement of every object had to be accounted for.

A chime sounded. Time to move into the observatory auditorium for the ceremony.

Just as Violet and Rez crossed the arched threshold into the thousand-seat arena with the brightly lit stage, they were joined by a breathless Shura and, just behind her, an apologetic Kendall.

"Hey. Sorry. Lost track of time. I was working in my lab," Shura said.

"You were supposed to be resting," Violet admonished her. They chose a row and filed toward a line of seats, first Violet and Rez and then Shura and Kendall.

"Couldn't sit still. I had this *terrific* idea," Shura answered, her voice rising with excitement, "about how we might be able to use the paintings to interpret . . ." She stopped speaking. She suddenly seemed to remember where they were and why they were there. "Oh my God. Sorry. I just—I've been trying to put it out of my mind. That's why I worked this morning."

"Me too," Kendall said. "I did the same thing. I've been in the police forensics lab since before sunrise."

Violet nodded. She'd dealt with her sadness over Mickey's passing in her own way, a way that had nothing to do with labs or experiments: She'd had a pint of chocolate-chip ice cream for breakfast. Her last act before leaving her apartment was to check her chin for smears of chocolate.

Geniuses have their *way of getting over grief,* she thought, *and I've got mine.*

"Tin Man's still not feeling well," Kendall added. "I told him to stay home."

And then they turned their attention to the stage.

Funeral services for robots were rare but not unheard of. When New Earth first was settled, they had been regarded as shady, bizarre rituals, and most of them were conducted underground. Rumors of a particular service for a certain beloved robot would arise, and people would gather quietly in obscure places to pay their respects. The resistance to such ceremonies died down as the truth gradually came to be acknowledged: The line between machine and human was a porous border. Robots had been selecting their own genders since 2247, even before the founding of New Earth, and after that, rogue programmers began to add small dashes of personality. It was still a controversial practice—older citizens insisted that uniformity was the entire point of robots—but that hadn't stopped creative programmers from sneaking in snippets of individuality.

Violet had been to two robot funerals—one for a very old BioRob that had been with Shura from high school through medical school, and another for a young ReadyRob who was destroyed in an asteroid strike on Higgsville.

But she hadn't known those robots the way she knew Mickey.

Her attention was drawn to the stage. A stir swept across the vast auditorium as two ReadyRobs rolled in, balancing a silver tube between them. That tube, Violet realized, was all that was left of Mickey after he'd been prepped for recycling.

The two robots set it down with great care and then whisked off to the other side of the stage.

"Hey."

A very tall, exceptionally disheveled young man had appeared at the edge of the stage, nearly tripping on the gathered drape. He walked to the center and repeated the greeting, looking out across the rows of myriad women and men and robots, shading his eyes against the stage lights with a flattened hand.

"Hey."

A murmur ran around and around the auditorium: *Dave Parkhurst.*

Rez leaned over and whispered to Violet, "That's Dumb-Ass Dave."

He was older than she had expected. Given Mickey's energetic spirit, she had assumed that the man who'd made him would be close to her age. But this guy had to be at least thirty. In other ways, though, he was exactly what she expected: skinny, awkward, with a greasy complexion and hair that hung down in his eyes and stuck out from the sides of his head.

Dave gripped the lectern with the bony, dead-white fingers of one hand. He was exceedingly nervous. He dipped his head and shuffled his feet and scratched the back of his neck and straightened his spine and then hunched over again. The whispers that had greeted his arrival had died down now. There was not so much as a stray cough. Everyone waited to hear what he had to say.

"We're here today . . ." He gulped. "We're here . . ."

Still he struggled. "We're here today to . . ."

He shook his head. That head, Violet observed, looked a little like a dust mop being shaken out by a ReadyRob.

"Okay." Now he seemed to gather himself. "Look, I'm no good at this. No good at all. But if anybody was going to talk about Mickey, I figured it oughta be me." He shrugged. "To begin with, I never called him Mickey. He was named later. By somebody else. I didn't like that name when I heard about it. It was short for *Mickey Mouse.* And it sounded kind of disrespectful, I guess I'd call it. Like he was being ridiculed. Well, Mickey knew that. He knew the truth behind his name. But he didn't care. He knew who he was."

Violet was aware of Rez shifting around uncomfortably in the seat beside hers.

"But I'll call him that today," Dave continued, "because that's the name he was known by. What did I call him, when I created him? Nothing. I didn't give him a name. I never do. If you work in robot programming, you learn pretty quickly that it's better not to name them. Naming them makes them too much like friends. Or sisters or brothers. And then it hurts too much—way, way too much—when you have to say goodbye. Let them go."

He licked his lips. "I knew Mickey was different. I could tell from the moment he first came online. And so I asked for permission to give him a personality. I saw something in him—a spark, a talent, a special spirit. And they said, 'Okay.' I could add a few lines of code in his production specs and I wouldn't lose my job. Mickey would be unique." Dave took a breath. "The bad jokes. The puns. The limericks. The riddles. Sure, people complained about all that. And the belches. And the farts."

Chuckles gusted across the auditorium.

"Yeah, I said the word," Dave went on. A grin replaced his somber expression. "At a funeral. I said the word *farts.* You see, I wanted Mickey to be this annoying, irritating guy. So people could focus on how irked they were instead of focusing on the fact that the earth where we lived for so many centuries is dying right below us." The grin vanished. "Yeah. That was the idea. Because it can seem pretty bleak sometimes, you know. Pretty dark. We had to *leave our own friggin' planet.* And now we're trapped up here. We're like kids on a homemade raft. It seems like a really cool adventure, right? Good times? But the truth is, unlike those kids on that raft, we can't go back home. We don't have a home. Not anymore. So here we are."

The crowd began to grow restless. Violet heard mutterings, the shifting of feet, some chain-reaction throat-clearings, a few random, perplexed *hmmmms.* They'd come here for a robot funeral, not a political lecture.

"Dumb-Ass Dave strikes again," Rez muttered.

Violet smacked his arm.

"Okay, I get it," Dave said. He took a long, sad look at the silver tube beside him. "Mickey. What a guy. I had to make his jokes really bad so that everybody could get them. They couldn't be cynical or sarcastic. They had to be the cheapest, lowest, rudest jokes you could think of." He squared his shoulders. "His first job was in the cyclotron over in Franklinton. They loved him there. Right, guys?" He looked down at a gathering of older-model robots in the first row. They buzzed and chirped. "Yeah. I know. When the knock-knock jokes got out of hand, that's when I knew Mickey was a hit."

Dave paused. "A few months ago, I heard that Mickey had

been sent to repurposing. He had some issues. His CPU was getting up there in years. I was hoping he could maybe become a swing set or some climbing bars. He loved kids. But it turns out"—Dave's face darkened—"somebody grabbed him from the recycle bin and used him for a while. That's when he got the name Mickey. Well, something happened to him. I don't know what it was. It's all a big secret, I guess. But whatever it was, I'm sure he was trying to help somebody. Because that's the kind of robot he was."

One more look at the silver tube. "Godspeed, buddy," Dave said. "Do you remember the joke you used to tell about Old Earth cemeteries? 'People are just dying to get in there.' Well, you don't have to worry about that; you won't go to any cemetery. They're going to make you into something useful. Count on it." Dave raised his right arm in a brief wave. Then he shuffled off the stage.

And with that, Mickey's time as an AstroRob had come to an end. However he might be used next—as the undercarriage of a tram car, or a component in one of the wind turbines that powered New Earth, or a part of the framework of a Uni or console—the job would not include consciousness, because the hardware required for artificial consciousness had been destroyed by the fire and could not be repurposed. Robots, like people, were given one life.

Whatever he was now, he wasn't Mickey anymore.

Violet stepped to one side of the lobby. Now that the service was over, a great wedge of mourners swept past, a mix of humans and robots funneled toward the big double doors, but she didn't want to leave quite so quickly. She needed a moment to think about Mickey, here in this place where he'd worked, here where his bad jokes and silly sound effects still seemed to reverberate.

She felt a hand on her elbow. She turned.

Kendall.

"Oh, hey," she said. "Pretty crowded, right? Mickey would've loved it."

"Got a minute to talk?"

He led her outside and down the stone steps and into the courtyard on one side of the observatory. In the center of the courtyard was a mobile statue. It was a holographic projection of Carl Sagan holding a book and pointing at the sky. Every few minutes, the image shifted, and Sagan was reading the book, or writing in it, or handing it to a small child.

"Is everything okay?" Violet asked. "I mean, I know we just came from a funeral and all, but you look a little grim."

Kendall didn't answer. He seemed to have something very important to say to her—so important that he couldn't find a way to begin.

When he did speak, it came slowly at first. "Sitting there, listening to Dave Parkhurst talk about Mickey, I just—" He stopped.

"What is it, Kendall? What's wrong?"

In a rush, he said, "Life's uncertain. For everybody. Even robots. And I just started remembering how much I love you. I know things didn't start out right between us—I had to lie to you, and I know how much that hurt you—but now, well, here we are." He looked into her eyes. "Do you think there's any chance that you and I could ever be together again? As more than friends, I mean."

Not this again.

"Oh, Kendall." She hoped he would glean her answer from the way she said his name. She said it with affection, yes, but not *that* kind of affection. Not romantic passion. She loved him, but they would never be lovers. She just didn't feel that way about him. She had once, but not now. She didn't know where the passion had gone, any more than she knew where Mickey's spirit had fled.

The universe, she reflected, abounded in mysteries large and small and in between.

"Okay," he said. He understood. The hopefulness in his face had melted away. There was sadness in his eyes.

Knowing she was the reason for that sadness deeply distressed Violet, but there was nothing she could do about it. Not unless she was willing to lie and pretend. And she wasn't.

Even if it meant she was alone forever, she wouldn't do that.

"I guess we'd better go," she said. "Catch up with the others. Shura wants to take everybody to lunch and then get back to the lab and pick up the pieces and figure out how to go forward."

"Yeah." Kendall glanced at his console. She could sense his discomfort, his desire to be anywhere but next to her. "Actually, I need to get back to the station. Tell Shura thanks, though. See you later. At the lab." And then he was gone, ducking through the throng of robots and people.

He wouldn't ask her again. She was certain of it. He had given it his best shot, and she had turned him down, and that was that.

Violet caught one last glimpse of him through a brief break in the shifting, murmuring multitude as he strode across the plaza in that purposeful way he had, head down, hands thrust in his tunic pockets. She remembered how many times she'd watched him cross the courtyard in front of Protocol Hall, back when she was in love with him. She could never have envisioned a time when the sight of Kendall Mayhew did not make her shiver all over, dreaming of his touch, of his kiss.

But that time had come.

Feelings changed. They were, she thought, like lightning in the summer dusk—real lightning, that is, like the kind on Old Earth that her father had told her about, not the artificial kind manufactured by the Environmental Control Center and slotted into the sky at regular intervals.

Feelings were like lightning that comes from out of nowhere, flashing and crashing and illuminating the sky for a brief moment and then disappearing, and all the wishing in the world couldn't bring them back again.

18

Return to Redshift

For the next three days, no one heard anything from Rez. He didn't answer console calls. His staff had been instructed not to bother him, and they followed those instructions, especially those who had been reprimanded by him in the past and still cringed when they remembered it. All anyone knew was that he had shut himself up in his office with the door locked. A band of light that showed underneath the door—and an indication on the observatory's meter of a higher-than-normal expenditure of energy—proved that he was doing *something.* His office wasn't as well equipped as his lab, but it had a computer. And as long as Rez had a computer, he could work.

Was he eating? Was he sleeping? Unknown.

Violet assumed that when the staff wasn't around, he left his regular office and slipped into his lab. She knew Rez, and she knew that whatever he was doing, it was related to the alien transmissions and Shura's paintings—and Rachel's chip.

For Rez, everything came back to Rachel's chip. It had to. The quest for its origin had even gotten him to put his exoplanet search on hold.

But why didn't he want their help? Why was he pushing them away? They were supposed to be a team, weren't they?

At least twice a day, Violet tried to contact him on his console. No reply.

Okay, Rez. Have it your way, she finally told herself. When he wanted them, when he needed their help, he'd call them back together, but not a second before. She was sure of it.

Because Rez was Rez.

Violet sat in her Senate office, behind the big brown desk whose many drawers were all still empty. For the life of her, she couldn't figure out what to fill them with.

It was the third day of Rez's self-imposed exile.

She had taken off her console and now absentmindedly rubbed her wrist in the spot where the console usually was.

This wasn't a job for a console.

Spread out in front of her were two sheets of paper. Everything she had written on the sheets so far she had quickly crossed out, either with a straight line or with a bunch of crazy, overlapping circles.

Nothing she'd written this afternoon sounded even halfway right. She knew what she wanted to say, but the proper phrases were just . . . beyond . . . her . . . reach.

The letter needed to be perfect in every way. That's why she had opted for pen and paper instead of her console. When the words were really important, she went retro. She liked the feel of a pen in her hand, plus the sound of that pen scratching along a square piece of real paper. Her father had told her about that feel, and that sound, and one day, just to please him, she'd tried it. He was right. Actual writing—forming letters and numbers with your own hand, in your own way, on a real piece of paper—was much more satisfying than using a fingertip to touch a console screen here and there.

Her console chirped. The sky-blue jewel told her it was Jonetta.

"Got some news," Jonetta said, "about the research you asked me to do. Can you meet me tonight? Won't take long."

She knew Jonetta hadn't found Ogden Crowley's console. If she had, she would have led with the news. So this had to be something else.

"Sure. How about Redshift?"

"Really?" Jonetta's voice was incredulous. "You want to meet *there*?"

Violet had fully expected her to question the location. Not only was Redshift the worst place imaginable to carry on a conversation—it was always loud and always dark and always crowded—but it held complicated memories for Violet, a fact that Jonetta knew all too well.

But Violet had her reasons.

"Yeah. I do. Oh, how's Tin Man?"

She hadn't told Jonetta about Rachel's chip, or, before that, about Rez's search for the exoplanet, or about the threat of New Earth's diminishing orbit. Jonetta was a good, trustworthy friend, but Violet kept her in the layer just outside the inner ring of her friends. She wasn't part of the core.

"He's fine," Jonetta answered. "Too restless to hang out at his house for very much longer, that's for sure. How'd he get so beat up, anyway? He wouldn't say."

"Wrong place, wrong time. I'll meet you at Redshift in twenty minutes, okay?"

Redshift.

If there were an unofficial HQ for anybody on New Earth between the ages of sixteen and nineteen, Violet often thought, it would be Redshift. A raucous dance club, a reliable hookup spot, a stage for the best new music, and the birthplace of the trendiest new drinks, Redshift was legendary. At night, the sky above it was shot through with the crisscrossing beams of its rooftop strobe lights, and the street that ran in front of it was packed with Unis and private cars and bobbing throngs of people. Through the golden double doors that marked the entrance would parade couples and threesomes and individuals—it didn't matter if you came by yourself, because nobody ever *left* that way—with the joy of bright expectancy on every face.

Violet had happily wasted many, many hours in Redshift over the last few years. She'd danced, she'd knocked back a fair number of Neptunia Nodes, she'd melted into the throbbing frenzy of the band's bass beat, a beat with which your heartbeat automatically synched up.

But she hadn't been to Redshift in months. Not since she had become *Senator* Crowley.

Which was precisely why she wanted to go there tonight for her meeting with Jonetta.

It was the same old Redshift.

Jumping lights, velvety darkness, laugher that erupted in great blurts of alcohol-fueled hilarity, music so loud that it made you want to rip your ears off and swaddle them in Bubble Wrap—but in a good way.

Violet spotted a high metal table with two stools at the far edge of the dance floor. She nabbed it. Except for the mini-explosions of light that pierced the room at erratic intervals, the club was blackout dark. In the old days, that was what she'd relished about the place. It was a melting, come-closer kind of darkness. It was a darkness that scooped you up and whispered, *You belong here.* She'd been comforted by this darkness over and over again, on nights when she was sure her world was unraveling for good.

Being back here, though, felt just a little bit strange. She'd outgrown this, hadn't she? Outgrown the need for thumping music and the oily closeness of sweaty bodies and the floating, magical feeling? She was way too old for the place, right? She was nineteen now, and a senator, and Redshift was—

"Hey, Violet."

She flinched. Jonetta had approached on her blind side, leaning over to speak in Violet's ear because the music was so loud.

"Jonetta, hey." She waved toward the empty stool.

"What?"

"I said, 'Hey.'"

"What?"

"HEY."

Jonetta nodded. "So now you get why I didn't want to meet here. I mean, come on," she said, raising her voice and carefully enunciating each word.

And then, a piece of luck dropped in their laps. The band took a break. It was a robot band tonight, and robot bands were always louder than human ones. In an instant, the fuzzy static and frantic, writhing guitar riffs were replaced by the ordinary noise of a club: talk, laughter, the constant clink of glassware.

"Just wanted to see the place again," Violet said. "Haven't been back since I took the Senate seat. It used to be my second home."

"Yeah. I know." Jonetta's voice had a sarcastic edge. As Violet's assistant at Crowley & Associates Detective Agency, she'd covered for her boss on many mornings when Violet was hung over after an all-nighter at this very club. Occasionally, Violet would fall asleep at her desk after an especially manic evening at Redshift.

"Those days," Violet said with a rueful sigh, "are gone forever."

Jonetta looked around. "Do you see any of your old friends yet?"

"Nope. Which is great. Buy you a drink?"

"No, thanks. Actually, I don't have a lot of time. I'm working on five different cases. Can you believe it?"

Violet could believe it. Jonetta was a better detective and businesswoman than she'd ever been. Which wasn't a stretch.

Detective—strike one. Senator—strike two. Would she ever find what she was truly meant to do? Violet shook her head. She needed to focus. This wasn't Career Day.

"So no luck finding the console, I guess," Violet said glumly. "Even in those new places you were going to try."

"Right. And trust me, I worked at it. Talked to everybody who'd had any contact with your dad in the last few weeks of his life, to see if they knew where he put it." Jonetta hesitated. Violet couldn't see the details of her face beyond its general shape—the club was too dark—but she could guess at the expression: thoughtfulness, a kind of quiet knowing.

"My guess," Jonetta added, "is that he hid it deliberately. It wasn't just misplaced. Your dad went to great lengths to make sure you didn't get his console. At least not right away."

Violet was about to react; that had been Evie Carruthers's theory, too, and it still rankled. A sudden spike of laughter rose from the other side of the room, followed by hoots and a lot of clapping and whistling.

All at once, she felt a hollowness opening up inside her. The laughter had reminded her of Mickey and his nonstop barrage of terrible jokes. And she really did miss the AstroRob. But there was more to it, too. There were other things she missed. She missed . . . *herself.* Herself—and days gone by. She missed the girl who, not too long ago, would've been on the other side of the room right now, laughing, dancing, raising hell, having fun. She had to be an adult now. She had to figure out what profession she ought to be pursuing. Oh, and while she was doing *that,* she also had to help her friends save New Earth.

Easy-peasy, Violet thought ruefully.

"Violet?"

She shook off the gloom. Returned her attention to the here and now, which meant returning her attention to Jonetta. "Yeah. Right here. Okay. Listen, my dad was an old man. He misplaced things. All the time. That's what old people do. They forget."

"Not a console." Jonetta's voice was firm. "And not if you're the founder and former president of New Earth, and you've been keeping a console journal for years and years, which you intend to donate to the New Earth History Museum someday. The director of Starbridge told me that. He also told me how carefully your dad kept track of it. He always had his console with him, even on the day he died."

Violet's mind flashed back to the last time she saw her father.

His heart had been failing rapidly. The head of the Starbridge nursing staff called her. *Come now,* the woman said.

Leaning over him as he lay motionless in his bed, taking his last weary, labored breaths, she had told him she loved him as she held his hand . . .

And there was no console on his wrist. She recalled that specifically.

It might have been in a drawer, of course. Or on a high shelf. In another room. But she'd scoured the apartment. And now so had Jonetta.

"It's right here in my notes," Jonetta said. Her voice drew Violet out of her reverie. "Hold on." She touched her own console, bringing up a lemon-yellow jewel. A second touch opened it. "So after our formal interview, the director was just making small talk about how important consoles are to life. How they're really an extension of our very selves. They contain the record of who we are. He said he'd made the same point to your dad, the day before he died. And your dad nodded and recited a poem."

"A poem?"

"Yeah. Well, part of one, anyway. The director didn't know where it came from. But your dad, he said, closed his eyes and started talking. The director recorded it and wrote it down. Here goes: 'That is the doctrine, simple, ancient, true / Such is life's trial, as Old Earth smiles and knows.' I looked it up. It's a line from a poem by an Old Earth poet named Robert Browning. Ring any bells?"

"My father always admired his work," Violet replied. "But as for how it relates to his console? Nope. Not a clue."

"Guess you don't have much time these days to read Old Earth poetry. What with being a senator and all."

"I don't have much time to do *anything* except wish I knew how to do a better job." Violet had surprised herself with that outburst. She hadn't intended to discuss this with Jonetta. "I guess," she continued, "I wanted to use this little visit to Redshift as a test. To see how it felt. To remember when I used to have fun."

"Fun?" Jonetta's eyes widened. "Is that how you remember it? Frankly, you seemed pretty lost back then, Vi." She used her old nickname for Violet—the one Violet hated—to rock her friend back to reality. "Drinking too much and hanging out with strange guys is not the behavior of somebody who's happy."

"I didn't say I was happy. I just said I had fun."

"Good point."

"So that's why I might do it."

"Do what?"

"Resign my Senate seat. I was drafting a letter of resignation when you called."

"*Who-o-o-a.*" Jonetta stretched out the word. "That's *huge,* Violet."

"Yeah."

Jonetta checked her console. "I'm late for an interview, but I'll cancel it if you need to talk. Just let me—"

Violet's console chirped. The black jewel was marked *URGENT.* It was Rez.

"Something big's happened," he declared. "I mean *big.* Come to the lab. Right now. I've called the others, too. They're on their way."

Everything else slipped out of Violet's mind: her father's missing console, her potential resignation from the Senate, the fact that she missed Redshift like you'd miss a bad-for-you friend who was nevertheless irresistible.

She slid off her stool so fast she could've created friction burns on her backside.

"Later, Jonetta."

Rez stood triumphantly in the center of his lab. His friends made a half circle around him: Violet, Shura, Kendall, Tin Man.

He had arranged Shura's paintings all around the tight space, propping the canvases on the floor, leaning each one against a black stack of computer equipment.

He looked terrible. His hair was bunched across his scalp in random oily lumps, the result of his absentminded plucking while he worked at his computer, and his eyes were ringed with red. Clearly, he hadn't used the time off to sleep, eat, change his clothes, or—*Like that would ever happen,* Violet told herself—shower.

He kind of... kind of smells *a little bit, too.* She wondered again at her weird choice of crushes.

But in an instant, those trivial concerns vanished. And she realized that, for all of his dishevelment, Rez was beaming.

Feet spread, hands on his hips, eyes feverishly bright, Rez addressed his friends. Hurriedly, his voice buoyed by excitement, he said, "I did it."

"Did what?" Kendall asked.

"Well, a bunch of things, but let's start with this. I know what the *HELP* message means."

Kendall seemed exasperated. "What's to figure out? Come on, Rez. You pulled me out of a staff meeting for this? The aliens—whoever they are—need assistance."

"Yeah," Violet said. She, too, was annoyed at being summoned on false pretenses, even though she'd left a bar instead of a staff meeting.

Shura was slightly perturbed as well. She put in a *Yeah* for solidarity's sake.

"NO," Rez thundered right back at them. "That is totally incorrect. Well, it's half right. But it's half wrong, too."

Silence.

"The aliens," Rez went on, "weren't just *asking* for help. They were also *offering* it."

More silence, but it was a different kind of silence now. It was a curious, tell-me-more silence.

"That's what I've spent the last three days figuring out," Rez said. "Using Shura's paintings, I was able to reverse engineer the alien language. I started with their emotions and worked my way up to their words. Words into sentences. And so on."

"How did you do that?" Violet asked.

"Art is *data.* It's just information in another form." Rez looked appreciatively at Shura. "I used your paintings and everything they told us about alien emotions and cross-referenced all of it with my cryptographic study of their language. Each time they tried to come up with one of our words to describe their emotions—remember *trillum* and *nogg* and *waw?*—I linked the word to a painting. Bit by bit, painting by painting, letter by letter, word by word, I cracked the code. I figured out the alien vernacular. Then I loaded it into my Simultaneous Translation app." He took a deep breath before continuing. "They sent us a real message, not just the bits and pieces of their emotions, a few minutes ago."

"Hold on," Kendall said. "Given the distances involved, it would take thousands of years for a message to get from them to us. This can't be coming in real time. It's impossible."

"No. It's not," Rez answered. "I mean, I can see why you'd think so, given twenty-third-century technology. But they're far ahead of us." He paused, trying to find a way to explain it.

When he started speaking again, it was, Violet realized, the first time she'd ever heard Rez explain something when he wasn't trying to sound superior, when he wasn't trying to put somebody else down because they didn't understand right away. His excitement at the new knowledge had made him leave all of that behind—the arrogance and the sarcastic edge, all of the things that had intensified after Rachel's death.

"Here's the deal," Rez said in the patient voice of a teacher. "When I started reverse engineering the signal, I discovered how they were communicating with us. Think of it as a Time Tether. Like the Virtual Tether that enabled them to send the images to Shura's imagination, the Time Tether syncs up two different epochs in time. Everything in the universe is really happening simultaneously. Time is just an artificial construct, a way of sorting things out and keeping track of them. Otherwise, it would be mass confusion—everything happening at the same time. The Time Tether taps back into that original simultaneity."

"I get it," Kendall said, snapping his fingers. "They've taken one tiny slice of the universe, the virtual link they created between their world and our world, and they restored it to the simultaneity of the Big Bang. Along this one conduit, their time and our time are synched up. Otherwise, to get a message to us, they would've had to have started sending it in"—he did the calculations in his head—"roughly 20 B.C., Old Earth time."

"Right." Rez seemed immensely relieved that somebody else understood. "The Time Tether is like a time-free zone. They speak, and we hear them. We speak, and *they* hear *us*—as if we're standing right next to each other, not separated by millions of light-years."

Shura rubbed her hands together. "Well, come on, then! Let's see what they have to say."

Rez grinned, his eyes glittering with excitement. "I'll upload it from my console."

All three of them crowded closer to his screen. A rush of letters, numbers, and mathematical symbols, interspersed with miniature versions of the vibrant images in Shura's paintings, tumbled across it.

"So what does it say?" Kendall asked.

"Watch." Rez executed a wide, dramatic, spreading gesture with his right arm. "I paused the translation until you got here. So we can all read it together."

One + One = One

A message from aliens.

A message from aliens.

This was the most exciting moment of Violet's life. She was fairly sure it was the most exciting moment in her friends' lives, too, but she couldn't verify that because nobody was talking. Awestruck, they stood there, waiting for Rez to work his magic.

He pressed a white jewel rising from the face of his console.

The image on the computer screen began to move again. The numbers and symbols and colors shifted, wavered, and transformed themselves into . . .

Into English. Plain, ordinary English. Standard alphabet, recognizable words, regular sentences. As the transmission surged in, Rez automatically translated it on his console and directed an image of the translation to appear on the screen.

All four of them read the message in a fraught, rigidly attentive, hold-your-breath silence:

I am Zander.

And I am Sonnet.

You are thinking, *Oh, so two are present there.* No. Only one. In the world in which I live, one plus one equals one. I will explain. Soon.

I am reaching out to offer you my assistance.

Sonnet sent emotions to you, and you transferred them into paintings. That was astonishingly clever. Your interpretations helped me understand how your language turns ideas and feelings into words. The words are mere vessels. I sense that you are translating my words into your language, even as I write them; likewise, I have mastered the rudiments of your communication system—the nouns, verbs, adjectives, adverbs, and the like—and soon I will be able to speak to you in English. For now, I appreciate the fact that you are able to translate my language into yours.

As I stated at the beginning of this message, I am Zander.

I am Sonnet.

As Zander, I THINK.

As Sonnet, I FEEL.

Based on my observations, it seems that your custom is to embed both—the intellect and the emotions—in a single individual. You unite thinking and feeling IN THE SAME PERSON. You may take that for granted, but believe me—it is quite extraordinary.

But I am getting ahead of myself. First I must tell you how I found you, and to offer my help to you in your endeavor.

On a routine patrol, our spacecraft came upon a tiny scrap of material—a chip, one might call it—of unknown origin. It was drifting amid the stars in a cloud of otherwise unremarkable space debris. Packed tightly inside this miniscule flake was an intriguing storehouse of data.

When I analyzed this data, I discovered that it was a complete record of the emotional memories of someone named Rachel

Reznik. Based on those memories, I deduced that she had been a young girl of exceptional intellectual gifts. Her chip contained the dreams and joys, the setbacks and triumphs of her life, a life apparently cut well short of the allotted time span for members of your species, based on what I have been able to glean from my cursory explorations.

I traced the chip back to you. It appeared to be tied to a technology known as the Intercept.

I am enchanted by this technology. While no longer active, at one point, it was able to capture the emotions swirling inside each individual, to store those emotions, and then to return them to the individual's brain in all of their intensity, all of their color and immensity.

I saw, based on what I read in the chip, that Rachel had a brother named Steven Reznik. And once I traced the chip back to its origin, I realized that this Steven Reznik was searching the galaxies with a telescope, using that primitive but marginally effective device to sweep the skies night after night, in hopes of finding a broken star—a star whose light is interrupted periodically by an orbiting planet. That planet could be your new home.

I know of just such a star. And I can supply the coordinates so that you might go there and begin your civilization anew. I have monitored your orbit and can report to you that Steven Reznik's calculations are correct: It is deteriorating steadily—much faster, actually, than your simple instruments are able to detect. That, I assume, is why Steven Reznik is so determined to find the broken star.

But there is another reason for my communication as well.

Perhaps you are asking yourself how we have managed to divide the emotions and the intellect so that each one of us is both one and two: Thinkers and Emotives. It came about after many billions of years of what you call natural selection. Those of us who were intellectual tended to gravitate toward our own kind. And the same for those who relied primarily on the emotions. Like was drawn to like.

Soon our civilization was split. Thinkers and Emotives were completely separate. Specialization has worked well—we are far more advanced than you are.

But now we Thinkers have decided—after a great deal of logical analysis—that our way, the way of dividing the intellect and the emotions into two different creatures, is no longer the most efficient design. It is cumbersome, and it is hampering our efforts to move forward. Our progress has slowed. It seems that without emotions to push them forward, our Thinkers are faltering in their efforts. We no longer have the motivation to try our experiments, to work hard for distant goals. We have no sense of wonder. We are efficient, but we do not dream.

This is not how we anticipated it would be; many, including me, thought the Emotives would need the Thinkers more than the Thinkers needed the Emotives. We were wrong. For our civilization to continue its progress, we must merge.

Thus it is time to bring thinking and feeling together.

It is time, that is, for Sonnet and me to be merged into one creature. And for all the others who are divided to undergo what we will call Fusion.

But how will this be done? My question is not about the technological specifications or biological imperatives of Fusion—those, we will easily master. We Thinkers are quite accomplished. Or at least we have been so far, until this unexpected pause.

My question instead is . . .

Forgive me. I find this awkward, but I must ask:

How will it be for me to suddenly FEEL? And for Sonnet, who is unused to sustained intellectual inquiry, to suddenly be awash in facts, information, problems demanding to be solved?

As Zander, I am a rational being. Sonnet is an emotional being. But as both . . . I do not know.

Sonnet is afraid of Fusion. I am not afraid—because fear is a feeling, and I do not feel. But let me say that I am concerned about the impact of these changes. If Zander and Sonnet can be successfully Fused, then others of our species will agree to undergo the procedure as well. If, however, there is a problem, I would rather that it be Sonnet and me who suffer, rather than the others.

Please do not think of this impulse as heroism. It is not. It is only practicality. Heroism requires emotion—one must feel that other lives are equally worthy to one's own—and I do not feel. Sonnet, however, is heroic.

Thus I would like to propose a bargain: You will send an emissary to my planet, to suggest ways that I might live with emotions as part of my being and ways that Sonnet might live with thoughts as part of Sonnet's being, and I will help you find your star.

At first, of course, I envisioned that I would come to your world and learn there, despite the vast distance between us. We have far more sophisticated versions of the technology you call a Virtual Tether. You have, I see, already deduced the chronologic one: The Time Tether is enabling us to communicate right now.

For travel, we use a Consciousness Tether. A single consciousness is attached to a faraway place or object, and transferred upon a secure conduit, while the vulnerable, perishable body is not involved.

But it is not feasible for me to come to you. My divided self makes the Consciousness Tether unworkable; the signal becomes too diluted when it is split in two. It lacks the power to make the long, long journey.

And so I ask that someone from your world come to mine.

I have studied your civilization, and I know that I must feel this individual's true essence in order to learn from your emissary. I must be in the presence of this unique spirit you call the soul—and the individual must be in the presence of mine. This cannot be accomplished through a communication channel, but only through the Consciousness Tether, only through a close approximation of what I understand you commonly refer to as face-to-face contact. I can offer technical assistance to enable this.

I will help you find your star whether or not you choose to help us. But I hope that you may agree. There is a symmetry to our searches. A rhyme to our respective quests. You will be giving us a new life. And I will be leading you to your new home.

Zander / Sonnet

The Decision

"I'm going."

Rez made his declaration before the others had finished reading the last line of the message. "I'm the only person who's right. Let's grab the specs they send and start installing the Consciousness Tether."

"Hold on," Kendall said. "You're our expert on Tethers. Nobody else around here is qualified to operate it. Suppose you go and we screw up and then can't get you back?"

"Science is a risky business," Rez answered nonchalantly.

"Oh, come on." Kendall's voice was slathered with disdain. "Get real. Who do you think you are—Sir Isaac Newton, doing ocular experiments by sticking a needle in his own eye?"

"No. I just think that—"

Violet clapped her hands a single time. "Nobody's going *anywhere,*" she said, "until we thoroughly discuss this. So you two can just quit arguing. To begin with, we've got to get a lot more data about this Consciousness Tether thing. Their home is thousands of light-years away. If something goes wrong, you could be stuck there. And even if you *did* make it home, the trip would last tens of thousands of years. Everybody you knew would be long dead. The world you knew would be—"

"Zander said there's a way," Rez declared, interrupting her.

Shura stepped in, shaking her head. "This is your doctor talking, buddy. Before anybody does anything like that, I'll need assurances from him—or them, or whatever—that the effects on a human body won't be serious or lasting."

Tin Man had been listening intently. "That's a good point," he said. "Even trips from New Earth down to Old Earth take a toll on the body."

"And there are other questions, too," Violet interjected. "Just what is it that this Zander guy actually *wants*? Lessons on how to feel?" She made a scoffing sound. "Right. Why doesn't he just read a romance novel from Old Earth in the twentieth century? My father told me about them; they were pretty stupid, but they were all about emotions."

"I think it's a little more complicated than that," Rez said. "They're an advanced civilization. And they're going to show us the star that might be *the* star. Whatever they want from us, I say we give it to them. They want their people to be more emotional? I can't really understand why you'd want that, but okay, fine. Their call."

"Not *more* emotional," Shura corrected him. "Just putting the feelings and the intellect on equal footing in one individual. You've never really understood this, Rez, but I get as much from my emotions as I do from my brain. My painting, which comes almost entirely from my emotions, is as important to me as my analytical skills."

Rez's face revealed extreme skepticism. But it was hard for him to argue the point, because Shura was among the most brilliant citizens of New Earth.

"Look," Kendall said. "It's obvious that I'm the best choice to go. I invented the Intercept. I can answer any questions they have."

Violet shook her head.

"Same objection as I had with Rez," she said. "You're too crucial to the technical work back here. Even with Rez in charge, Shura and I don't have the knowledge to help run the Tether. It's too risky." She turned to Rez. "So the orbit is decaying? You're sure."

He nodded glumly. "Absolutely. The numbers are irrefutable. And our new friends just confirmed it."

"But if we find the star, there's a chance that one of its planets might be habitable?"

"A very good chance."

"Would we be able to transfer everybody on New Earth there? Before the orbit decays and New Earth falls out of the sky?"

"Yes. Well, maybe. But we'd need a lot of help."

"Like the kind a superior civilization can provide."

"You got it." He looked at Violet eagerly, as if he'd closed the deal. "So I get to go to Zander's planet, right? We're all agreed?"

"No," Kendall said, answering before Violet had a chance to. "If anybody goes, it's me."

Violet let them squabble and name-call and step all over each other's sentences for a good two minutes. Then she raised a hand, asking for quiet.

"You're both wrong," she said. "*I'm* going."

She wasn't a genius.

She didn't have the kind of dazzling brain that could solve a dozen math problems while simultaneously discovering a new chemical element and testing the atmosphere of a recently discovered planet.

She wasn't an inventive prodigy like Shura. Or a superbly accomplished scientist like Kendall. Or a computer mastermind like Rez. Or somebody brave and strong like Tin Man. Or a visionary leader like her father.

She wasn't brilliant at all.

She was, in fact, kind of ordinary. And she knew it. She'd failed at her business. She was a second-rate senator, even though she tried hard to be a better one.

But she could pull this off. She believed that down to her toes. And she had a very good reason for wanting to give it a shot, a reason she could not share with them. Yet.

"I'm going," Violet repeated.

Her friends turned, one by one, and stared at her. Their expressions ranged from horrified (Shura) to shocked (Kendall) to suspicious (Rez) to curious (Tin Man).

"No matter how calm and smart this Zander sounds," Shura said carefully, "something like a transfer of consciousness would be totally experimental from our end. And maybe dangerous."

"We don't even know if it would work," Kendall put in. "Spirit? Soul? Essence? There's no precedent for it."

"Um, yeah," Violet said. When she was nervous, she tended to get sarcastic. "I think that's what *experimental* means, right?"

"The Virtual Tether almost killed me," Shura reminded her. "And I wasn't even sent anywhere. I just had to stand here and be the recipient of the signal—and paint. And I still almost exploded in a massive fireball, along with the lab itself. This is much more complicated. We'll be using the Consciousness Tether as a sort of transportation system. We don't know how much the human body can stand. Or if Zander can really make his planet hospitable. You could land there—okay, your *essence* could land there—and your body could die instantly back here. Or two seconds later."

Violet was irked. Clearly, they didn't think she was up to the job. And they were hiding their lack of confidence behind a show of concern for her safety. "Come on, Shura. Yeah, we had a bad scare when you were hooked up to the Tether. But really, what are the odds it'll spring some unforeseen surprise on us *twice?* It's just not going to happen."

None of them would meet her eyes.

I'm right. They think I'm incompetent.

"Look, Violet," Rez said. "I don't want to be insulting. But you just don't have the background for this. How will you tell Zander about the Intercept? What if he asks a highly technical question?"

"He won't. He already told us that it's not the technical part he's after. He's got that down. He wants the feeling. The feeling of—well, of feeling. He doesn't know what it's like to have emotions. When he does, when he goes through the Fusion—that's what he called it, right?—he wants to know what he's in for."

Her friends weren't budging. Rez stared at his computer. Kendall's face was a stubborn version of the word *no.* Shura's eyes were filled with wariness and uncertainty. Tin Man was studying his boots, not sure of whose side he should be on.

"This is about technical expertise," Rez stated. "Nothing else."

"Yeah," Kendall said.

"Glad you guys finally decided to agree on something," Violet said. "Just wish it wasn't *this.*" She crossed her arms. "Frankly, though, I don't care what you think. I know I'm right. We can't spare any of you. You're all needed right here in the lab to make this work. And I'm telling you, *I can do this.*"

Yes, she could force them to go along with her decision. She had more political authority than anybody here. Rez was head of the New Earth Science Authority, and Kendall was head of the New Earth Security Services, and Tin Man worked for Kendall, and Shura ran the Innovation Lab, but Violet was a senator.

At least for the time being. It was the one thing she hadn't screwed up yet.

But she didn't want to win the day by pulling rank. She wanted them to understand that certain kinds of knowledge had nothing to do with computers and algorithms, or with telescopes and microscopes. She wanted them to agree, with their own free will and not by being forced into it, that what had truly created New Earth wasn't just physics and math—as necessary as those things were—but curiosity and imagination. Things that everybody possessed. They had to learn how to access them.

"Hold on," Violet said. "I'll be right back." She moved toward the porthole and, before her friends could react, she'd opened the hatch and dropped out of sight.

No one said a word. They had no idea what she was going to do or where she was going to go. She'd thrown them such a curve by volunteering to go to Zander's planet herself that they were still in a bit of a daze.

She was back in three minutes. Being a fast runner came in handy at the oddest times.

None of the four of them seemed to have moved while she was gone. They still stood in a half circle: Shura, Rez, Kendall, and Tin Man, looking flummoxed and troubled.

Violet was holding something behind her back.

With a flourish, she pulled out a small, intricate object. It was the orrery from the observatory's conference room: the carved wooden sun, surrounded by the planets, each painted a beautiful color and attached to a thin, delicate metal rod. The clockwork mechanism concealed in the round base would, when the tiny crank was turned, make the planets revolve around the sun just as they did in the heavens.

"Before anybody had ever heard of computers or spacecraft or any of that," Violet said, "*this* is what filled them with wonder. They didn't know anything about quarks or neutrinos or supernovas or black holes. All they knew was how they felt when they looked up at the sky at night. And they took that emotion and they put it right here." She lifted the orrery a bit higher. "So it's not only about what you *know*. It's also about what you *feel*."

She waited. She couldn't read their faces anymore. Shura's frown had gone away, and Tin Man didn't look quite so concerned. Kendall and Rez, too, seemed a little less aghast. But that might have just been fatigue. They were all tired. She might have made no headway at all.

Shura looked at Rez and Kendall and Tin Man. They gave her a single nod. She nodded back.

At that moment, Violet realized that she'd done it. She had convinced them to let her go.

"Not to get too personal in front of the guys," Shura said, turning to Violet with a grin, "but if I were you, I'd go pee before we hook you up to the Consciousness Tether. No telling how long you'll be stuck on that planet—and who knows what kind of bathrooms they'll have?"

Pathways and Banana Peels

Violet took a long look at the chair that Rez and Kendall had rigged up to accommodate the New Earth half of the Consciousness Tether.

And by 'New Earth half,' she thought with a flicker of anxiety, *I mean, um*—me.

When a Tether was used for robots, it was a relatively simple process. The receptors were plugged directly into a CPU. And when the Tether had been employed to channel Sonnet's emotions into Shura's paintings, that, too, had not been especially difficult; it was a one-way road, with no necessity to send anything from Shura back to Sonnet.

But to use a *human* subject for a Tether—much less this totally new kind of Tether—was strange and exhilarating. Violet had read news stories over the years about Tether experiments with dogs and cats and even a parakeet; the parakeet wound up being able to calculate probable trajectories for meteors hailing from the Canis Major constellation, while at the other end, the computer began to tweet a pretty little song.

A human, though, was a very different problem. It was dauntingly complex. So complex, in fact, that Violet could sense the expectancy rippling through the lab as Kendall and Rez settled her into the chair, Kendall on her left side, Rez on her right. Their excitement at the prospect of this new challenge was palpable. Their eyes were wide and bright, and their movements seemed to crackle from an extra energy source. Any animosity that had simmered previously between them had vanished, replaced by the sheer joy of attempting a feat no one had ever tried before:

Using a human at one end of a two-way Tether.

Was she scared?

Shura had asked her that an hour ago as she worked her way through Violet's pre-mission physical exam, Tin Man reading out the numbers while Shura handled the instruments.

Violet's reply had been blunt: "Hell, yes, I'm scared!"

Shura had patted her shoulder. "Okay, buddy," she'd said. "You just passed the psychological portion of today's exam. Because you damned well *should* be scared. If you weren't, I'd recommend that we scrub the mission."

And they had both laughed.

To make sure they weren't disturbed by some nosy staffer while they rigged up the Tether, Rez had sent out an observatory-wide console message. He'd explained that he was busy with his own project and was not to be disturbed. His colleagues were so used to his quirky pronouncements that they shrugged and went about their business.

The chair was positioned in the center of Rez's lab. It was an ordinary kitchen chair, made of dark blond wood with six slats across the back, a square seat, and four sturdy-looking legs. A couple of gouges were visible in the wood. It didn't have arms.

"You couldn't maybe have dug up a nicer chair? Like maybe one with arms?" Violet asked. She tried to make her voice sound playful, but she knew her nervousness was showing through.

"It's only a vessel. It's totally irrelevant," Rez answered absentmindedly. He was hunched over his computer as he made some last-minute calculations, his body rooted deep in his red armchair.

"Yeah," Shura said archly, "but I can't help but notice that *your* chair has arms, Rez."

Violet felt a surge of appreciation; her friend would always have her back.

"Come on, everybody, we've got to focus here," Kendall stated. He concluded his final tests on a snarly nest of routers bubbling out of a portable medical cart that Shura had assembled so that she could monitor Violet's vital signs during the long journey—even though, on this particular journey, Violet would not be leaving the chair.

"There," Kendall said. "Ready to go. Is the cart in the right spot, Shura?"

She nudged it a little closer to Violet's chair. "Perfect."

Violet sat back in the chair, wiggling her shoulders. "How long will I have to be in this thing? What if I get a cramp or something?"

Rez stood up from his armchair and turned around to face her.

"Your body will feel as if only a few minutes have passed," he said patiently. "With a human subject, the Tether should last approximately six hours, but it won't *seem* like six hours. It will be six hours back here, and six hours will pass, but you won't experience it that way. So your body won't cramp from being in one position. Got it?"

Violet appreciated his explanation. She knew that Rez and

Kendall were still a little leery of letting her be the one to make the trip.

Someday, she'd find the words to explain to them why it had to be her. She had something very important to tell Zander. Something only she—Violet Crowley, ordinary person, definitely a nongenius—had figured out. A theory that would sound so incredibly wacky and out there to her friends that they'd stare at her and ask if she'd like to lie down for a while.

She felt Tin Man's hand on her shoulder. It was a good feeling.

"You're going to be fine, Violet. Piece of cake," he said.

Looking up at him, Violet realized that she'd completely forgiven him for his earlier slipup. The forgiving had happened while she wasn't even aware of it. He was a part of the team again.

Shura's voice was calm. "I'll be right here the whole time, keeping an eye on your heart rate and respiration and blood pressure. And besides, if I could let an alien take control of my paintbrush and almost get burned to a cinder from a power surge, then *you* can travel a few million light-years to have lunch with that same alien, right?"

Violet gave Shura a grateful smile. Her friend could always settle her down.

"Just about ready," Rez said. He'd gone back to work after his little lecture to Violet. "Kendall?"

"Yeah. All set over here."

"Tin Man? Make sure the router indicators are all showing green."

"I'm on it."

The atmosphere in the lab echoed what they'd gone through when Shura was preparing to paint the alien emotions—with the tension ratcheted up by a factor of at least a thousand, Violet estimated.

Kendall flipped a switch on the tripod. Then he flipped the

one right next to it, followed by the one next to that one. And then he flipped them all back again. He was handling his own nerves by testing the system over and over again.

Violet looked down at her trousers. And below that, to her sandals and painted toenails.

"Maybe I should've dressed better," she muttered, half sarcastically, half for real. "I mean, what are you supposed to wear when you're traveling across space and time? I'm thinking that socks might have been a good fashion choice."

Rez cleared his throat, which was his signal for everyone to hush up and pay attention. He was ready to initiate the Consciousness Tether, synching it with the signal Zander was sending forth from his own planet.

"Don't forget, Violet," he said. "We need to get a complete set of coordinates for the broken star. And when it comes to the emotional stuff, well, go easy on him. Think of your first taste of a new feeling. Or a new anything. Even if it's great, it can be overwhelming."

"Will do."

Kendall gathered the excess cable into a loop. While he wound the cable round and round on the spindle, he talked to Violet, trying to sound casual. But she knew better. "Let's go over this one more time," he said. "You don't have to do this, you know. We can shut the whole thing down right now. Nobody would blame you."

Violet nodded. Yeah. She knew she could back out. But a wonderful calmness had settled over her in the past few seconds. This was the right thing to do. She knew it. She'd faltered in the time between saying, "I'm going," and sitting down in this deceptively normal chair, but now she had steadied herself.

She felt centered and resolute. She even felt a kind of golden serenity.

She trusted her friends, even when they argued with each other or got a little full of themselves. She trusted their brains, and she trusted their hearts.

They might accidentally put her in a place of danger, but they would never leave her there. No matter what, they would not abandon her. In a sense, they were going along with her on this fantastic adventure. She was the one on the rickety wooden chair with no arms, the one whose consciousness would soon be pinballing through the galaxy, but they were along for the ride in spirit.

"I'm good," she said to Kendall.

He gave her a thumbs-up. And then he backed away. He had work to do—technical work, the work that would make this all happen. He and Rez, plus Shura and Tin Man, too, would be gruelingly busy as long as the Consciousness Tether link lasted.

This is their *leap of faith as much as mine,* Violet thought. She closed her eyes.

Each was giving what they had to give. They were doing it for themselves and for each other, yes, but they were also doing it for New Earth.

For home.

"We're a go," Rez said. "Tether initiated. Countdown in progress."

Violet felt a weird sensation in the soles of her feet. It was a kind of funny prickling, as if she were walking barefoot on fresh-cut grass. The blades of grass were short and spiky. It was not painful, but it was . . . interesting.

Yeah. That was exactly the right word.

Interesting.

Voices faded. She heard faint, trailing tendrils of words—words like *System calibrated* and *On my mark* and *Now!*—but the words grew fainter and fainter and fainter. She tried to envision the faces of her friends—Shura and Kendall and Rez and Tin Man—but now the specifics of those faces began to fade, too. They grew smaller, until they were mere dots in her mind.

She was alone. She was leaving them all behind.

And now, ironically—or did she mean *impossibly*?—she was even leaving herself behind.

It was as if her life were peeling away from her, like the skin of a banana being stripped, off, section by section. You started at the top and you found a seam and . . .

You peeled . . .

And peeled . . .

And your life fell away in these long, identically sized segments, friend by friend, year by year, memory by memory, thought by thought.

All at once, her torso felt tight, as if somebody had tied a rope around her and was yanking on it. She opened her mouth to say, "Hey, that *hurts,* guys," but she discovered a peculiar fact about her current state of existence:

She had no mouth.

Furthermore, she had no face.

She did not, it seemed, have a body at all anymore. The peeling was complete.

She was a beam of light, a bundle of particles—or was it waves? Strangely, it was *both*—surfing a pathway with no beginning and no end. She felt . . . *giddy.* She felt drenched in hope. She felt the purest, most sinuous sensation she had ever known. It was like drinking from a clear stream in which the stars were reflected, and when she looked up from the stream into the heavens, she realized that she was actually *in* the heavens themselves.

It wasn't a reflection. It was reality.

She'd had it backward her entire life. Everyone had it backward.

It wasn't the moon's reflection you saw in the ocean; it was the moon itself.

Everything was the opposite of what she'd thought it was. Up was down, right was left, light was dark, inside was outside. She wasn't Violet Crowley anymore—Violet *who*?—but a small chip of infinity.

She was small, yes, but without this specific chip—without *her*—infinity could not exist. She was the key to everything.

Wait—*everyone* was the key to everything. It was all part of a vast and beautiful plan.

Wait, that didn't make sense. How did that make sense?

Suddenly, it didn't matter that it made no sense. She let go of sense. She said goodbye to gravity and to logic. She opened her mind as wide as it would go, like a window thrown open to catch the morning breeze.

She rose. She dreamed. She soared.

PART THREE

Music from a Broken Star

Zander's Planet

he crashed.

Violet had no body, and so the notion of crashing into solid ground—like a kite when the wind dies down—made zero sense.

But that's what it felt like: a long fall (*Oh nooooooo*) and then a jarring *thwump.*

Or at least that's what it *should* have felt like, if she'd had a body.

Which she didn't.

Or did she?

Because if she didn't, then why did her butt ache? And why was she dizzy? The word *ouch* darted around in her head, a link in a chain of unuttered sounds that went something like this:

OuchOuchOuchOuch

She felt the way she'd felt three years ago during her first forbidden trip to Old Earth, when somebody had knocked her down and then punched her in several places.

Except that she couldn't feel that way, not really, because

there was nothing for anybody to knock down, right? And no place for anybody to punch.

"Welcome, Violet."

Had she dreamed that?

No. Apparently, someone really had spoken to her. She sensed the presence of the words as much as she heard the sounds. When she replied, she found that she didn't actually need a mouth—or a tongue or a larynx or lungs or the body that commonly went with them—in order to speak.

Weird.

But kind of cool, too, if she was honest about it.

"Hey," she said. She didn't even bother to ask herself how she could talk without having a mouth. It was what it was.

She was floating in what felt like a warm bath. Her eyes were open, but she couldn't see anything—no landscape, no colors, no faces—and she found that she didn't really care.

"How was your trip?"

"Not too bad." There. She'd done it again. She'd spoken.

The truth was, her trip had been amazing. Extraordinary. It had felt like hours, like days, like seconds, like a lifetime, like a hundred lifetimes, and it felt like all of those things, all at the same time.

"Good," the voice responded. "I'm Zander. And Sonnet is right here, too."

Surely he didn't expect a handshake. Because, inconveniently, she had no hands.

She took a moment to analyze the voice: It was strong and clear. Stilted, a bit formal, with few contractions. Occasionally a nugget of slang would pop up as if his study had revealed that slang tended to put people at ease.

"I don't want to freak you out," Zander said, "but it's probably good that we get one thing out of the way. The trip here is many, many light-years away from your planet. Had you tried to come in a conventional way—in a spacecraft—you would not have survived the journey. Each light-year is 5.9 trillion miles. Not even cryobiotic technology would have worked. It's far too long for a human body—one of your species—to be suspended while vital functions like heartbeat and breathing are suppressed."

She nodded. Or she *would* have nodded if she'd had a head.

Why was he telling her this? She understood. They had gone over all of this back in Rez's lab, before the first electrode was plugged into Kendall's tripod and then to the Tether's uplink.

"Your visit will not be long," Zander continued, "but I need to caution you. I advise you not to think about it, after this preliminary phase of our conversation."

"Think about what?"

"About the fact," he said, with a tinge of reluctance in his voice, "that if you looked up in the sky at this moment, turning your gaze toward the spot where you would expect to find New Earth, you would be looking at a place that no longer exists. Your family and your friends no longer exist. They have been dead for millions of years."

Violet felt a sharp wave of terrible grief. Shura, dead? And Kendall? And Rez? And Tin Man? And Jonetta? How—

"But of course," Zander went on hastily, "they are not dead. Not really. They still exist. And it's also true that they don't exist, that they've been dust for a long, long time. Both are correct. Do you know about Schrödinger's cat?"

"Duh." She didn't mean to sound like a smart-ass, but really. Physics was a required subject in New Earth schools.

"Good." Zander hadn't reacted to her disdainful tone. Maybe his world didn't do sarcasm. "I downloaded and translated the work of your major thinkers while you were on your way here, and I have to say, that Schrödinger fellow was onto something.

"The same principle," he continued, "is at work here. All the people you know back home are alive *and* dead. And you are there, and you are here, too. Both realities exist simultaneously. Think of it this way: You haven't left that lab on New Earth at all. The Consciousness Tether brought you here, but only as a prosthetic version of your mind and your will and your personality. As a beam of pure energy. And without having to drag along that annoying, needy appendage known as a body.

"What makes Tether travel difficult for the individual," he concluded, "is not the technical or the physiological aspect. It's the psychological one. It's the idea that billions of years have gone by, while you have remained static. That millennia have passed for the people of New Earth, but they haven't passed for you. It's an uncommonly challenging thought to get used to. So please, don't look up. Don't think about distance or time. While you're here, just *be*."

Violet sucked in a deep breath. *How can I be taking a deep breath when I don't have any friggin' lungs?* she thought, growing a tad frantic.

And then she let it go—both the breath and the anxiety. Her concern over the incongruity of her situation just wafted away from her like a fever that breaks at the end of a long night.

From here on out, she needed to be able to talk to Zander without stopping every few seconds to ask herself, *How am I doing this?* So she'd just do it.

Moreover, she would accept the fact that she seemed to be floating in a large glass bowl of something warm and nice. It wasn't specifically wet, but it wasn't *not* wet, either. It supported her, but it didn't feel sticky or gross.

A crucial question occurred to her. "What if the Consciousness Tether breaks?"

In a solemn voice, Zander replied, "Either you would die instantly or the second reality—the one in which billions of years have passed and everyone and everything you ever knew has disappeared—would be the only truth. You would be marooned here. You could not go back home because your home would be gone, having dissolved through the long, long fall of the years. The place where you came from would be no more. It disintegrated and became stardust millennia ago."

She nodded.

"Now that you understand," Zander said, "we can proceed."

"I'm still not sure I do."

"Understanding is overrated."

It took Violet a moment to realize that Zander had made a joke.

"What I mean," he added, "is that it's not necessary to comprehend all these nuances of space and time and the oblivion that waits for all living objects. You are here. We can help each other. But first . . ."

She waited.

A soft, undulating feeling slid over her like a spring rain. Before she knew it, she had arms and legs again, and a midsection, and even a face. A body, in other words. It felt a little odd, as if she'd put on somebody else's clothes by mistake, and while they generally fit, the sleeves of the tunic were a little short, and the trouser cuffs were a little too long, and the underwear was maybe a bit snug.

Tunic? Trousers? Panties? Where did these *come from?*

Violet tugged at her right sleeve. She moved her shoulders—*Hey! I have shoulders again!*—and she moved her feet a few times, marching in place.

Yeah. A body. Cool.

"Okay," Zander said. "Let's go."

Violet blinked. The man who'd just spoken was standing beside her. He had a body, too, and—*um, thank God*—he was fully clothed. He was a medium-sized young man with wispy blond hair and a pale, sharply angled face from which a pair of bright green eyes looked out. It took her a moment to realize that there was someone behind him. A smaller young man stepped out from Zander's shadow. He had wavy, shoulder-length brown hair that fell in crinkled folds around a dark smudge of a face. Violet couldn't make out any specific features. It was as if the features—mouth, eyes, nose—were waiting for a signal to arrange themselves. Both hands rested in the pockets of his gray tunic. He glanced at Violet, and then his gaze went straight to the ground.

"And this," Zander said, "is Sonnet. My Emotive. I am sorry to say he won't be able to greet you back. He hasn't learned your language yet."

"I sort of assumed he'd be—I mean, she'd be—female."

"Would you prefer that?" Zander asked.

"No. I mean, yeah, sure. I mean, it doesn't matter." Violet was confused.

"Not a problem. Sonnet?"

In the second it took for Violet's eyes to go from Zander to Sonnet, Sonnet's features resolved. It was clear now that Sonnet was female. Violet wasn't sure how she could tell—nothing had really changed—but a slightly different energy emanated from Sonnet now.

"From perusing your records," Zander said, "I can see that gender makes a great difference in your world. It's irrelevant here. But I assure you, whether female or male, Sonnet is happy to make your acquaintance. I know that, of course, because she's me. And I'm her."

Violet nodded. "I know." She didn't know how she knew, but she did; there was an obviousness to the fact of Zander and Sonnet that made their duality seem like just another part of the landscape.

The landscape.

She looked around. There was a landscape now. Where had all this come from?

They stood in a narrow, grass-floored valley surrounded on all sides by rocky outcroppings, some gray, some rusty red, some black. Beyond that, the craggy, snow-jacketed peaks of a massive mountain range were barely visible. The sky was white. No clouds, no birds.

It seemed to Violet more like a page torn out of a book of dreams than an actual place.

And maybe that's what it was. Maybe Zander was simply projecting some random geographical details that would seem familiar to her, elements he'd picked up in his recent study of New Earth and of Shura's paintings. He'd get around to adding trees and birds and lakes later if he had the time.

Why not show her the place for real?

Maybe he thought she couldn't handle that, couldn't absorb the true nature of his planet. Who said other environments would necessarily come in a recognizable form? As trees, streams, clouds, soil?

"Where's everybody else?" she asked.

"Like Sonnet, they're a little afraid of you. They asked me to be your host. They know you are helping me with Fusion, and they eagerly await the time when I pass along what I learn. We all must go through it."

Fusion.

Never mind that the name of their crucial ritual sounds like a band at Redshift.

"Okay," she said. "I'm pretty harmless, except when I'm mad, but okay."

Zander raised his hands, palms up. "Our time is short. Let us get right to the point. Please tell me. How do you live with both? With all that you know and all that you feel? It seems . . . too much."

"Well, it is. A lot of the time, it is. It's *way* too much."

"What do you do?"

She'd known this question was coming. And she knew what she wanted to say, but it was so peculiar that she wasn't sure she had the nerve to say it.

"Listen, Zander, my friends would think I'm absolutely nuts for what I'm about to tell you."

"'Nuts'?" Apparently some portions of slang were still unknown to him.

"Yeah. Crazy. Unhinged." Violet grinned. "But you know what? I don't care. The real reason I wanted to make the trip, even though my friends all thought they were better qualified—and frankly, they probably *are*—is because of the idea I'm going to tell you about right now. Maybe it will help you figure out what to do with emotions."

He waited. There was no curiosity in his face. Curiosity, Violet realized, was an emotion. If Sonnet were visible—she'd ducked back behind Zander—doubtless her face would show keen anticipation.

Zander, though, was interested in what Violet had to say. He was interested because it was related to survival, and survival was advantageous. In the last few minutes, she'd figured out how to read him.

"Okay," Violet said, plunging in. "I told you I took physics, right? In school? Well, I'm not supersmart. Not like Rez or Kendall or Shura. But sometimes it's not about being brilliant. Sometimes being brilliant can be a *hindrance* to understanding if the understanding needs to come from emotions instead of just brainpower.

"Physicists have been trying for centuries to figure out a single theory that will unite everything. In fact, that's what they call it—a TOE, or theory of everything. Right now, we've got one theory that works for ginormous things—things like stars and planets—and another theory that works for tiny things. Things smaller than atoms. Things in the quantum universe. But what unites the two? Lately, I've been thinking maybe it's . . . emotion. Maybe emotions are a unique form of energy. One that we've never gotten to the bottom of. Because nobody's considered it as just that—as an energy source in the universe. We still just think about emotions as love and hate and fear and greed and all the rest of it. Not as fuel. Which they are."

Zander considered her words. "Perhaps. How will that help us, though, when we Fuse?"

"I don't know. I've never mastered it myself. I've never been able to move past my emotions; they always get me into trouble. In fact, I'm not sure why you're so hell-bent on changing your system. I don't know why you want to have both the emotions and the intellect in a single individual. I mean, if I could do that—if I could split myself in half, with one side of me doing the thinking and the other side handling all the feelings—I'd sign up in a heartbeat. I'd do it."

Zander's voice was grave. "I was not exaggerating when I first communicated with you and your friends. We have stopped progressing. Our civilization has come to a standstill.

The status quo is not working. At this rate, your world will catch up with us in a few hundred million years."

"Wow. Unthinkable." Violet smiled. She couldn't tell whether or not he understood her sarcasm. Didn't matter.

"Hence our determination to Fuse." He touched his fingertips to his forehead like a man with a nasty headache. Violet realized he was thinking. Thinking ferociously hard. "Fuel," he said, saying the word out loud as if he were calculating the probability of her thesis being correct. "Emotions as fuel."

"Yeah. And that's why the Intercept was more than just a technology. More than just a device. Kendall's invention tapped into the very core of the universe, extracting the greatest power source ever known—the greatest power source that ever *could* be known." She took a breath. "At first, we didn't know what to do with the Intercept. As you've seen, our civilization is still a work in progress. We're way behind yours. And so we did the wrong thing. We turned the Intercept into something small. Just a way to control citizens. Like a better gun or a bigger jail. And then we corrected our mistake."

Sheepishly, she added, "I guess you could say we *over*corrected. Because we shut the whole thing down. And that wasn't right, either. The Intercept needs to exist. When you found Rachel's chip, you realized what emotions could do. All the possibilities. All the amazing, astonishing things that emotions can create."

"How do you know these things?"

Violet's reply came in a flash. "That's just it, Zander. I don't know those things."

"Then how—?"

"I *feel* them."

His face changed several times as ideas moved through his mind. It was, Violet thought, a little like watching the sea creatures moving through the water in the aquarium in Mendeleev Crossing.

"So feeling has a kind of intelligence behind it, too," Zander said.

"Yeah. I guess that's a good way to put it." She pondered. "And it works the other way, too. Thinking has passion in it." She ticked off examples for him: Rez's love for computers. Shura's devotion to creating vaccines and paintings. Kendall's excitement when he was working to reduce crime on New Earth. Tin Man's diligence in helping him. And the way *she* felt when she was looking for her true calling and not just doing what other people thought she should do, because of who her father was.

"Fusion will not be painful, then?" Zander asked. "Some of our Emotives are worried. Sonnet is terribly frightened. I can tell her that it will be smooth and easy, yes?"

"Nope. Trust me, you're going to be a mess at first. You're going to be sad and crazy and happy and weird. You're going to have to do what I did when they sent me here on the Tether. I had to let go. And just ride the ride."

"Ride the ride."

"Yeah."

"There is no shortcut? No way to get through the parts that cause the sadness? And just keep the good parts?"

"No shortcuts." A picture flashed in her mind: Neptunia Nodes, all lined up on the bar at Redshift in their fancy little glasses. And the nights she'd mowed down the row of drinks, trying to dull the pain of whatever was troubling her at the time: an argument with her dad, or her unrequited love for Kendall, or—later—her failing detective agency, or letting down the people who'd told her she would be a great senator. Or, or, or.

"Well," Violet admitted, "there *are* shortcuts, but they don't really work. They seem like they do, short term, but no. No shortcuts."

She sensed that he was sorting it out, sifting through what she had said, and getting input from Sonnet along the way. She could feel the energy going back and forth between them, between Thinker and Emotive.

"All right," Zander said. "We have to hurry. You must go back to New Earth right away."

Alarmed, Violet looked around. Had she missed an active volcano or an imminent tsunami? "What's going on?" she asked.

"Your friend who is searching for the star. He doesn't have much time."

"You mean Rez."

"Yes. The New Earth orbit is deteriorating much more quickly than he has projected. He must find a new planet right away. I wish it could be here, but that is not possible. You cannot breathe our air. Our gravity would instantly crush the bodies of your population. Your deaths would occur within seconds. And living inside a Consciousness Tether is unacceptably limiting."

"Wow. Okay, then."

"I apologize for not warning your friend sooner. But I only comprehended the urgency myself in the last few seconds."

"What?"

"I have now completed my review of his calculations. It is a highly complex problem; the variables are almost infinite. But now I have factored in all the probabilities. I was working on it while we talked."

You're quite the little multitasker, she thought.

A flickering light appeared in the sky, gradually resolving

itself into recognizable shapes: the skyline of New Earth. Violet realized that Zander was showing her a time-lapse projection of what the immediate future held for New Earth.

With a sickening lurch, the buildings began to buckle. The ground split apart, making wide gashes that swallowed trees and cars and shrieking people. Fires broke out as energy-generating facilities were crushed. Explosions were frequent and catastrophic.

The angle of the projection changed. Now the perspective was from farther away, looking back at New Earth from a distance. The magnificent civilization created atop the crumbling old one was now crumbling itself—and not gradually as Old Earth had done over centuries, but rapidly.

In seconds.

Violet watched. She felt disbelief, and then horror, and then fear, and then something beyond even fear: the cold, all-consuming terror of watching everything she had ever known and loved sink to ash right before her eyes.

"How long?" she whispered to Zander. She hadn't meant to whisper; her voice just wouldn't get any louder.

"Weeks. At the most. My original projections were wrong. I failed to account for the arrival of a massive blast of solar wind that will require an exponential acceleration of the heavy magnets used to maintain your orbit. That, in turn, changes all the calculations."

"So there's no hope."

"For New Earth's survival? No."

"Oh my God." She was overwhelmed by the enormity of the news. She felt sick, and for a fleeting moment, was afraid she might throw up.

Can you puke if you don't have a stomach?

She was about to find out.

"However," Zander said.

Violet perked up. The nausea slid away.

"I believe," he continued, "that I've found a potential site for New Earth. At least a star with a very plausible planet. One with an atmosphere that can sustain your population, along with copious raw materials. I believe you could transfer your population there within the time frame—before catastrophe strikes, that is."

"Great. So give me the coordinates so I can pass them along to Rez and—"

Suddenly, Violet felt as if someone had grabbed her lungs and ripped them out of her chest and thrust them between two heavy boulders. Her lungs were being pulverized.

She couldn't breathe. She couldn't move. She couldn't think.

She gasped for air, but there was no air.

She was dying.

Marie's Mistake

Rez slammed the keys on his computer keyboard as fast as he could, desperate to find the right combination of commands that would reverse the last ten seconds.

"You cut the Tether!" he yelled. "You *idiot*! You *moron*! You—"

"Stop it," Shura interrupted him. "She's a robot. She didn't know what she was doing. Let's focus on restoring it."

"We *can't* restore it!" Rez replied, still yelling, but now he'd transferred his wrath from the AstroRob to Shura. He was still fighting the keyboard, too, even though he knew it was useless. "The line's severed. Violet's got about two minutes left. Maybe less. *Look*."

Shura was already looking. She didn't need Rez to tell her that her best friend was in mortal peril. Violet's body had been resting peacefully just a few seconds before, eyes closed, head tilted back, hands clasped in her lap. Her breathing was deep, regular, and relaxed. Shura had been dutifully monitoring her vital signs: heartbeat, blood pressure, brain wave activity, oxygen levels in the blood. All normal.

And then Violet's body had begun to jerk wildly. She flung herself forward and then from side to side, back and forth, back and forth. Her eyes were still closed, but her body shook and writhed. She struggled to breathe. Her hands flew to her neck, and she clutched at it, clawing frantically for air.

"What's going on?" Kendall shouted.

Mickey's replacement, an AstroRob that Shura had nicknamed Marie in honor of her favorite Old Earth scientist, Marie Curie, was the culprit. She was young, and this was her first assignment. She had mistakenly fed the wrong coordinates into the Consciousness Tether's energy conversion chamber, causing a spike in the power feed. The Tether had initiated its automatic shutoff protocol.

Violet's body was now entirely at the mercy of the environment at the other end of the Tether: a cold, bleak, impossibly distant planet that was totally incapable of supporting human life.

"Oxygen levels dropping!" Shura called out. "She's going into shock."

"No, no, no." Rez's voice edged toward panic. He'd stopped punching buttons. He drew his hands back from the keyboard as if he was afraid of it. He thrust his head in his hands. "I can't lose anybody else. I *can't.* Not after Rachel. I—"

"Stop it," Shura admonished him. "We need to focus. Kendall?"

He was at the tripod, desperately trying to find a way to reinitiate the Tether. He switched out wires and changed circuits, both hands busy with one stratagem after another.

Violet gasped. Eyes still closed, her body bucked and flailed. Her consciousness was light-years away, but her body was right here—and it was perishing.

"Marie," Kendall barked, turning away from the tripod and

his useless maneuvers there. "Unlock your CPU. *Now.*" He began disassembling the AstroRob's middle coil. "Stand by. I'm taking your power core."

Marie's voice was calm as she gave him directions. "You should select circuits fifteen through seventy-seven. And then one hundred and forty-two through eight hundred and five." She knew why he was doing what he was doing, and she wanted to guide him quickly to the correct circuits. They both understood that she would not survive the ransacking. She was narrating her own death. "Watch out for the red wires. And don't let the blue wires touch the green ones."

Kendall tore off the sheath that protected the AstroRob's circuitry. He rooted around in a wilderness of chips and power cells, grabbing what he could grab from the grid levels that Marie had suggested. In cupped hands, he carried the components to the tripod as a shower of sparks popped and fizzed from the AstroRob's strewn-about parts. He jammed the chips and wires into the spaces between the tripod's receptors.

It was crude, it was imprecise, but it was their only chance of saving Violet.

"Don't just *sit* there, Rez!" Kendall shouted. "Get back on your computer. We've got to bring the transplanted energy cells online! And *fast*!"

Startled, still wiping tears off his face, Rez protested, "But what about the power differential between a robot's cells and a human being's if we don't run a—"

"Just keep the signal going. I'm making a temporary patch," Kendall said, cutting him off. "We can splice into the signal at this end and use the cells to transfer it back out to Zander's planet. If we're lucky."

"Forget luck," Rez muttered as he scooted his chair back up to the control panel, fingers skittering across the keyboard.

He was attacking his panic the only way he knew: by working. "It'll take a friggin' *miracle.* Not luck."

"Her vital signs are in free fall!" Shura called out. "Tin Man, get Marie out of the way. I need more space over here."

They worked frantically, the four of them, knowing that the next few seconds would mean the difference between life and death for Violet.

With a series of rapid clicks and a long, loud buzz and then a siren-like yelp, the patch seemed to be taking hold. Violet's vital signs began to stabilize.

Shura, Kendall, Rez, and Tin Man all realized they could stop what they were doing. The patch had worked.

There were no fist bumps, no high fives—just a moment of quiet triumph.

"Whew," Tin Man said. He wiped the back of his hand across his forehead. "I'm sweating. That was too close for—"

His sentence was cut off by a shrieking alarm on the tripod. Violet's blood pressure was dropping again. Her arms and legs had resumed their violent shaking.

"I can't believe this! It's happening all over again!" Shura cried out. "The transplanted cells aren't holding. The toll on her body—she can't take much more—"

Kendall took Shura's shoulders in his hands. He looked into her eyes as he spoke in a rush. "You're working on a Graygrunge vaccine, right? Didn't you tell me that?"

"Yeah. Jumping viruses are a major threat to computers and human beings alike, and so I—"

"Okay. So there in your medical bag, the one you carry around all the time, do you have any samples of Graygrunge?"

"Yeah. In case I have a spare moment to work on the vaccine. But they're sealed up and completely safe. They can't escape."

"Actually," Kendall said. "I'm hoping they *will* escape. At least one of them."

"What the—"

From his spot by Violet's chair, Tin Man's voice rang out, "Guys, hey, she's turning blue. You've got to hurry!"

Kendall was still talking to Shura. "Listen. Grab the Graygrunge vial from your bag. Break it open and give it to Rez. Let's get it in the system."

"You want to *introduce* a virus into our computers?" said an incredulous Shura. "Are you out of your mind?"

Rez answered before Kendall could. "Wait, I get it. I see what you're trying to do, Kendall. Graygrunge will infiltrate the system faster than we could ever get a rescue program up and running. It'll serve as a bridge to carry the signal. A makeshift Consciousness Tether. A temporary fix until our own patch is strong enough to hold. Once Violet's safe, we can worry about getting rid of our old pal Graygrunge."

Shura, digging frantically in her bag, muttered, "I think you're both nuts, but given Violet's condition, I'm not really in a position to debate you." She pulled out a small translucent box. Inside the box was a set of five glass vials. She plucked out the first one on the left. The hand-lettered label said GRAYGRUNGE. Below the words was a skull and crossbones.

She handed it to Rez. "Better you than me."

In seconds, Rez had cracked it open. The tentacles raced along his keyboard and dove into his computer's central core, reaching and stretching. "And now," he said as he watched his screen change, "let's see if the signal is willing to hitch a ride with a virus at the wheel."

Shura had returned to Violet's side. She held her friend's hand. Tin Man was on the other side, and he took Violet's other hand. Kendall stood behind Rez's chair, keeping track of the virus as it branched out, linking the broken-off tether to the sections of the computer still in contact with Zander's planet.

There was nothing else they could do. The virus bridge would either work or it wouldn't.

"How's she doing?" Rez called over his shoulder.

"Better!" Shura declared, her voice ragged with relief. "Respiration levels are stabilizing. Blood pressure, too."

Violet's head had settled back against the chair again. The shaking had subsided.

"Her breathing is still shallow, but at least she's breathing," Shura added. And then she fell to her knees, exhausted from the effort of holding herself together through the crisis.

Kendall started to help her up, but Shura waved him off. "Give me a minute," she said. "I can't stand up right now. My knees are kind of wobbly."

From across the room, Rez's voice was a little sheepish. "Um, guys? Sorry I lost my cool. I mean, the crying and all."

"You know what, Rez?" Shura replied. "I'm not sure we could still be friends if you *hadn't* gotten so upset. This is Violet we're talking about, and she damn near died. She was seconds from asphyxiation." The thought was too much for her. Shura had tried to rise while she was speaking, but she slid back down to her knees again. "Still too wobbly."

Kendall took a deep breath. "She's okay for now, but let's get her back here."

"What if she's not finished?" Rez inquired.

"Doesn't matter. That jury-rigged Tether is way too fragile. It could blow any minute." Kendall looked over at Marie. Tin Man had dragged her into a corner. She was a mess: flat on her back, wires spilling out of the ripped-open coils. The odor of singed circuitry was unmistakable. "Some of those parts can be salvaged," Kendall said. "I just hope the robot repair crew's able to fix her up."

"Hey, Shura," Rez said. He was trying to keep his voice at a normal level, but the anxiety was back again. "Now that Violet's okay and all, any idea how I can get rid of Graygrunge? A few more seconds and the virus will stop being just a friendly little bridge; it'll start shutting down our systems."

Shura came over to him. "Thought you'd never ask." The prospect of work had restored her.

She elbowed him away from the keyboard and punched in a strip of code. And then another. One more. With a *pffittt* sound, Graygrunge whisked off the screen.

"What was that?" asked a totally impressed Rez.

"A suppression code. Carting that virus sample around with me really paid off; I've made a lot of headway, working on ways to thwart it. I don't quite have a vaccine yet, but I will. And soon."

Fusion

Violet awoke with a start. Her lungs were burning, but at least they seemed to be functioning again. She took a breath. Not a deep one, but a breath.

Another.

She didn't want to push her luck, but she tried a third.

All good.

I'll never take breathing for granted ever again, she thought as relief swept over her.

Her arms and legs had returned to her, too, along with that handy capacity to breathe. It all occurred in a finger-snap of time. She felt almost normal again . . . or as normal as it was possible to feel when one's hypothetical self was visiting a planet in a distant galaxy and chatting with a being that had temporarily assumed human shape to facilitate conversation.

"You're back," Zander said blandly. "Sonnet was worried."

Weren't you *a little bit concerned, too?* she was tempted to ask until she remembered that worry was an emotion. Emotions, for now, were Sonnet's job. Not Zander's.

"I'm okay now," she said. "So what happened?"

"As nearly as I can determine, the Tether was somehow disrupted, but your friends back on New Earth must have fixed it. And in a timely fashion, too; otherwise, we wouldn't be having this conversation. Sonnet would be mourning your loss, and I'd be wondering when they might send the next emissary."

Cold, but honest, Violet thought.

"You must leave very soon," Zander continued. "But perhaps you might like to witness the opening stages of Fusion."

She very much would, but she hesitated. Frankly, the ritual sounded as if it might be . . . well, at little *private.* Fusion: There was a definite sexual connotation to the notion of two beings blending into one.

She'd feel like a voyeur.

If they don't bring that up, should I *bring that up?*

Yeah. She definitely should.

"You sure it's okay?" she said.

"Yes."

"Maybe you'd better check with Sonnet." Shame and embarrassment were emotions. Sonnet was the go-to guy/gal for those.

Zander offered her a curt nod. He was quiet for a moment. She heard whispering and then an answering flurry of whispers from Zander to Sonnet.

"She doesn't mind. She said it is fine for you to watch," Zander said. "The total Fusion will require a much longer period of time, because we must go slowly. These will be great shocks to the system. But Sonnet is quite pleased for you to witness the first step."

"Great."

She was tempted to ask if any popcorn was available, but held back. Apparently, Mickey had influenced her more than she knew.

Time passed . . . maybe. She wasn't sure. This place did funny things to time, stretching it out and then wadding it back up into a tiny pellet, and then dividing it up into separate pellets, and then consolidating all the little pieces again into a little ball, and then bouncing the ball.

Zander did not move.

Just when Violet had convinced herself that he'd changed his mind—no Fusion today, ladies and gentleman—she saw that he'd closed his eyes. Sonnet stepped out from behind his back. She looked all smudgy again; her eyes, too, were closed.

A soft radiance enveloped the two bodies. A light wind had started up; Violet felt the air grazing her skin.

Spring, she ruminated. *That's what this feels like—spring on New Earth.*

Something was happening. But there was no crash of cymbals, no flourish of trumpets. Violet had no access to what was really going on here, beyond her own raw observation and basic intuition, both of which seemed to have called in sick today.

There was barely of a ripple of movement on either creature's face. It was a quiet epiphany.

And it was—the realization came to her along with that soft riffle of wind, the one that danced lightly across her skin—the most beautiful moment she had ever been a part of. Somehow she *was* a part of it, too. She wasn't just watching.

Sonnet was thinking for the first time.

Zander was feeling for the first time.

For each, it was absolutely enchanting.

Sonnet's brain was streaking through billions of fields of stars, and each star was a thought, a theorem, a hunch, a proposition, a certainty: photosynthesis and Brownian motion and penicillin and calculus and longitude and igneous rock and gravity and dark matter.

Zander's brain was zipping with equal abandon through billions of fields of *other* kinds of stars, and each star was a feeling, and each feeling was inspired by a symphony or a soliloquy or a heartbreak or a dance or a dream or the precise angle of sunlight on the face of one's beloved on a summer day.

And that, Violet knew, was just the beginning. That was the faintest, briefest taste of the wonders that awaited each one of them, a sumptuous bounty of all the things they had never known before. Once they knew them, they would not be able to live without them, ever again.

Was it over? It seemed to be over, but she couldn't be sure.

Okay, yes, it was over. The Zander who spoke to her was himself again. Sonnet had vanished, ducking back behind him. Many more such sessions would be needed in order for Fusion to hold; Fusion, after all, was a process, not a singularity. Zander had explained that.

"And now," he said, "we must conclude your visit. Under the present parameters, you are getting very close to the outermost limit of the safe zone. I have encoded your Tether's return feed with the latest coordinates for the new star. So it's time to part. Although . . ."

"What's up?"

"I have a proposition."

"Sure," Violet said breezily. "Name it." Maybe he wanted a selfie with the three of them.

"Stay."

"Pardon me?"

"Remain here with us. Teach us more about emotions."

Violet was stunned. Was he kidding? "Well, to begin with, there's the small matter of me not being able to breathe your air. Oh, and being crushed like a bug by your gravity."

"We can work around those obstacles. With a single person—not an entire population—it would be possible. We could devise a way to enclose you and protect you from—"

"Whoa. Time-out. Sorry, Zander; there's no point in trying to brainstorm this. I'm a New Earth girl, all the way."

"But you will be leaving New Earth, anyway. Your world is doomed."

"Just the physical part. And that's the least of it." Violet hadn't known she felt this way until she heard herself saying it. Saying it felt good. "What really matters are my friends. Shura and Rez and Kendall and Tin Man. Those guys are the reason why it's home. So thanks for the invitation, but it's time for me to go now. We've got a lot of work to do back there. Getting ready to relocate and all. God, I'm getting tired just *thinking* about all that packing."

Why wasn't she more upset about Zander's news, about the updated timetable for the demise of New Earth? Now she knew: Because no matter where they went, she and her friends would go there together. Home wasn't a planet. Home wasn't New Earth or Old Earth. Home was the place where her friends were.

"If you change your mind—"

"I won't."

She almost thought that Zander looked disappointed. But that was impossible, of course. Disappointment was an emotion. And emotion wasn't his thing.

Yet.

Simple, Ancient, True

At last, she was alone.

From the moment she'd returned from Zander's planet, Violet had been surrounded. Shura insisted on performing a thorough physical exam before she could even get out of the chair, to guarantee there were no lingering effects from the Tether breach. Rez downloaded the numbers proving the updated rate of decay of New Earth's orbit, and then began work on the coordinates for the new star. Kendall was ravenous to know Zander's reaction to the Intercept. And Fusion: They wanted details and explanations. More, more, more.

Violet felt a little bit like a buffet supper. They were elbowing each other out of the way to take what they wanted.

Yes, the crisis was real, and yes, they would have to begin planning immediately for evacuation to a new planet.

But there was something she needed to do before she could think about all that lay ahead. To accomplish this task, she had to find a certain book.

And she had to be alone.

She located it right away.

It was in the first drawer Violet checked in the spare room of her apartment. She knelt in front of the long row of small blue ovals in the wall and touched the first one. The drawer slid out, revealing the most important elements in her father's life: His books.

Ogden Crowley had maintained a vast library. Not the modern kind, with digital versions of every published work in history, but the old-fashioned, paper-and-ink-and-binding kind. When he died, the books became hers. She knew she ought to display them, arrange them in neat rows, organized by author and title and subject, but she hadn't done that yet. She hadn't found the time.

No, that wasn't the real reason. That was only an excuse.

The *real* reason she hadn't put the books on shelves yet was because the thought of doing it made her too sad. Her father's death was still too fresh in her mind.

And now her delay looked like a smart move. She would only be packing them up again now for transport to the new New Earth.

The volume she was looking for was right on top. She'd expected that.

The Complete Poetical Works of Robert Browning. A beautiful book. Handsome red leather, raised gold lettering on the cover and spine.

When Jonetta told her what Ogden Crowley had murmured to the Starbridge director in the final days of his life, it had stirred something in Violet's memory. The words *simple, ancient, true* awakened something in the back in her mind, something tucked behind the swirl of her daily activities: her Senate duties, hanging out with her friends, all the things—some important, some trivial—that comprised her life. And after that, of course, they'd taken a definite back seat to her preparations for a voyage to another galaxy.

Simple, ancient, true.

The book smelled musty and old, but she didn't mind. When she opened it, she had a general notion of which gilt-edged page she should turn to. She didn't need to check the index.

And there it was. A poem titled "Among the Rocks." She read it to herself all the way through once, and then a second time; the words were like old friends. When she was a little girl, her father had read this poem aloud to her many, many times. This one, and others, too. That was their favorite thing to do together, especially on rainy nights. Ogden Crowley would settle in his big armchair with a book on his lap, as comfortable as it was possible for him to be with his wounded leg, and Violet would sit cross-legged on the floor next to him. He would read aloud to her in his low, rolling, sonorous tone. Sometimes, if the poem was too long, she fell asleep, but her father never got mad about that.

The poem was about the fall season on Old Earth. She read the first stanza to herself for a third time:

Oh, good gigantic smile o' the brown old earth,
This autumn morning! How he sets his bones
To bask i' the sun, and thrusts out knees and feet
For the ripple to run over in its mirth;
Listening the while, where on the heap of stones
The white breast of the sea-lark twitters sweet.

The three words her father had uttered to the director came in the second stanza:

That is the doctrine, simple, ancient, true;
Such is life's trial, as old earth smiles and knows.
If you loved only what were worth your love,
Love were clear gain, and wholly well for you;
Make the low nature better by your throes!
Give earth yourself, go up for gain above!

Violet pondered. What did it mean? Why had he chosen this poem? And how would it help her to find the console?

Because now she was absolutely certain that that was the point of her father's seemingly casual remark to the Starbridge director, the one with *simple, ancient, true* embedded in it. He had totally expected Violet to make inquiries as she tracked down his console. He hadn't left it in plain sight, where anybody might find it; even though it was password-protected, the authorities had ways of breaking even the most rigorous security system. There was something in his console that he wanted her to discover—but only her. No one else.

He had known very well that, in tracing his movements and statements in the last few days of his life as she sought the console, Violet would hear the three words, and they would strike a chord with her. She would recognize that the lines were from a Browning poem.

And she would come here to check it out.

Here, to this room, to this drawer, to this book.

But what could it be? What was the clue that he wanted her to—

She glanced up from the page toward the drawer in which she had found *The Complete Poetical Works of Robert Browning.* And then she remembered.

On a day shortly before her father died, he had asked if they could have tea at her apartment. As weak as he was, he wanted to share a final time with her—and not at Starbridge, he'd said, which was comfortable but was also sterile and soulless.

So they had come here. To her apartment. She had made two cups of tea, one for her father, one for herself, and they'd sat at her kitchen table and had a wonderful conversation. It wasn't heavy and sad—nothing about death or pain. It was light and loving. They'd talked about Violet's mother, Lucretia Crowley, who had died when Violet was ten. Her father told Violet how proud Lucretia would have been of the young woman Violet had become.

In her heart, Violet doubted that—she was a screwup, right?—but she hadn't corrected her father.

They talked about the Intercept, which had seemed like such a splendid idea in the beginning but had ended up being a very bad idea. In turning emotions into weapons, it became another way for the government to control the citizens.

Her father, though, had had more to say about the Intercept. He told Violet that he'd begun to believe that the idea behind it was right, after all. Emotions contained an important power, a power all their own, a power that human beings had yet to even come close to appreciating. Someday, he said, they would understand emotions better. Emotions were part of the vast mysterious forces in the universe.

They might even be *the* force.

And that, Violet recalled as she knelt on the floor in front of the open drawer, was the seed of the idea she had passed along to Zander: Emotions were the lost link between the forces that ruled the quantum universe and the forces that controlled large things like galaxies.

Still facing the drawer, something caught her eye. She smiled. Why hadn't she noticed it when she first pulled out the book?

Because I was so damned eager to read that poem.

There, atop the next volume in the closely packed drawer, was her father's console. He must have placed it there the day he'd come for tea. Maybe it was when she left the kitchen to go to the bathroom or to take a call from a member of her Senate staff. Whatever. He had slipped it into the drawer and then put *The Complete Poetical Works of Robert Browning* on top of it, knowing she would follow the trail of words and end up here. Right here.

The override feature was keyed to Violet's DNA. Other than her father, nobody else could open the console. When she touched the rising green jewel, it automatically unlocked.

She listened for the soft click that would tell her that the message was ready. All she had to do was initiate playback.

She hesitated. Did she really want to do this? What if her father had been hiding a terrible secret?

Yeah. I want to do this. Because I have to know.

Fleetingly, she wondered if this was how Shura felt when she pushed toward a breakthrough in her lab, one that might have cataclysmic consequences. Or Kendall in his lab. Or Rez in his. They had to discover the truth, even if the truth was hard to live with.

Maybe, Violet thought, this is what courage really meant: not fighting great battles with terrifying weapons or going to a strange planet on a Consciousness Tether. It meant searching for the truth and, once you found it, dealing with it. Either kind of truth: a scientific one or an emotional one.

She took a deep breath.

She activated the playback function.

Another jewel rose from the face of the console. It was a

soft coral color, which surprised her; she'd assumed that her father's last message would be embedded in a primary-color jewel. A bold red, say, or a deep blue, or a brassy yellow.

But no. It was a pastel, the color of the delicate whorled interior of a seashell or of the last sunset of your life.

She touched the jewel.

Ogden Crowley clears his throat. His breathing is a rhythmic rasp. The low, pleasing baritone of those long-ago rainy nights is long gone; old age has replaced it with a clotted, reluctant bramble of sound.

He clears his throat a second time, and then he begins:

> My darling girl. If you are listening to this now, it means that I have died and you have found my console. I knew you would figure out where I hid it—you, and you alone. What I have to say is only for you.
>
> Of course, if you choose to share it, that is fine. I know you have good friends, and maybe you will need to tell them what you are about to find out. Once I reveal the truth, it no longer belongs to me. You may do with it what you choose.
>
> I know that New Earth's orbit is decaying much faster than even our best scientific minds have predicted. Until my retirement, I controlled the data. Afterward, it was too late; they were using incomplete information. I kept the essential numbers—the correct numbers—from them so that they would not piece together the truth.
>
> New Earth does not work.
>
> My dream of creating a world that lives above the known world is a false dream. I was wrong. I should have listened to

my opponents in the first place—the ones who advised that we should relocate to an entirely new planet.

But I was too attached to Old Earth. I could not leave it behind. I wanted to keep it in sight, even as we built the new world on top of its bones.

I have lacked the courage to admit my mistake.

I discovered my fatal error several years ago, when a manuscript was found on Mars by one of our mineral trawlers. According to this document, written by a long-dead Mars citizen named Scaptur, the civilization on that planet was once much like ours. And their solution was the same as mine: construct a New Mars, high atop the old. A gleaming new world. Most of the citizens relocated there, with only a few remaining on the planet's surface.

First gradually, and then suddenly, the New Mars orbit failed.

It crashed onto the surface of Old Mars, and both civilizations—New and Old—were destroyed.

That will eventually happen to New Earth as well. I knew it, but I could not bring myself to divulge it. I am the founder of New Earth. The father of New Earth. People trust and respect me.

Before my discovery of the Tablet of Scaptur, I put the Intercept in place to make New Earth perfect. To keep it safe and beautiful. When the Intercept did not work, I could not confess to yet another mistake. Two mistakes—two unforgivable errors in judgment—would destroy whatever authority I had left. My legacy would be in ruins. My life's work exposed as a lie.

I could not leave New Earth unprotected. I could not admit my mistake during my lifetime—but I could make amends in my own way. I began stockpiling the materials that can be used to transfer the population of New Earth to a new planet. Energy, specialized pods, technical apparatus—I have heaped them up in a secret location for the day they will be needed.

I am dying. So I am recording this for you, Violet. By now, your friend Steven Reznik has surely discovered the decay in the orbit. And your other friends—Shura and Kendall and Tin Man—will help you find a new planet. The equipment I have assembled will help you get there.

I have put the location coordinates for the supplies at the end of this message.

You and your friends will save the world. I am certain of it. In fact, my remaining silent about New Earth's sure doom is a perverse tribute to the abilities of you and Rez and Shura and Kendall and Tin Man. You are well able to solve this. I can die knowing that New Earth will survive—somewhere.

I hope you can forgive me for my weaknesses, Violet. I am an old man, but I have a young soul—a soul too immature to rise above ego and petty arrogance.

If the Intercept were still operational, and you and Rez were sitting in Protocol Hall, monitoring my Intercept feed, you would see a blend: deep regret and sadness, and also fear, because death is the great unknown. But the most powerful part of that blend, the one that rises above all the rest like a star on the near horizon, is love. Love for New Earth.

Love for my little girl.

My Violet.

The recording ended.

She tapped the coral-colored jewel. It drifted down and then winked out.

She shut off the console. She slipped it into a trouser pocket.

Violet was filled with so many emotions that she wasn't sure she would ever be able to sort them all out. There was anger—her father had withheld the truth from the very people he'd promised to take care of—but there were other feelings, too.

Pity, for one thing. She pitied him for his vanity and his pride, his unwillingness to admit that he'd made a mistake. Well, two mistakes, if you included installing the Intercept.

And there was also gratitude, because in the end, he had made preparations for the journey to a new world.

But mostly there was love. She loved him. He was human—gloriously, ignominiously human, which meant he was both good and bad. It meant he was a thinker and a dreamer at the same time. He had ideas, and he had emotions, too. He was Zander—and he was Sonnet.

Just like everybody.

Violet stood up. Time to go. She needed to help her friends organize the mass evacuation from New Earth. And now she had something to contribute.

Homeward Bound

DemoRobs were totally different from other kinds of robots. The other varieties—AstroRobs, BioRobs, TechRobs, ReadyRobs—were like siblings, sisters and brothers who had grown up in the same house. They all looked very similar, from the silo of flexible cylinders to the central casing wrapped around their silicon hearts.

The DemoRob, short for Demolition Robot, was nothing like that.

Violet stood in the magnificent entrance hall of the observatory. In front of her were four rows of gleaming, seething, can't-wait-to-get-cracking DemoRobs.

Prior to this moment, she had never seen one in person. Neither, she suspected, had her friends. They stood alongside her, equally intimidated.

"Wow," was all Violet could think of to say, as lame as that was.

"Yeah," Kendall said.

"Yeah," Shura echoed, rubbing the back of her neck. It was

sore from staring up, up, up, at the DemoRobs, which were enormous—twenty times larger than a typical robot. The machines had had to disassemble themselves to make it through the doorway and then reconstitute in seconds.

DemoRobs were rare, being expensive both to manufacture and maintain. And their programming made them nasty and dangerous. No Dumb-Ass Dave would ever have been allowed access to a DemoRob.

A DemoRob, true to its name, was created to demolish. It was specifically engineered to smash, wallop, crush, shred, rip, wreck, and pulverize.

And after it had done all those things, the suction/cleanup feature would scoop up the tons of detritus and suck it into a side compartment, whereupon it would be further ground up into ash.

Thus a DemoRob not only killed. It also removed all evidence of the murder.

They were a little scary to behold: the ten separate pincers on each one, five to a side, were adorned with razor-sharp blades that could revolve millions of times per second, generating a blur of pure destructiveness. There was no pity in the two slits designed to look like eyes.

"Are you sure about this?" Kendall asked. He cast a dubious eye across the four rows of what were, essentially, killer robots.

"Of course," Rez replied.

"There's no other way?"

Rez glared at him. "If you can think of an alternative, then be my guest."

"I just asked."

"Well, I'm not thrilled about it, either. I just don't know what you want me to do about it."

"Guys. Come on," Violet said. "We're all exhausted. Let's keep it together, okay?"

It was late afternoon, and the light tumbled in from the curved glass ceiling. Etched on the glass were calligraphic quotations from the thinkers and visionaries whose work had led to the miracle of New Earth, sometimes directly, sometimes indirectly.

There were excerpts from the writings of Newton and Galileo, and from Einstein and Heisenberg and Leavitt and Planck and Atwood, and from Sagan, of course, the observatory's namesake, and there were lines from the six people who had been immortalized in the names of the cities of New Earth: Stephen Hawking, Michael Faraday, Dmitri Mendeleev, Madeleine L'Engle, Rosalind Franklin. When New Earth was being created, Ogden Crowley had insisted that public spaces be used to honor scientists and writers from long, long ago. Some people had argued for the inclusion of more recent scientists—Melinda Stratton and Penelope Hemlepp, for instance, the discoverers of the jumping virus—but Violet's father said no.

He wanted these names.

These were the spiritual mothers and fathers whose ideas had truly given birth to New Earth, back in the doomed, final centuries of Old Earth.

And now New Earth itself was doomed.

Rez had given them a quick briefing just after they arrived at the observatory. Everything was ready.

The materials that Ogden Crowley had secretly gathered were crucial. Without them, Rez explained, they could not have made the deadline. With them, there was a chance. A real chance. When Violet had led him to the hidden warehouse the day before, and he began pulling the tarps off the giant pods, his face had lit up. Discovering the stockpiled energy reserves had made him even happier.

The pods, each capable of carrying five thousand people, had begun their departures from the transport site that morning. Each citizen had received a pod assignment and a boarding pass, stamped with a time at which to arrive for embarkation. The entire process would require sixteen hours, and groups of pods gathered along the horizon before the final stage. They would be hurled away from New Earth like rocks in slingshots, following the precise trajectory required to arrive at the planet in approximately nine years. The landing process had been planned with similar exactitude by Rez and Kendall, with assistance from Zander. At that point, people would be awakened from cryogenic sleep.

And then the real work would begin—the task of establishing an entirely new civilization from scratch. But their parents and grandparents had done it before, and so they could do it again.

Not everyone wanted to go. The people on Old Earth had been offered the chance to leave, too; a few agreed, and they had been brought up to New Earth to join the lines for the pods, but most stayed. Here on New Earth, it was generally only elderly people who resisted, claiming they were too old to start all over again. A few others were openly contemptuous of the projections that Rez had made public. They professed disbelief in the prediction that New Earth's orbit was deteriorating at a much faster rate than had been foreseen. That New Earth was, in effect, galloping toward the edge of a cliff.

The doubters, the skeptics, the deniers, the people determined to stay, could do as they pleased. They had that freedom.

Once the last pod was jettisoned from New Earth, they would be trapped here, lashed to a dying civilization like a captain tying herself to the wheel of a sinking ship. When New Earth's fall began, it would accelerate quickly, and they would ride it down to its final fiery landing on Old Earth.

Rez had requisitioned the DemoRobs to tear down the largest and heaviest physical structures on New Earth, to cut down on friction in the orbit. They would start once all the transport pods carrying the rest of the population had departed.

He wanted to do right by those who had chosen to stay, no matter how ridiculous he found their view. He would strip New Earth bare, making it as light and as aerodynamically sleek as it could be to delay the final fall as long as possible. The work of the DemoRobs would buy the holdouts a few extra hours. Maybe even an entire day.

A single day, Violet had thought, when Rez first told her his plan. *How would I spend one day, if there was a chance it might be the last day I'd ever have?*

She wasn't sure.

Now she asked herself the question again as she stood in the vast echoing space in the shadow of the massive telescope, along with twenty-four DemoRobs and five friends: Shura, Kendall, Rez, Jonetta, and Tin Man.

My last day? I'd spend it with these guys. Absolutely.

She smiled. The realization had made her happy. As it was, they had plenty of days ahead of them. They were going to a new planet, and they would make a new life there. But it was their choice. The skeptics had made another one—which was their right.

"I've given them the timetable for the DemoRobs," Rez said. "It'll be up to them to stay out of the way. They understand."

"How can they understand?" Shura said. "They don't really

believe New Earth is dying. Why would they approve of your tearing most of it down once we're out of here?"

Rez shrugged. "I don't know. Based on my final conversation with their leaders this morning, I'm sort of convinced they *do* believe it, no matter what they say. They just don't want to do anything about it." He checked a few coordinates on his console, then resumed his musing. "Maybe it's like those people on Old Earth, right before Violet's dad created New Earth. Toward the end, they *had* to have seen what was happening. They had to know that the ice caps were melting and the oceans were gorged with plastic and the air was so polluted that you could taste the poisons in it. The world was dying right before their eyes. But they insisted they didn't see it because they didn't want to change. Better a pretty lie than an ugly truth, I guess."

An alarm sounded on Rez's console. He silenced it and faced his friends.

"The countdown's started," he said. "I'll set the coordinates for the time-delay deployment of the DemoRobs. Shura, you and Tin Man will be in charge at the transport site. Violet, you and Kendall need to go up to my lab and shut down the computers and power sources. While you're there, send a message to Zander that we're on our way to the new home he picked out for us. And thank him again. If he hadn't found that broken star for us . . ." He let his sentence trail off. "But he did. And we're going."

Tin Man was already on his way out the door. Shura lingered for a moment.

"One more thing, Rez," she said. "Yeah, Zander found the star. But don't forget who found Zander. It was Rachel. Rachel's chip is what brought Zander to us. Otherwise, you'd still be frantically searching for that star while our orbit decayed. Rachel led us to our destiny."

Rez's face was blank. He was holding back a great torrent of emotion, a fact that would be apparent only to the people who knew him best.

"She was brilliant," he murmured. "She would've changed the world. She would've—"

"Hold on," Violet said, interrupting him. "You're always talking about how smart Rachel was. And she *was* smart. No question. But sometimes you act as if that's the only thing you're mourning—her intelligence."

"She was a genius. The world lost a lot when she died."

"Yeah. But I'm not talking about what the *world* lost, Rez; I'm talking about what *you* lost. *You.* And not because of how smart she was. Because she was your little sister, and you loved her."

Rez started to speak. He couldn't. He waited a few seconds, and then he tried again. His voice was clipped and businesslike. He was, Violet knew, trying to keep his feelings hidden behind a show of gruffness. That's what he always did. But she knew the truth.

"Let's get moving," he snapped. "Lots to do."

Violet flipped the toggle switch on the control panel. She was just about to flip the toggle switch right next to it when Kendall put his hand on top of hers.

"Hang on," he said.

She was mildly annoyed. They had begun the shutdown protocol in Rez's lab. Surely Kendall wasn't going to bring up the whole why-can't-we-be-together stuff. Here? Now? Today of all days?

"Kind of in a hurry here," she said. "We're got a million things to do. And then we've got to get to the transport site. Our pod number's coming up soon."

"Yeah. But give me a minute."

Mystified, Violet shrugged and backed away from the control panel. "What's up?"

He didn't answer right away. She was just about to repeat herself, only with a lot more annoyance packed into her voice, when he spoke.

"I'm not coming, Violet."

"What?"

He was kidding. It had to be a joke, right? It wasn't funny, though. Who did he think he was? Mickey?

"I'm not getting in the pod," Kendall said. "I had a long talk with Zander last night on my console. They'd like to learn all about the Intercept. More than what they already know. And I'm going in person, not on the Consciousness Tether."

"You—you can't do that." She was suddenly frantic. She realized Kendall was serious. "No way. You'd be dead by the time you arrived. It takes about ten thousand human life spans to get there."

"They're sending a ship for me. It's scheduled to get here just after you guys leave. We'll use suspended animation for part of the trip, as long as it's safe. When my vital signs start to show the wear and tear, Zander has a plan for the next few thousand years or so. They'll put me into something called biostasis conversion chronology. Time will pass, but my mind and my body won't feel it passing at the same rate that it's really going by. When I get there, I'll be fresh and ready to go."

"And you trust their technology?"

"Yes. I do."

She was feeling increasingly desperate. "You have to tell the others."

"No. I don't want to argue with them. Especially not Rez. He and I fight a lot, and he can be a real SOB, but he's got a sentimental streak. Especially now. He'd be pulling out all the stops to get me to change my mind. Besides—I've already turned off my console."

Violet felt tears coming into her eyes. "You can't survive on Zander's planet. The atmosphere is all wrong. That's why we couldn't transfer New Earth there. We'd all have to live inside bubbles."

"Zander has a plan for that, too," Kendall said quietly. "I don't understand it yet, but he assures me I'll get used to whatever device he comes up with. Not a bubble, but something that protects me from the planet. Enables me to breathe. It's true that I'll miss the wind on my face. Or being able to touch the ground and really *feel* it. But I can survive. And I'll spend the rest of my life with Zander and his colleagues, explaining how I created the Intercept. Describing what it's like to live with the ability to think *and* feel. It's still so new for Zander. He's not sure how to handle himself."

Violet was openly weeping now.

"Is it worth it, Kendall? With all that you'll be giving up?"

"I've lost my parents. I've lost my brother." With his eyes, he added, *And I've lost you, too, Violet. You're still alive, but you don't love me the way I love you, and you never will. I feel that pain every day.* Out loud, he went on, "I'm the perfect choice to be the permanent ambassador from New Earth to Zander's planet. I've got nothing more to lose."

Violet felt a sadness that reached so deep inside her that she was sure it had taken root in the soles of her feet. But she believed to her core that people had the right to decide what they wanted for their lives. It was the most fundamental freedom in the universe.

"You need to go now, Violet," he said solemnly. "They'll be waiting for you at the transport site. And I've got work to do here. Zander gave me instructions on how to prepare for the ship they're sending. Once I go, there's no return. The path will seal up behind me. It's a one-way trip."

"No. No, Kendall. Please." She clutched his arm.

He gently removed her hand and then held both of her hands in his. "I've made up my mind. This is how I want it to be."

He turned away from her.

"Kendall," she said. "Wait."

She took his arm again—not grabbing at it frantically this time, not trying to change his mind, but because she wanted to have a final connection. She wanted to make a memory—a memory of how it felt to be close to him.

He turned back.

She kissed him. They had kissed only once before—a long, long time ago, back when everything was different, back when the Intercept ruled New Earth, back when the yearning went in the other direction: She loved Kendall more than he loved her.

This kiss, like that one, was filled with as much sorrow as joy.

Joy for what they were: good friends who had enriched each other's lives.

Sorrow for what they would never be: lovers, partners, united for all time in a fierce bond of mutual passion.

"When I look at the stars at night," Violet said, her voice barely a whisper, "I'll know you're out there."

"And I'll be looking back at you," he said. He smiled. "I probably won't wave, though. I doubt if you could see me."

She laughed. She was glad he'd relieved the tension with a joke.

"Sounds like something Mickey would've said."

"I'll take that as a compliment," Kendall replied. "He was a good friend."

They were quiet again. The quiet wasn't awkward; it felt exactly right, somehow, as they gazed into each other's eyes and thought about all they had been through together.

But the pressure of the situation—they both had other places to be—caused Violet to cut into that silence. She would never see him again. There were so many things she wanted to say. So many things she *needed* to say.

Too many things to get them all said in this brief span of time.

So she gathered up all of those things as best she could. And she realized, as she did so, that the words she was about to say contained enough energy to fuel the mighty furnace of the stars and to keep the planets spinning in their elegant orbits and—the most immense and difficult task of all, a task that dwarfed the others—to move a single human heart, changing the universe for all time.

"I love you."

The four of them stood next to the giant pod that would take them away from everything they knew, everything they had ever known.

Violet, Shura, Rez, Tin Man.

They were the last passengers on the last pod.

All around them, the beauty of the New Earth sunset filled the sky with the colors of fire: amazing reds and gee-whiz golds. The members of the Color Corps had already boarded a pod; this sunset was a natural one.

Along the horizon, visible now only as tiny black dots, thousands of giant pods hovered. They were awaiting the final pod. At that point, the propulsion systems would engage, flinging them in unison into deepest space.

Violet had told the others about Kendall's decision. They did not understand it, any more than she understood it, but they had to accept it. It was too late to go back to the lab and say goodbye to him. He had designed it that way, Violet realized. It was how he wanted it.

"We have to go," Rez said, tapping his console. He boarded the pod. Shura went next, and then Tin Man.

Now it was Violet's turn. She stepped forward. She paused. She had one foot on the metal threshold of the enormous vessel while the other foot still rested on the surface of New Earth. There were a few words she needed to say to herself while she was still touching this planet, this world. The words were a link to her past. Another kind of tether.

Her father had recited the words to her when she was a little girl. He had done it just after he'd told her the story of New Earth—a story about courage in the face of the unknown. It was fitting then. It was even more fitting now.

"*Per aspera ad astra,*" she murmured. It was a line from Virgil, an Old Earth poet from long, long ago, who spoke an ancient language called Latin. She added the translation: "To the stars through bolts and bars."

And then it was time to go. The stars were waiting—and so were her friends.

Acknowledgments

As this journey rounds to a close, I am compelled to thank Alexander Key and Ray Bradbury, authors of, respectively, *The Forgotten Door* and *The Martian Chronicles*. The first time I read those wonderful books, I felt the world shift beneath my nine-year-old feet; doubtless *The Dark Intercept* was born then. I can only hope that, through the death-defying magic of words and stars and time, in some dimension richer and less linear than ours, the spirits of those two writers know how very much their work meant to me—a bespectacled, curly-haired girl growing up in West Virginia, a girl whose happiest hours were spent in the Gallagher Village Public Library at the bottom of the hill.

Thanks once again to Ali Fisher at Tor, who made each book in this trilogy better, and to Lisa Gallagher, longtime source of expertise and encouragement.

This book is dedicated to Ruth Thornton, my Latin teacher at Huntington East High School. Ancient Rome now lives only through its writers—but as Mrs. Thornton taught us, that is enough. That is more than enough.

CPSIA information can be obtained
at www.ICGtesting.com
Printed in the USA
LVHW041926111119
637009LV00002B/221